UP FROM THE BOTTOMLESS PIT

UP FROM THE BOTTOMLESS PIT

PHILIP JOSÉ FARMER

Meteor House

UP FROM THE BOTTOMLESS PIT

by Philip José Farmer

Meteor House
ISBN 978-1-945427-17-6
First Trade Edition

"When they have finished their testimony, the beast that comes up from the bottomless pit will make war on them and conquer them and kill them." (Revelation 11:7)

FOREWORD

An Uncanny Accuracy

In 1970 Philip José Farmer announced he was working on a novel about the effects of pollution twenty years in the future; but this book, which he called *Death's Dumb Trumpet*, never materialized. Still, Phil did not abandon the idea of a speculative novel about the environment. As early as 1974 Phil had another idea, a novel then titled *The Dragon's Breath*. It was to be a story that would address the nexus between humanity's addiction to petroleum and concern for a habitable environment. With long lines and pain at the pump a daily concern in the mid-1970s, Phil had every reason to believe his new novel would resonate with both his American reading audience and the world at large.

Phil submitted a draft of the novel to Judy-Lynn del Rey at Ballantine Books. The forthcoming book was announced in various publications, much to the excitement of Phil's fans. Then Ballantine contacted Phil and requested an extensive rewrite, suggesting that he blame the catastrophe in the book on the story's protagonist. Phil complied with the rewrite, though he retooled some of the plot details along his own lines. Still, Ballantine felt the story—now titled *Up from the Bottomless Pit*—did not meet their needs. Another rewrite was requested, but by this late date in 1978 Phil was too frustrated to go on and he offered up the science fiction epic *Dark is the Sun* to Ballantine instead.

Somewhat ironically, *Up from the Bottomless Pit* might carry more weight today than if it had been published in the late 1970s. In the book, Phil anticipates with uncanny accuracy the rough ride U.S. agencies such as FEMA have since had in responding to extreme crises, as well as the necessity and dangers of consolidating such bureaucratic power. In this vein, *Up from the Bottomless Pit* is more than just a rip-roaring eco-thriller—it is also science fiction prognostication at its best.

Christopher Paul Carey

INTRODUCTION

THE IDES OF MARCH

As I write this introduction to Philip José Farmer's prophetic *Up from the Bottomless Pit*, the World Health Organization has just declared a pandemic, and the coronavirus is falling like the shadow of a racing cloud over the United States. Most of us feel we are living at the beginning of an apocalyptic novel, in a state of foreshadow and suspense. You who are reading this opening paragraph know what has happened since March 15, 2020—literally the Ides of March—but I do not.

At this moment, I am glad for all the science fiction I have enjoyed over the last fifty years. Storytelling has always been a way to prepare us for the future, as well as to inform us of the past and present. Science fiction, specifically, is the literature of the future, and as often as not, that future is some version of dysfunction or upheaval. Through such literature, I have experienced alien invasions hurtling at humanity from beyond our galaxy and totalitarian regimes rising up from the depths of our own dark hearts. Global warming has irrevocably changed the face of the Earth, as have comets and Artificial Intelligence. My life has been upended many times over by solar flares, nanotechnology, time travel, nuclear war, and yes, pandemics.

Of course, it would be hubris to say that any amount of reading and writing has prepared me for the suffering and grief of a real pandemic. But as someone who has lived by the sword of reading and writing, I have to say again: I am grateful for the power of all those imaginative acts, all those tales of prophecy, destruction, resilience, and survival.

Up from the Bottomless Pit is the sobering and sometimes thrilling story of an environmental disaster, one that has gone unexplored in the literature of apocalypse but that is certainly possible in the real world of apocalypse. Early in this story, the narrator states, "Everything had been considered; everything was safeguarded." We readers have to smile—and sigh.

Inevitably, in Farmer's account of this plausible disaster, society's failure and lack of will to truly safeguard the environment results in a cascade of effects. Many of the characters in the novel are surprised by the interrelated nature of our planetary systems and by our human dependence on them. As their priorities shift—casual extramarital affairs and job promotions become suddenly less important—they are forced to ponder the connections between the oceans and the atmosphere, Arctic sea ice and coastal cities, forests and human respiration. It all sounds so familiar. Many of our leaders in the 21st century seem similarly uninformed and would be similarly surprised.

Human nature, of course, is at the heart of Philip José Farmer's work, and one thing we learn from reading his body of stories and novels is that human nature is not a simple matter of good or bad. In extreme situations, faced with the possibility of their own death, his heroes and heroines do not behave like self-sacrificing and overly-competent movie-stars on screen, not even when all the action is taking place in Hollywood, California, with the city of Beverly Hills burning south of Sunset Boulevard. The villains, too, are more nuanced, often believing they speak for the greater good of other people or the greater glory of their particular God. This, too, sounds familiar.

"No wonder humanity was in such a mess," the narrator in *Up from the Bottomless Pit* muses, "Out of every hundred beings, there were at least ten fools. No, make that at least twenty."

On this Ides of March in 2020, I stand balanced between optimism and pessimism, not only about current and future pandemics but also about global warming and other threats to life on Earth. The Ides of March comes from the Roman calendar and was celebrated as a day for settling debts. In 44 B.C.E., this was the date the Roman Emperor Julius Caesar was assassinated, changing the course of history. "Beware the Ides of March," wrote William Shakespeare in his *Tragedy of Julius Caesar*. "Beware our own foolishness," Philip José Farmer seems to be saying in the novel you are about to read and enjoy. In the end, my temperament leans toward optimism. Perhaps if we can truly imagine our foolishnesses, we will work harder to prevent them.

Sharman Apt Russell

ONE

"Don't blow your top," Malone's expression said.

James Cable knew that was good advice. But he'd been under high pressure for a long time. This conference was doing to him what a rotary drill did to cap rock. It was boring—in two senses. Irksome and useless. And cutting straight through his self-control to forces which had been waiting a long time to get out.

He gripped the edge of the table as if it were himself he was holding onto. In a way, it was.

"O.K. I'll say it again, though I shouldn't have to. The ruptures caused by the earthquake have been located. The flows have been capped. The new fast-drying slurry sealed them off quite effectively. It wasn't the drilling that caused the flows. It was a natural phenomenon, the quake. As a matter of fact, it was fortunate that the rig was on the spot. We stopped the flows that much sooner, and the spill didn't amount to much.

"There's really nothing for the good people of Santa Monica and Venice to worry about. Their beaches aren't going to be polluted. Not any more than they are now, anyway, and that's not Cal-Pax's fault.

"As for esthetic objections, what the hell. The platform is three and a half miles out. Once the drilling's done, the oil flowing—if there is any—the platform will move on. The pumps will be under-surface. Nobody can see them even if they sail over them.

"The geological setup is a freak. There are two deposits of oil, one shallow and relatively small. The cap rock over it is thin, and that's why the quake made fissures so easily. Deep down, about 20,000 or so feet, there seems to be another deposit. The cap rock over it is quite thick. But our experimental laser burner has gone through it like a knife through cherry pie."

He paused and managed a thin smile. "Well, that's an exaggeration. But laser drilling goes about five times as fast as conventional drilling. And core samples indicate that there may be a vast deposit under this double-domed cap rock."

"It's really not necessary to go into that all again, Jim," Malone said. "The point is, the one we should stress to the public, the point is that we have new blow-out preventers. The old ones were designed for pressures up to 10,000 pounds per square inch. They were more than adequate. The new BOPs can take 15,000 psi. And we're using two. No way can there be a blowout."

"We need more oil," Cable said. "And more. And more. Eight billion one hundred thousand barrels this year. Next year, more. The Arabs are threatening another embargo . . . the coal miners are going on strike . . . again. Well, why go over that again. Every second counts, and I'm being held up . . ."

"Too bad," Meisser said. "But this conference is absolutely necessary. Too much public pressure, and the ecofreaks have a clout out of all proportion to their numbers. If it hadn't been for that damned Alaskan quake, and the spill there, they wouldn't carry so much weight. But how can you predict an act of God? And then we have another quake off Santa Monica . . ."

"Everybody's punching the repeat button," Cable said. "Why can't we get a decision now? This minute?"

"I agree one hundred and one percent," Malone said. He was six foot six, fifty-four years old, and president of the West Coast branch of Cal-Pax Petroleum Products, Inc.

"I have work to do, too. And there's no doubt that this laser drilling is going to up production tremendously. Once we get going, expand, we might not even have to depend on foreign oil. We have all the oil we need here. Getting it is the problem. But we can drill five times faster now. We'll get that oil, and we'll show those damned camel-riders what's what!"

He looked at the faces around the table.

Thaddeus Meisser, liaison for the Department of Energy and Natural Resources. Six foot two, lean, long-faced, hook nosed, and tight-mouthed. About forty.

Dr. Randolph Feesher, Cal-Pax's top geologist. Tall, pudgy, double-chinned, blob-featured, wearing thick bifocals. About thirty-five.

Dr. Horning, the oil expert for the secretary of the DENR. A handsome black man of forty.

Warwick, the state of California's oil expert. Short and blocky. Fifty or so.

Georgeman, the Environmental Protection Agency's representative. Short, massive-headed and pipe smoking.

Near the table sat Mrs. Myrna Adkins. Malone's private secretary was taking shorthand notes since it had been agreed that the conference would not be taped. Mrs. Adkins was a tall handsome woman of about fifty. His father would have called her full-figured, Cable thought. She was a widow with a twenty-two year old daughter who was getting her M.A. in political science and Arabic at UCLA. There was much speculation about Malone's relationship with Adkins. His passion for the bottle and huge breasts was no secret. Cable, though thirty-four, considered this fifty-year old woman to be very attractive. So she had a few lines in her face.

Horning said, "Mr. Tengel,"—meaning the secretary of the DENR—"is very concerned about conservation."

You said that more than once, Cable thought.

"But conservation has to include more than preservation of the physical environment. It includes people, too, and people have to have jobs, have to have fuel to get to work, heat their homes, etc."

Get to the point, Cable thought. Everybody, by their expressions, was thinking the same. Though, come to think of it, this was the *real* point.

"There is a known supply of 190 billion barrels of crude oil in this country's outer continental shelf. Getting it out fast enough has always been the problem. This laser drill promises to do it, to make us much less dependent on the foreign oil-producers, anyway."

"So, from what Mr. Cable and Dr. Feesher tell us, I'd say that it's quite safe to drill there. Maybe we might have another quake and more faults might show up. But Cable did a good job of stopping the flows before they did too much damage."

"At a cost that Cal-Pax absorbed," Malone said.

"Which will be padded on to the consumer, unfortunately," Horning said. "And the consumer is raising hell about it now."

With the election coming up next year, Cable thought.

"But, all factors considered, we must have oil, must have independence. So, I'm going to decide right now, since time is of the essence, and I have authority from Mr. Tengel to speak for the department, that we go ahead with the drilling. Now. As of this moment."

"What about you, Dr. Warwick?" Malone said.

"There isn't any doubt about what the governor and the majority of state representatives think," Warwick said. "There'll be a lot of screaming from Senators Shink and Jones. But they don't carry enough weight. As for the ecofreaks, well, they can be ignored. What we need is some good propaganda. True propaganda, of course, no lies. But there's no need to lie. This decision is, all things considered, good for the nation. More than that. Urgently mandatory."

"O.K.!" Malone said, and he rose. "You all handle your end, and I'll see that Cal-Pax handles its end. We've got some damn good PR men, and the other industries'll put out some bulletins, too. They have as much interest in this as we. We'll work together. For one thing, we can say that when the laser drilling gets going, the price of petroleum will probably, *probably*, note, come down. That'll make a lot of people ignore the ecofreaks. Maybe they might get mad enough to bust up some of those picket lines."

"I'll call the secretary," Horning said, also rising.

Cable got the impression that Horning was going to confirm a predetermined decision. Tengel knew what was going to be said, what the outcome would be. But the ritual had to be performed. Meanwhile, he was wasting his time, everybody's time, because of the semi-magical quality of ceremony.

"What about Senator Caraman?" Meisser said.

"He'll make all the noises he thinks necessary for public consumption," Horning said. "But he's fully aware of the unemployment in the plastics industries in his state. They need oil, and we can promise them that. We can, can't we?" he added, turning to Cable.

"I think it's safe to say they'll be up to their asses in oil," Cable said. He grinned slightly. "That's language they'll understand. Too bad you can't use it in the news meetings."

He was to remember that statement for a long time to come.

Malone said, "What about a toast? Ordinarily, I don't drink during business hours"—Mrs. Adkins looked at him and lowered her head—"but this is a special occasion. You're eliminated, Jim, since you'll be getting back to work right away."

Cable didn't see the logic in this, but he didn't want a drink anyway.

The others nodded agreement, and Mrs. Adkins walked toward the concealed bar. A voice spoke over the intercom on the desk and she detoured to answer it. Malone went to the bar himself, opened the panel, and said, "What's your pleasure, gentlemen?" He looked very happy.

Adkins said, "Mr. Cable, you have a call. You want to take it outside?"

He said, "Thanks," and crossed the huge luxuriously furnished office and went through the door. Mrs. Adkins' secretary, an overly coiffured and dressed blonde said, "Over here, Mr. Cable."

His expectations that it would be from the rig left him unprepared when he heard the voice. "Lee?" He said sharply. "How'd you know I was here? And why . . . ?"

The voice was, when under control, a deep contralto. It was now shrill with incipient hysteria. It usually was when she talked to him.

"The TV said you were at the conference. I didn't want to disturb you, but I can't ever seem to get you at home. Where are you . . . ?"

"Working, mostly, damn it!" he said. "And you *are* disturbing me. What is it this time? Give it to me quick! I have to leave right away."

"It's the plumbing," she said, her voice shaking. "The toilet's backed up. And . . ."

Cable looked at Ms. James, who looked back down at the document on her desk. He spoke more softly.

"Call a plumber, for Christ's sake!"

"But you're always questioning the bills, and I don't know who's good and who's expensive, and . . ."

"We're not married anymore," he said. "You'll have to do things like that yourself. And there's no reason why you can't. Thirty years old, nothing to do except take alimony . . ."

"And take care of your daughter," she said. The hysteria had died a little; when she got angry, she became cool. For a while. Then the shrillness abruptly took over again, like a tablecloth snatched off a table by a magician. Why hadn't he married a woman who wasn't so childishly dependent? There must be millions who knew what to do, thousands who could probably fix the plumbing themselves.

"Call *X-spurt Plumbing*," he said. He regretted it at once. There he went again doing it for her when she had to learn for herself.

"You won't come out and fix it yourself? It's so much cheaper, that way."

"I should take time off . . ." He stopped. This could go on, if not forever, for hours.

"You're too transparent. Is the toilet working or is this just a way to get me out there? It's no use, Lee."

The phone clicked. He replaced the receiver. Ms. James smiled tightly at him. He hesitated, wondering if he should go back in to shake hands goodbye. Why waste the time? He started for the door and heard Malone's voice.

"Hey, Jim, you can't go yet!"

He turned, saying, "Why not?"

"I meant to tell you. You're supposed to go with a TV crew. WBC is going to film the operation, doing a documentary. The crew'll be here in a few minutes. They'll go with you on the company chopper. Come on back in. I changed my mind. A little booze won't hurt you. It'll settle your nerves. You look mad, like your shorts were on backwards."

"I don't have time to baby-sit that TV mob," Cable said, walking toward him.

"It's good publicity. They might even be on hand when you strike it," Malone said. "You don't have to give them a Cook's tour. Turn them over to your assistant, what's his name? Reynolds?"

"Yeah," Cable said.

He entered, deciding he'd have a small scotch after all. Taking it from Adkins, he walked to the window and looked out.

He didn't feel like small talk or shop talk either. What could he do about Lee? Being reasonable, being angry, hanging up on her, hadn't done any good. He couldn't get it through her head that they had nothing in common except Katie. He'd found that out shortly after their daughter was born. He and Lee had been attending the University of Texas when they had met and fallen in love. Lee was one of the most beautiful girls he'd ever seen; at thirty-two she still turned heads in a city full of striking women. Nor had she been helpless and moody then. Something had happened after Katherine was born. The doctors said it wasn't post-partum depression. But something had changed her character, something that must have been in her since childhood. She couldn't help it. On the other hand, continuing to live with her was wrecking both of them and destroying Katie. Not that the divorce was much better for Katie.

Across Wilshire Boulevard was Hancock Park. He looked down at the tar pit, the tiny relic of what had once covered much of this area ten thousand years ago. A dozen tourists were by the wire fence, rubbernecking the cement tableau inside. Two huge mastodons standing on the shore, a male and a baby. The baby's trunk was stretched out in soundless trumpeting for its mother. She was half-embedded, sunk in the dark watery liquid, helpless and hopeless, doomed to sink and strangle. She was like the hundreds and thousands of animals and birds that had been caught in the sticky but yielding bitumen pitch. A little further down the pit side, two cement saber-tooths snarled, longing to go after all that meat but aware that they, too, would be caught if they did. Later, after they had forgotten the danger, they might venture out on a part of the surface covered with fallen and blown vegetation. They would sink, too, and scientists ten millennia later would dredge up their bones and mount them in a museum.

Cable remembered when he had first come to work for Cal-Pax.

This building hadn't existed then; HQ for Cal-Pax had been in Santa Monica. Shortly afterward, the buildings on this block had been torn down and a forty-story monolithic structure covering the entire block had been erected. On his first visit to it, he had gone across the street to see the Museum of Los Angeles and to walk around the park. The bust of General Hancock didn't interest him much. The largest tar pit, which was only relatively large—it disappointed tourists who'd envisioned a lake—and the smaller ones were pitiful remnants of the once vast tarry swamp. But there were places on the lawn where the dark oil-odorous stuff oozed out.

It had seemed to him that the tar was just waiting for a chance to regain its ascendancy. A passing thought, and no doubt it occurred to most of the more imaginative visitors. However, this valley was founded on oil. The earth beneath Beverley Hills was being sucked dry by slant-drills and small pumps, looking like dinosaurs that couldn't get enough to drink, working beside children's playgrounds. More and more of these windowless steel buildings were going up. These attracted the questions of the tourists, who couldn't see how people could live in such viewless narrow apartments. They were surprised to find that these concealed pumping machinery.

At this height he couldn't see the pickets on the sidewalk unless he opened the window. And that couldn't be done in this tightly sealed air-conditioned building. They were being watched by the police, but there had been several minor turbulences in the past few days. The oil flows after the earthquake had brought them out in droves. Except when it had unseasonably rained two days ago.

He wouldn't have to go through the jeers and catcalls and the waving of signs. He'd be taking the company helicopter from the roof of the building.

Malone said, "Hey, Jim, you're not being polite!"

Cable turned. "Sorry."

Adkins ushered in a woman. She was almost six feet tall, slender, and looked about thirty. Her blonde hair was short, and though Cable preferred long hair on a woman, he thought the pixie cut looked good on her. She had the bones for it. Her jumpsuit, how-ever, would be dirty before she was long on the job. Her eyes were large and electric-blue, but she didn't look like any Kewpie doll. She looked tough and self-assured.

"Jim, come here," Malone said. Cable approached.

"Ms. Gill. Dorothy Gill. She's boss of the camera crew. Ms. Gill, our chief engineer, James Cable."

She held out a long slender hand with unpainted nails.

"Hello, Mr. Cable. I'm ready when you are."

Her voice was pleasant, though cool. This pleased Cable, who disliked the hail-darling-well-met phoniness of so many mass-media people he'd met.

Malone laughed and said, "There's a straight line if ever I saw it."

"It separates the sheep from the goats," she said. "Or the wolves."

Malone opened his mouth, an expression passed over his face, and he said, "Jim'll take care of your people, Ms. Gill." Cable saw what had happened. Adkins' look had warned her boss to watch his mouth. He put the drink down and said, "O.K. That's enough until quitting time, and that's a long way off. She's all yours, Jim. And that's not a straight line but an order."

"Mr. Malone seems to feel pretty good," she said.

"The word is *go* on the drilling," Cable said. "After you. Unless you're one of those who resent the old-time chivalry."

Her thick dark-brown eyebrows went up. "Whatever turns you on," she said emotionlessly. "I could care less. Anyway, we're not on a date." She smiled as if there was little likelihood of that.

Maybe she didn't like engineers, he thought.

She had turned and was going out of the door ahead of him. Slim hips. She probably had good legs under that baggy cloth. She wouldn't interest Malone. Her breasts were too small.

Cable shouldn't have been thinking such thoughts. He had a job to consume all his time and energy. But she certainly seemed to be the opposite of Lee.

TWO

Wells Martin, chief day shift cook, waited in the shack by the white circle reserved for choppers. For fourteen days he'd supervised and helped cook meals for twenty-five men. Sometimes, when the big shots or TV crews visited, for thirty or thirty-two. Soon he'd be handed his paycheck and he'd be off for six days to Los Angeles. His apartment on Orange Street would be waiting for him; it'd been cleaned up the day before by the woman who took irregular care of it. She was honest and had been trusted with a key by Martin for five months now. However, the last time he'd had off, he'd arrived to find his apartment as dirty as when he'd left it. And that was *dirty*. Tabitha had pleaded sickness, and he'd gone along with her, though he suspected the sickness could be diagnosed as a whiskey hangover. Not that she had ever touched his booze, but he'd smelled it once on her breath when he'd been home while she was cleaning.

Or maybe she had missed that day because she had found a new lover. She talked a lot during the few times he saw her; she'd confessed that she occasionally took in boy friends. She had three children, was on welfare, but augmented her income by cleaning. Uncle Sam, of course, never heard about this. Martin didn't blame her. He'd been on welfare a couple of times when he was married and knew that the monthly checks were just too small to do anything with. Except stay at home and slowly starve. Or eat bread and dog food, and even that was too expensive.

He looked at his watch. The chopper should land in about ten minutes. It might have been held up, though, since it was bringing in that hard nose Cable and a TV crew. The rumor was that the head of the crew was a woman, a good-looking but cold bird. Too bad he'd be off while they were filming; he'd sure like to see himself on TV. But maybe they'd still be shooting when he came back. He didn't really care. He wasn't going to stay here, trade off with another cook, just to get his picture taken. Not when he had three swingers lined up for tomorrow night. These promised to be first-rate Kansas City cuts. They weren't the usual fat asses and weirdoes you met by advertising in *The Free Press* or *The New Staff*. His buddy, John "Oscar" Wilde, knew them. He'd recommended them and had arranged by phone for them to party at his place. Oscar had sent photos of them through the mails. They were all beautiful. Two blonde AC/DCs and a curly redhead that Oscar said was a real stud.

Martin hummed the latest hit by The Pawnshop Balls. If only the chopper didn't get held up because Cable was held up by that conference. If it was, he was going to complain to the shop steward. He had a lot to do to get ready.

By him stood the forty-year-old fart named, believe it or not, Abel Baker. Martin wondered what Baker would say if he knew what was going on in his mind. Probably nothing. He was a family man with five kids, doing his best to add to the over-population problem. He was a good worker, but he didn't swear or talk dirty or drink or smoke. His wife, according to what Martin had heard, was a nag and a drag. She was the one who'd converted him to that freako cult, the Soldiers of Jehovah. It's been good for him, in a way, since he'd been on the road to the DTs and couldn't hold down a steady job. But, man, what a holier-than-thou the big prig was. And what did he have to look forward to on his days off? A skinny flat-chested broad with a mouth that never stopped, going to church twice on Sundays, spending his free time passing out pamphlets at the corner of Wilshire and MacArthur. Old Baker had shoved his literature and the Bibles on the workers, too, until they complained, and Cable and the steward had put a stop to it. The Bibles were mostly Gideons stolen from hotels and motels. Martin had said something to Baker about this once. But that didn't faze Baker. He'd said it was his Christian duty to get the Book into the hands of those who'd read it. Statistics showed that very few guests ever bothered to open the Gideons. So it was all right to steal them if they were personally placed in the hands of those who might read them. God wanted it that way.

Martin hummed, and Baker read his pocket Bible. The others waiting in the shack told dirty jokes, grabassed, or argued over the Rams and the Bears.

The roughnecks and Reynolds, day-shift engineer, were gathered around the drilling rig. They seemed to be excited about something. Maybe they were about to strike oil. Martin wasn't interested enough in the drilling part to know what was going on. He had enough to keep these big bellies happy with tender steak, mashed potatoes and gravy, and cherry pies. But it was impossible to work on a drilling platform and not absorb some knowledge about operations. He did know that this was experimental, that a laser beam was being used instead of the usual diamond-tipped rotary. The drilling had gone fast. It'd taken only two weeks to get 20,000 feet instead of the three months of conventional drilling. If there was any oil down there, it should be hit pretty soon. All this expensive work wasn't being done just to test out the laser, no matter what kind of bull the company was putting out. There was supposed to be both oil and natural gas down there. Seismic and core-drill exploration had indicated that. As if that wasn't enough, the quake had opened up a few faults here and proved that there was at least some oil under the cap rock. It might be little and low pressure. It might be a lot and high-pressure. The pressure didn't matter. There were two BOPs, blowout preventers, on the pipe where it entered the mucky sea bottom three hundred and sixty feet below. They were new, from what he'd heard, and each could take 5000 more psi than the best old ones. And the old 10,000 psi BOPs were supposed to be infallible. There just wasn't going to be any of the gushers you saw in the movies about oil drilling. The oil companies had made sure of that after the Santa Barbara Channel disaster of 1968 or was it 1969? Who cared what the date was? The only date he was interested in was he one in his pad two days from now.

"They're going to make a trip," Baker muttered. He was looking at the men working under the twenty-story high rig.

"Me, too," Martin said, and he laughed at Baker's puzzled expression.

He understood Baker's reference. "Making a trip" meant that the drilling was being stopped while the 90-foot long drill strings were removed. These had to be hauled out, uncoupled one by one, and stacked by a crane on racks. Then a new section would be added to increase the length of the drill strings. And the tedious time-consuming process of putting the strings together, one by one, would start.

Ordinarily, this had to be done whenever a core sample was to be taken, a drill-bit replaced, or another casing added. However, the laser drill did not wear out. It burned away the hardest rock as long as electricity was supplied through wires leading up to the generator on the platform.

Just now a core sample was to be taken, and so the strings were being hauled up. The laser burner would be taken off, and the core-sampler burner put on. This differed in that a number of small lasers ringed the corer. When it reached bottom, its lasers would burn out a cylinder of rock. The cylinder would still be attached to the rock at the base. But the lasers would then descend on the ring to the base, turn at right-angels, and sever the base. Extensions would slide out under the base, and the secured core would be drawn up to the surface.

Laser drilling was a strange operation, one which bothered the old-timers. They couldn't get used to the absence of the rotary table and the "kelly."

One thing hadn't changed. "Mud" still had to be pumped down the hole. This heavy gooey stuff was made of water, clay, and thickening chemical compounds. It was forced through the drill's stem, the hollow pipe attached to the burner, and up the well between the drill's stem and the laser-made hole. It controlled the pressure within the well, sealed the rock strata until steel casings were put in place, and supported the sides of the hole. In conventional wells, it carried the rock chips cut by the bit back to the surface.

Lasers burned all the rock, so there weren't any chips. Moreover, they burned the mud, too. So the laser worked on an automatic on-off system. It stopped every four seconds for two seconds to allow some mud to get by the beam. This process required about three times as much mud as the ordinary process. And that meant that the mud supply cost three times as much.

But, all in all, discounting the expense of the laser itself, the operation was far cheaper than usual. Smoother, too. There was no quivering of the platform caused by the powerful drive needed to spin four miles of steel pipe.

If there was oil down there, the four-mile high column of mud, weighing hundreds, maybe thousands of tons, would keep the oil from rising.

As if that wasn't enough, two BOPs were attached to the pipe at the sea bottom. The BOPs, Martin knew, had rubber rings inside them. Pressure from moving parts of the metal containers would close the openings with the rings if, by any chance, the oil did blow the mud out and come roaring up.

No chance of that. Automatic alarms would go on if the pressure suddenly became threatening. A man at the master control panel in a shack near the rig would punch a button. And two BOPs with a combined pressure of 30,000 psi would squeeze down like Uncle Sam on a tax dodger.

Everything had been considered; everything was safeguarded.

Martin chuckled. He was going to blow for sure this weekend. No BOPs for him. He didn't need safeguards. All he had to worry about was the siph and the clap, and so far he'd been lucky. Only had the clap twice. He didn't have to worry about one of the party being a sadist either. They were all gentlefolk; they didn't need a whip or a fist to get their kicks.

He whistled a bar from "Up Your Cosmic Creek, Geek," another of The Pawnshop Balls' hits. He stopped and said, "God's in his heaven and all's right with the world, heh, Baker?"

"What?" Baker said, blinking stupidly at Martin from behind thick glasses.

Martin repeated. Baker, scowling, said, "God's always in His heaven. But the Prince of Darkness holds this world tightly, young fellow. And he'll do so until the Soldiers of Jehovah bring light to the darkness."

Oh, oh! Martin thought. He said, "Forget I said that, Abel-Babel, old buddy. No sermons, now. I feel too good."

Abel's mouth tightened, he wouldn't say any more until he got off the copter port on top of the Cal-Pax building. Their pay was portal-to-portal, and his time off didn't start until he got off the chopper. He didn't want any more complaints to the steward.

Martin stepped out into the breeze and looked at the sunlit skies. The one o'clock sun flashed off of something to the west about a thousand feet up. That would be the chopper, and soon he would be departing with the others. He for Heavenly Come and old Baker for Kingdom Come, he thought. He chuckled again. Too bad he couldn't tell Baker that, but the old guy might take a swing at him. The SOJ claimed to be Christians, but they were as belligerent, and sometimes as violent, as old Samson among the Philisteins. Philisteens? What was the difference?

"Hey," somebody said. Martin turned. Everybody was looking at the roughnecks around the drill. They were excited about something. Reynolds was looking inside the door of the shack and was shouting something. The wind carried his words away from those in the shack.

"Geeze, maybe they struck it!" a roughneck named John Smith—would you believe it?—said.

Smith looked as happy as if he'd never seen a strike before. Strange about these roughnecks. They must be in love with their long slender drills. Old Freud could say something about that if he was still alive, Martin thought. Penetrating into old Mother Earth, really giving her the shaft. Love and hate, though the hate was more like greed. Why, Smith is actually slobbering. Look at them goggly eyes!

He felt the platform quiver under him.

"What the hell?" Smith said.

The faces by the drill were wide-eyed and pale, their mouths dark holes.

"Earthquake!" Martin said. "Jesus! Maybe this is the big one they predicted!"

"No! No!" Abel shouted. "It's . . ."

He did not get to finish whatever he meant to say.

No one did.

THREE

Alfred Chang, the cameraman, sat in the seat on the right of the pilot. His camera, a revolutionary design weighing only thirty pounds, minus film, was at his feet. The apparatus for carrying it on his shoulder was jackknifed beside the camera. Behind him sat Cable with Gill on his left. Behind them sat Chang's assistant, Grey, and Gill's assistant, Belmont. Of the twelve seats, only six were occupied.

Cable hadn't said much. He was occupied with the details of the work to be done and with a report to make. He hoped that Gill would think that he was silent because the noise made talking difficult. Apparently, she thought so or else had her own problems to consider. But when the rig became more than a vague triangle on the white-capped surface, she leaned over and shouted.

"Is that platform really as big as BP's *Sea Quest*?"

Cable's eyebrows rose. Evidently she had done some research or had some done for her. But of course she would. Very expensive TV crews didn't go blind into their assignments. For all he knew, she'd even studied the layout of the platform, all its functions, and had scheduled her work as if she were arranging a parade through Manhattan.

"No," he said, "it's somewhat smaller. The third largest, though. It's the semisubmersible type, floats on pontoons above the site to be drilled and then lets water into the pontoons. The pontoons sink to a depth of eighty feet, and the platform is then anchored. It's in three main parts, only has three legs . . ."

He stopped at her knowing grin.

"You're aware of all this?"

31

"Not of everything by any means," she said. "But I've read about a dozen books on offshore and deep sea drilling. And Cal-Pax's PR people gave me some bulletins on the *Dylan*. I was told that you'd cooperate in every way. But I was also told that you were a very busy man, and Reynolds—he's your second-in-command, isn't he?—would be my faithful guide. I'll try not to get in your way. Though, from the looks of you, you'd probably tell me quick enough if I did."

"I hope I don't look *that* grim," Cable said. He could feel the flush on his face.

"No. Not quite," she said, and she laughed.

"We will be following you around some," she said. "And be giving some of your background. It was necessary to get a biographical profile of you, of all the people of any importance there. We asked for a psychological profile, but the company refused without your permission. A matter of civil rights, I guess. No, I know. Apparently, you refused."

She was looking at him quizzically. He said, "I don't see it's anybody's business but mine. Not that there's anything damaging in it. If there had been, the company wouldn't have hired me."

"I'll bet you're a conservative Republican," she said. "Steady, a very hard worker, thrifty, and temperate in your habits."

"Right so far," he said, "though it wouldn't take a genius to deduce that."

He was definitely feeling uncomfortable.

"You look a lot like Charlton Heston."

"I look like James Cable. Are you planning on making me the leading man in your documentary?"

"Star of the stage, screen, and platform?" she said, and she laughed again.

Cable leaned over to look past the pilot and Chang at the instrument board. They had dropped five hundred feet. The *Dylan* was about three-quarters of a mile ahead. Its tender, looking small below by the side of the gigantic structure, rocked at anchor in a mild swell. It was too far yet to see the vague bulks of the submerged pontoons, but when the chopper was close, the two on this side would be huger than whales.

The platform itself was sixty feet above the surface.

The seas, gentle or violent, would not rock the giant platform. The waves raced below the floating rig, striking only the hollow pillars connected to the pontoons and the steel shaft which descended from its center into the water and to the bottom. And deep into the cap rock. And, he hoped, now close to the bonanza, the oil-bearing sedimentary rock. Though it might strike instead natural gas. Not if calculations were correct, it wouldn't. But luck played as much a part in this as science.

He had been afraid that oil would be struck while he was absent. Reynolds or any of the engineers were more than competent enough to bring it on in. But he wanted to be there when the "kill," he often thought of it as the "kill," happened. It was wildly exciting, even though he restrained himself from any show of exaggerated exuberance.

However, the pilot, who was in constant radio contact with the platform, would inform him if the strike was made before they got there. And in a few minutes he'd be getting out of the chopper, going down the steps into the big housing/cooking/supply quarters, out onto an open deck, across it to the building below the rig, up the exterior steps to the rig deck, and then to Reynolds. And it shouldn't be long before all this work was rewarded.

His anticipation was suddenly dulled. Would he have to take care of the WBC crew first? Yes, he would.

He leaned forward again and checked the altimeter. Three hundred feet. He leaned back. He didn't think he was especially introversive, but since his divorce he had been doing some inward looking. This monitoring of the chopper's instruments meant, he thought, that he was trying to exert some sort of pseudo control. He always wanted to be the master of the situation, in control. He couldn't be when he was in a chopper.

But watching the instruments was a sort of magic ritual. He was the pilot, if only vicariously.

The pilot, who had been talking into the mike, turned his head. He shouted something. Cable leaned forward again.

"Reynolds said to tell you they must've struck it! The pressure gauges are going up!"

"Oh, damn!" Cable said. "O.K. Get us down as fast as possible."

"I always do!" the pilot yelled. "But safety first!"

Dorothy Gill screamed in his ear.

"What in hell's wrong?" he shouted.

He looked at where she was pointing. Ahead, level with them, 90-foot stringers, sections of steel pipe, turned end over end.

Then they were gone. A grayish-black fluid was spreading out before the copter, gobs of it falling away from the main mass, strange shapes forming, dissolving as the wind carried them away.

These disappeared, their place taken by a thin pillar of straw-yellow liquid. At its top, just a little above the copter, it unfolded, fell back, became a golden spray.

Condensate, Cable thought automatically. But he didn't believe it.

The pilot worked his hands and feet as if he were dancing in a discotheque. The craft swung away, turned, tilted. At five hundred feet, Cable could look down and see the whole situation.

Five hundred feet!

Stringers and condensate had been blown by an inconceivable pressure half a thousand feet into the air.

Below, the base of the yellow glass shaft had suddenly become a green-black. And then the darkness mounted, like dirty mercury in a thermometer. The pillar was an iridescent green-black from bottom to top with some flickers of red, yellow, blue.

Abruptly, the pillar became a flying thing, collapsed, spread out.

It had been cut off—if only for a moment—at its base.

He couldn't see all that happened, but he could imagine, even in his numbness.

The pipe leading from the sea bottom to the platform must have been blown upward too. Incredible as that was, it had been expelled. The spout had then struck the underside of the platform, had been bounced off back onto itself and the sea. But only for a moment. That ravening force had begun breaking up the massive steel structure, striking the plates and girders as if it were a solid shaft of something harder than steel. Which, given its narrow diameter and its pressure at close range, it was.

What was left of the drill tower was toppling.

Then the ragged triangular structure of the platform itself broke in the middle. And the two parts turned inward, folding like the pages of a book put aside to be read no more.

Over it and around it, fallen oil spread.

There were no men visible on its top, none visible on the black rolling surface of the sea. They would all be dead, smashed or drowned.

The broken sections, turned on edge, sank. The gusher, now free, soared up again.

Droplets of oil appeared on the windows of the helicopter. The pilot cursed and took the craft up and away. Unable to see through the now thick film, he lowered the window by his side and looked out. His passengers cranked down their windows to see what they really didn't want to see.

Cable, for the first time, became aware of the odor of oil. He must have smelled it before this, but the demands of the eye had overridden those of the nose. Even at this height of eight hundred feet, the odor was heavy and sickening.

Cable could see the giant pontoons rising like slick black sharks. The upper edges of the platform sections disappeared, and the pontoons rolled belly-up. They began drifting southward, urged by the swift current of oil.

Gill had given one long scream. Now she was clutching Cable's arm with one hand. The knuckles of the other hand were in her mouth.

The tender? Where was the tender?

There it was, heading for the shore, its decks and hull completely covered, shining green-black, its wake white as its twin diesels worked at top speed. It was out of the oil-fall, and now it was curving around. It slowed, and men came out on deck, slipping on the liquid, and extended poles with white rags at their end to wipe the oil off the glass across the bridge. The commander, navigating blindly, by the feel in his sea legs, had gotten his ship away from the danger. Now she was hove to, prepared to render assistance. But there was no one to help.

The pilot twisted and handed the headset to Cable. "Malone."

"Jim! Is it true?" Malone bellowed in Cable's ears.

"It's the oilman's worst nightmare," Cable said, with an effort keeping his voice calm. "Worse than that. It's absolutely unprecedented. The pressure is unbelievable. It's going down a little now, sinking back slowly. But it was five hundred feet high, Mr. Malone. Five hundred above the sea surface, that is. Eight hundred and sixty, about, counting its thrust through the sea itself. From the seabed, I mean. I think, though I've no way of checking it, that the pipe from the bed to the platform was torn off, too. Torn off, Mr. Malone. The BOPs might as well have been made of cardboard."

There was a silence for a moment. Then Malone, speaking more softly, said, "The secretary of the DENR called me a few seconds ago. He'll be patched in with us. I want you to describe, as best you can, just what happened. And what's happening. How much oil is being spilled?"

"Just a minute," said a familiar voice. "Tengel speaking, Cable. I'm at the White House. The president is listening in to this. Is it true that the well is totally out of control?"

"As of the moment," Cable said. Then, "And for some time to come."

"About how much time?"

"It's too early to evaluate."

"I know," Tengel said impatiently. "What I want is an eyeball estimate."

Cable looked down again. He said, "Well, I'm just guessing, you know. But, based on what I see, I'd say that approximately one thousand one hundred and thirty or so barrels a second are coming out. Since a barrel is 42 U.S. gallons, that makes, let's see . . . 47,460 gallons a second."

"A second?"

Cable knew the question was rhetorical, but he said, "Yes. If this keeps up, and I don't see how it possibly could, but if it keeps up, the oil'll be pouring out at a rate of . . . let's see, wait a minute . . . 2,847,600 a minute. Which means that in an hour, 170,856,000 gallons will be in the sea!"

"Oh, my God!" Tengel said. Cable could hear a similar exclamation. From the president?

"Just a minute," Malone said. "Adkins is using the calculator. Here, Jesus! That's 4,100,544,000 gallons in twenty-four hours! Over four billion! That's incredible, impossible! Jim, you sure that you're not so excited you're exaggerating?"

"It's possible," Cable said coolly. "It's only a guess. But even if I should be off a billion, which isn't likely, well, the magnitude . . ."

"Just a minute," Tengel said. "My secretary is calculating the output for the year. Oh, here. Oh, my God! It's 1,496,573,560,000! Almost a trillion and a half gallons! But that can't possibly continue at the same rate! No well has ever come close to that. So—I think we can assume that the flow will diminish very soon. But even so, we've got a catastrophe on our hands. The *Santa Barbara* spill is nothing beside this, nothing!"

Tengel breathed in deeply and then said, "What're the chances of capping it, Cable? How soon, I mean?"

Tengel was a knowledgeable man. He had not worked for the oil industry, one of the reasons he was picked for the position of secretary of the DENR. No conflict of interest. But he knew the history of the petroleum technology and for a layman was well acquainted with its technology. Thus, he knew the answer. But he could not keep from asking.

"We don't *have* the means to cap it," Cable said. "Not now, anyway. We'll have to think of something new."

There was a strangled sound, and Malone said, "Cable!"

Cable didn't reply. Malone could protest all he wanted. He knew the truth as well as Cable, and there was nothing to be gained by optimistic statements. If Malone wanted to make them, he could do so. But he'd make a fool of himself. And of his company.

He looked at Chang. Chang had been filming the platform as the copter approached, and he must have caught everything from the beginning. His films could be studied later, but it'd be locking the garage door after the car was stolen.

Dorothy Gill was pale and her eyes were wide, but she no longer seemed stunned. She was speaking in a low voice into a pocket recorder held close to her mouth as she looked out the window. He wondered briefly what her thoughts were. This would be the biggest scoop in her life. Johnny, or Joan, on the spot. What she didn't know, probably, was that her films would be confiscated on landing. Tengel would want to see them first before he allowed them to be shown. There'd be screams from WBC, from every news media in the country. Not that it would do them any good. The secretary wouldn't want the country sent into a panic. Though how he . . . oh, well, why should he bother about that? He had, Cal-Pax had, a job to do. But could the company do it alone?

He felt something in him grow cold. Cal-Pax couldn't do this alone. Just the cost of cleaning up, if the well stopped flowing at this very second, would bankrupt the company. It had lost about a hundred million dollars in labor and equipment when the *Dylan* was destroyed, and this was a bagatelle compared to what it would have to spend. And all those men . . .

They were now a thousand feet up and half a mile away, upwind, and he could still smell the strong odor.

"Hey, Jim, you still there?" Malone bellowed in his ear.

"Here," Cable said. He looked northward. The gray shape of a Coast Guard cutter was approaching from the east. And several dots above it must be helicopters. They'd hold Coast Guard personnel, government officials, and TV reporters.

"How high's the spout now?"

"Still going down. About three hundred feet high now. I'd estimate that it'll be level with the surface in about twenty minutes. If it keeps subsiding."

"That's something, anyway," Tengel said. "Has the oil drifted enough so you can give me an extrapolation? I mean, where will it touch shore first? How soon?"

"The current's about two and a half knots, from the last report I heard," Cable said. "The oil's spreading, of course, but I don't think it's going to spread to the beaches of Santa Monica. It'll come in at or near Venice. And the smell's strong, sir. Very strong. It's not up to me, of course. But I'd advise that the beaches be cleared. I mean, the houses along the shores, too."

"Cable!" Malone said. "That's not your concern! The company can't be held responsible for that statement, Mr. Tengel . . ."

"The civil authorities will be advised, if you're worrying about passing the buck," Tengel said coldly. "Mr. Cable, what will be the effect of the oil? Inland, I mean?"

"The winds are from the ocean this time of year," Cable said. He was aware that Gill was watching him now. She was still speaking into the recorder, probably repeating his words. "The oil is being carried shoreward. It's sort of a right-angle triangle now, the apex being the gusher itself, of course. The isosceles is extending straight toward Venice now. But it won't be a triangle long. Despite the wind, the oil is also spreading outwards, seawards. And the isosceles is bending, bulging. At the rate the oil is spreading, I'd say that in about four hours the oil will first hit the beach. At somewhere around Venice Boulevard. But I'm only eyeballing it, of course."

"Is the stuff highly inflammable?" Tengel said.

"I don't know how much natural gas it contains," Cable said. "But I wouldn't take a chance until we can make some tests. Core samples indicate a high gas content. I sure as hell would clear all cars off for a distance of about half a mile inland. And shut down any factories, home fires, you know, stoves and so forth, within a half mile. Get any navy craft out of the harbors. Make sure no private craft operate anywhere near the oil. Until we know for sure."

Tengel was silent for about three seconds. Then, "Of course. Very well. We're in contact with the mayor of Los Angeles, the other mayors, too, and the governor of California. We'll get going on that right away. But it'll be a hell of a job . . ."

His voice faded. Probably he was speaking over another transceiver. He wasn't going to waste time telling Cable what he already knew.

"Jim," Malone said. "Stay there as long as the fuel holds out. Get down as close as possible and study the situation. Keep up a running report. When you've got everything, get back here. This is a hell of a bad situation, Jim. It'll look bad for the company, though God knows we took every possible precaution. But you know how the public is about the oil industry. They want more and more oil, and we try to give it to them, but if anything goes wrong, then they scream. And there's been too much talk about nationalizing us."

"I'll give a running report," Cable said. "We've got gas for about two more hours. Oh, by the way, did you tell Tengel that we have a TV crew aboard? They've been filming this from the start."

"Jesus, I forgot!" Malone said. "O.K. I'll tell him."

"Never mind. I heard that," Tengel said. "I'll have men at the landing port—it's on top of the Cal-Pax building, isn't it?—to pick up the films."

"One more thing. Ah, I don't want this repeated to anyone unless he's authorized to hear it. But . . . could the BOPs have failed because of sabotage?"

"*Sab . . . !*"

Cable looked at Gill, who was listening intently. She couldn't hear Tengel, of course, but she could learn much from what Cable said.

"No!" he said. "At least, I don't see how it could be. Look, I can't speak openly just now. You understand? But I'd say no. That pressure is natural even if it's a freak. No. No human intervention caused that. Except for the drilling itself, of course."

"The drilling," Tengel said. "There you are. But how would anyone have known? Never mind that for now. I'm hanging up now, Cable."

Cable removed the headset. Dorothy Gill said, "Hey, what was that about my films?"

"The DENR wants to see them as soon as possible."

"I suppose it does," she said. "But they'll have to wait. These have to be rushed to the studio. Do you realize WBC has the only complete pictures from beginning to end?"

Cable didn't say anything. Why argue about it now? The DENR would pick up the films as soon as the chopper landed. He had more important things to consider than her reactions. Even if she looked as if she wasn't one to give up without a knock-them-down-drag-out fight.

"It's a real Glory Hole, isn't it?" she said.

"That's as good a name as any."

FOUR

A t four A.M. Cable parked his car in the garage beneath his apartment building. The Hanover Arms had been built two years ago in West Hollywood. Its tenants, with much justice, referred to it as The Hangover Arms. Most of them were young, single, and given to staying up until late hours. The building's walls were too thin and the occupants too noisy for Cable. But he spent so little time in it that he had not yet been forced to look for a quieter place.

He was so tired that he briefly went to sleep in the elevator on the way up to the sixth floor. He was too weary to resent the music blaring three apartments from his. While he fumbled with the key, a door down the hall opened, and a woman stepped out. Somebody closed the door behind her. She reeled toward him, stopped on seeing him unlock his door, and said, "Say, aren't you Jim Cable?"

He looked up. "Yes, what about it?"

"Shaw-saw you on TV," she said. "I din't realize I was living so close to a sh-celebrity. Is it really as bad as you said it was?"

The telephone in his room began ringing. Cable paused. If that was Malone or reporters . . . He might just go back to his car to sleep.

The woman came close. Her eyes were red, and she breathed gin. At another time he might have paid more attention to her.

She was wearing a semitransparent gown, had nothing on beneath, and one breast was bare. Not bad to look at even with her messed-up hair and glazed eyes. Though that was all he'd have done, look, even if she had made a pass at him. She must be loaded with sperm and, statistically, probably with gonorrhea. Unless she was one of the lesbians that had lately begun moving in.

"It's bad," he said, stepped in, shut the door, locked it, and shot three bolts. The woman beat on the door. "Let me in! I want to talk to you, get the straight stuff! It's scary, you know!"

"Go to sleep. Read about it in the morning!"

He picked up the phone. "Cable speaking."

"Jim! I've been calling you all day. I did what you told me to, I didn't call your office. But I've been out of my mind ever since I saw the five o'clock news. That blowout happened just before you landed on the platform, didn't it? My God, what if you'd been a few minutes earlier!"

"I wasn't," he said. "Listen, Lee, I'm dog-tired. I've been talking to the reporters and the company's officials and the DENR secretary, the president, too, and about fifty Cal-Pax people. I have to get to bed right now. I'm supposed to be back at Cal-Pax at eight with another long, long day staring me in the face. So . . ."

"I'm not doing this for me," she said. "It's for Katie. She's scared too. She says that if the oil keeps on going, the whole Pacific'll be covered. And there won't be any air for us to breathe. She's only a kid, but she knows more about this ecology stuff than I do, and . . ."

"I'll talk to her when I get a chance," he said. "Oh, by the way, our trip to Catalina Island Saturday'll have to be cancelled. I don't know when I'll see her next. But she'll understand."

"*I* don't!" she said. "You see little enough of your daughter as it is. And she *is* your daughter, despite your nasty insinuations. She's going to be tremendously disappointed . . ."

"Damn it, Lee!" he said. "She'll know why I can't take her. It's you that doesn't understand. You don't want to. You just want me to come over and pick her up so you can get a chance to dig at me about coming back to you. You put Katie up to talking to me about it, too, and it spoils our whole time together. You don't really care about her, you just want to use her as a weapon against me."

There was silence. Lee's voice, when it came, was rising. "You're a cold cruel man, James Cable! I don't know what I ever saw in you! You've got a slide rule for a heart and an IBM computer for a brain!

I'm going crazy with loneliness and you don't give a damn! Your daughter's going crazy, and you could care less!"

Cable held the receiver away from his ear. There was nothing he could say that would put sense into her. She could, and would, go on for hours like this. Maybe, though, if he scared her enough, she'd quit.

"Listen to me, Lee!" he shouted. "I have no time for personal problems! If I, we, don't cap that hole, there won't be any personal problems for you or me or Katie! Or for anybody, understand! We'll all be dead! Katie was right, but I'll bet she didn't go into hysterics about it! Now, listen to me good! I'll call you and I'll see Katie whenever it becomes humanly possible! Meanwhile, I'm going to be working day and night to stop this oil flow! So, don't bug me any more unless it's really an emergency, a desperate one, and I don't mean something like what plumber do you call! Understand! Goodbye!"

He slammed the phone down, started for the bedroom, stopped, and waited for the phone to ring again. It did, as he had known it would. She'd keep ringing until he answered it.

His anger cooling off somewhat, he began to feel guilt. Harshness was necessary; it was the only thing that would make her leave him alone for a while. Nevertheless, he always experienced some irrational feelings of regret and guilt. Or if not guilt, shame. Whatever it was the psychologists talked about. He didn't remember the distinction between guilt and shame. What difference did it make? He didn't like what he was feeling. If only she'd accept the inevitable. What kind of a woman was she to take his abuse, his dislike of her, and still try to get him back? If only she'd meet some man who'd fall in love with her. But that man would have to be staggering blind not to realize in a short time how clinging, how dependent, how nearly psychotic she was. She couldn't help it, something had twisted inside her, changed her after Katie was born. But she wouldn't go to a psychiatrist, even though he'd offered to pay for the treatment. She insisted that he was the one who needed therapy, not her.

He strode to the wall, unjacked the cord, and the phone stopped ringing. He wouldn't, however, put it past her to take a taxi out to see him. She'd done it once, two months ago. And there had been a scene he could not recall without cringing. The neighbors had called the police, and for a while it had looked as if they'd both be taken down to the station. She had finally agreed to go home, and he'd had to talk to the manager to keep from getting thrown out. Not that he really cared, since he intended to leave sometime anyway. He had done some complaining about the noisiness of the tenants himself. But the manager had only said that he knew this was a place for swingers when he moved in. He had no right to bitch.

Cable took a small alarm clock out of a drawer and carried it down to his car. He crawled in, locked the doors, since burglars had broken into the cars several times, cracked open the front window, and set the alarm. He fell asleep at once, wakening sluggishly when the clock rang. In his apartment, he shaved, showered, and put on a business suit. He turned on the 24-hour news channel to watch during the bacon and scrambled eggs, toast with butter and cherry jelly, an apple, and two mugs of black coffee. The program had been on for ten minutes and was still going on when he left. Its single subject was the Glory Hole, credit for the phrase being given to Ms. Gill. He saw himself again in the anteroom of Malone's office, answering a barrage of questions from the reporters. Though Gill's films had been taken into custody as she got off the copter, they had been released two hours later. An Air Force jet with a copy aboard had taken off for Washington while WBC was showing its film to a stunned world. Tengel had wanted to suppress the film until he had studied it, but he had bent before the storm of protest from the news media.

"According to word just received, Robert Tengel, the secretary of the DENR, is discussing with the president the setting up of a new federal bureau, as yet unnamed. More details on this later, though it's obvious that the bureau will have one goal. That is the capping of the Glory Hole. And now for an interview with Mr. Alfred Malone, president of Cal-Pax Petroleum Products."

Cable went into the bathroom, coming out just as Malone's red face faded from the screen. He turned the set off and left for the Cal-Pax Building.

On the way, the car radio informed him that the oil was washing along the beach from one block north of the end of Venice Boulevard and south to the projection of land along which the Palos Verdes Drive ran. This was about a quarter of a mile from a point opposite the marine land of the Pacific. It had covered about twenty-five miles of beach, and only a heavy rain of an hour and a half had kept the fumes from spreading for a while over the entire area of Los Angeles. Cable could smell the sickening odor now, overriding even the exhaust fumes he normally would have smelled with the window open.

According to the radio, the oil stream was at its widest off of Redondo Beach. The weather satellite showed a breadth of twenty-five miles. Cable swore. Twenty-five miles across! Of solid oil!

The gusher was gone, a fact Cable already knew. It had subsided about one o'clock in the morning. Now only a heavy bubbling was evident. The latest estimates had it that about 850 gallons a second had been flowing steadily since then.

Cable made a quick calculation. That would be 51,000 gallons a minute. So, in an hour, 3,060,000 gallons. In a twenty-four hour period, 73,440,000 gallons. During the first twelve hours, there had been about 48,816,000 gallons poured out onto the ocean. Add the approximately 21,360,000 gallons since then. That made 70,176,000 gallons now covering the sea off Los Angeles.

And there was no sign that it was slowing down.

According to the reports he'd heard before he went to bed, and was hearing now, there had been plenty of panic along the beach. The radio and TV stations had gone onto an emergency status and were warning the people on the shores to get out. *At once.* The police and fire departments of the whole metropolitan area had moved every man available to make the evacuation as swift as possible. The Civil Defense personnel had been summoned to help. National Guardsmen had moved in. Citizens had been awakened by loudspeakers on vans and by knocks on their doors. Main arteries: Venice, Washington, Culver, Lincoln, Century, Imperial had been cleared of traffic for the refugees. Later, the boulevards and main streets south of these as far as Long Beach had been taken over. For a quarter of a mile inland, not the half-mile originally ordered, the inhabitants had been roused.

There were those who refused to leave, there always were. Like it or not, they were forced to go. Those who put up a struggle were arrested and taken off in police cars and vans. The invalids and those who had no cars, old people mostly, were put into trucks and vans or assigned to private cars which had room for them.

The giant Marina del Rey south of Washington Street was cleared. This ran inland, curving up north from its outlet to the ocean. Those who wanted to take their boats and go south before the oil stream reached the outlet, were allowed to do so.

Radio, TV, and loudspeakers on vans warned that no smoking was permitted. The danger of fire from natural gas and other evaporatives blowing onto land was not thought to be high. Or at least it was not admitted that it was. But there was no use taking chances.

At this time, ten minutes after eight, it was believed that all inside the quarter-mile beach area had gotten out. Even those who had evaded the police and the National Guard had been driven out by the sickening odor. Now, all those within a half-mile of the beaches were voluntarily leaving. This was adding to the traffic problem; the Santa Monica and San Diego freeways were jammed. Warnings had been issued to people normally using them to stay home if it was at all possible or use the alternate routes of the city streets. Thousands had ignored this with the expected result.

Among these were an uncertain number of sightseers and would-be looters. Reports of looting and vandalism came in from the police and firemen. This was heaviest along the Marina, which was populated by those wealthy enough to afford yachts. The police had orders not to shoot unless fired upon because of the danger of igniting the gases. Several incidents occurred where the police and looters exchanged shots, but the gas was too tenuous—at this time— to be flammable. Two policemen were killed, five wounded, and seven looters had been slain. About thirty had been caught; it was estimated that sixty had been chased but had escaped. One National Guardsman was accidentally wounded by his sergeant.

An incident which was played up by the news media was to become even greater in significance in the not too distant future.

Two policemen in a patrol car came upon four men rowing a

boat in the marina. Warned to get out immediately, the men obeyed. Suspicious, the policemen questioned them and then frisked them. They brought from their pockets automatic pistols, .38's and .45's, and some religious pamphlets. These had been published by the SOJ, the Soldiers of Jehovah. The SOJ was well known by now, though in the first few years of existence it had not attracted much attention. Generally, they were considered as just one more of the many lunatic cults that infested southern California. But they were not Johnny-come-latelies. Their history went back to the early nineteenth-century. At that time a wave of belief in the end of the world swept through western Christianity. Its main strength was in the rural Protestant areas and especially in the United States. A man named Miller had attracted thousands to his preachings, and when the day predicted by him for the world to end came, thousands gathered on mountaintops or high hills to witness the fiery judgments. Nothing happened. But the prophet, instead of being discredited, got his followers to believe that he had merely mistaken the date. Several years later, they collected on the high places to wait for the skies to roll up like a scroll and death and damnation for the unbelievers to descend. Again, nothing happened. The prophet died, but his successor said that the date was somewhat in the future.

Though many dropped away, the original organization flourished, continuing to attract others. The Testifiers of Jehovah grew in rural areas and among the strongly fundamentalist in the cities. Like the Mormons, they were zealots dedicated to missionary work. In 1960, they numbered two million in North America and an equal number abroad. It was in this year that the cult began spreading the word that the world would end in 1975, and on this they based their faith. As 1975 approached, they increased their zeal. Their faithful spent most of their spare time proselytizing, passing out literature on street corners and going from door-to-door. They got considerable publicity at the end of 1975, much of which was derisive but which also brought at least two hundred thousand converts. The predictions of Judgment Day were not quite as specific as those previously made. All that would be admitted was that, sometime in 1975, the earth would surely perish, the dead would all be given new bodies, and those who had the true faith would inherit heaven, which was actually old earth reconstructed into a paradise. The evil resurrectees would all go to hell forever. The Testifiers, unlike most Christian sects, did not believe in spirits. A dead man was a dead man, and he would know nothing until the day God gave him a new body and sent him to dwell with the sheep or the goats.

They were also extremely militant, believing that violence was morally justified if done in the name of God and of the Testifiers. Evil was a vile thing to be crushed no matter what the means used.

January 1, 1976 arrived. The world was, as usual, in a mess, but the Day had not come. The Testifiers had stuck their collective neck out and it had been chopped off. At least, that was the assumption. Surely, the sect would now disintegrate.

A majority did quit the organization, but there were diehards who insisted that God had only put off the Day. He had expected more from His soldiers; He had expected them to help bring about the Day through militancy. Instead, they had sat by, waiting for Him to do everything. And so He had humiliated them, discredited them. His faithful must prove they were His Righteous Soldiers by action against the Enemy, not by a show of prayers and passing around of pamphlets. If necessary, and it was, they must become martyrs in His name. They must testify truly with deeds.

And so the Soldiers of Jehovah was born. Their leader was Miller Breck, a veteran of Viet Nam, widower, father of seven children, owner of a small publishing firm, a radio station, and a string of self-service laundries. He was also, for a while, mayor of the Tennessee town in which his publishing house and radio station were located. He attracted worldwide attention when he announced, during a broadcast sermon, that communists, socialists, and left-wing terrorists should be slain on sight. Moreover, atomic warfare was to be prayed for, since this would bring about the Last Days.

The SOJ was on the lists of the FBI as a subversive organization. It was suspected that it was responsible for the killing of a number of young terrorists, of hardened criminals, and of the man who had run for president on the communist ticket. What chagrined the FBI was that the SOJ had succeeded in locating subversives and criminals who had eluded the FBI. They were further embarrassed when the house in which a group of Mafia dons was meeting was blown up. The FBI had the conference under close surveillance, yet the killers had slipped in and out under their noses.

Some arrests of SOJ members had been made, but these had been released because of lack of evidence.

Most of the public, though not in sympathy with the theology of the SOJ, approved of their aims and methods. After all, they were only murdering murderers.

Much of this approval was lost when the FBI did succeed in identifying an Army general in a critical position as a secret member of the SOJ. He was in command of a number of ICBMs in a Western state, and though he could not independently give an order to launch the missiles, he was a very dangerous security risk. He was hastily but quietly retired instead of being brought to trial. A newsman discovered this and published the information despite efforts made to suppress his report.

The publicity forced the federal government to prosecute, and the general was fined and sentenced. The jail term, however, was suspended, it being thought that the loss of his pension benefits and the disgrace were enough punishment. Two months later, he disappeared, apparently into some underground station of the SOJ. This could not be proved, of course, and there was some speculation that he might even have been killed by his organization because he knew too much.

The police who collared the four suspects knew all of this. They called in for a backup car and started to manacle the four men. Two men stepped out of a nearby house and shot the policemen. The six eluded pursuit, but a search was made in the marina near the spot where the boat had been. The drag brought up a large bomb loaded with thermite floating a few feet below the surface. It was enclosed in bags which could be inflated by a mechanism activated by sonar. And it contained a detonating mechanism which could be set off by radio. It was obvious that the bomb was to be raised and exploded after the marina was filled with oil.

Cable, hearing this, shuddered. Samples of the oil analyzed early this morning showed that its natural gas content was extremely high. A bomb such as the SOJ had planted ought to start a fire that would sweep over the entire stream if weather conditions were right. A jet airplane falling onto it, a flash of lightning could do just as well. He didn't know why the authorities were keeping this from the public. Perhaps they were afraid that the information might attract more psychotics than could be handled.

FIVE

Stepping into Malone's office, Cable was surprised to see Dorothy Gill. He was also pleased, which made him wonder why. She was good to look at but somewhat cool and a little too tough for his tastes.

Or was she?

She seemed to know what he was thinking. "I'm assigned permanently to Project Glory Hole," she said. "Sheer luck, being Joanie-on-the-spot. I became famous overnight, and so the BOC appointed me as official photographer/recorder of the project. My boss at WBC cried a lot, but he agreed to give me my old job back when this is finished. The other networks are raising hell. They claim favoritism, but they don't have a leg to stand on. I'm not working for WBC, and only an employee of BOC is permitted to film the goings-on of the inner sanctum. So, here I am!"

She gave him a completely warm smile.

"Congratulations," he said. "I'm completely confused. Just what is BOC?"

Malone, approaching, heard him. "History was made while you slept, Jim. BOC stands for the Bureau of Crises. The president announced it this morning. Didn't you hear of it . . . of course you didn't. Haw, haw! Listen," taking Cable's elbow and guiding him toward the conference table—"here's a good one. Tengel was going to name it the Bureau of Technological Crises and Hiatuses. He can be a windy bastard, you know. Then someone pointed out what the initials would be. BOTCH, haw, haw!"

51

"I hope that's not a bad omen," Cable said.

"For an engineer, you're pretty superstitious," Malone said. "Take that seat there, next to Mr. Meisser."

Malone looked as if he hadn't been to bed at all, but he was vigorous enough. He leaned against the table with his opened palms and said, "Ladies and gentlemen. We're all here, so the quicker we get started the better."

He went on, "Most of you know what's going on, but for the benefit of those who don't, like Jim here, I'll fill you in. The Bureau of Crises is only a few hours old, but its top organization has been fixed, and a chart of responsibility levels is being made with all due haste. Congress, as you know, is being called back from its Christmas holiday. It'll ram through legislation right now, making the BOC legal and funding it. Tengel is going to give them the facts; he'll lay it on them that it has to be a survive-or-else program, no holds barred.

"There isn't time to wait until a new organization is all set up. So the president and Tengel and the Ways and Means committee, and God knows who else, sat up last night at the White House. They decided to make use of the facilities on the spot. So, Cal-Pax—its California offshore facilities anyway—is being commandeered, requisitioned. As of three this morning, Cal-Pax is part of the bureau. There's been a cry for nationalizing the petroleum industries, you know, and Cal-Pax thought maybe this was the first step. But the president has promised there won't be any of that. The BOC is just using Cal-Pax on an emergency basis. When the crisis is over, Cal-Pax will revert to normal operations. Of course, we have interests all over the world, and we can't stop supplying oil and gas to the public. But the western branch will be dedicated to capping the Glory Hole.

"We have been promised the full cooperation of all military services, especially the Navy. I'm a reservist, rank of commodore, and I'll be serving as such. In addition to my position as president of Western Operations. But I won't be wearing the uniform, no need for that."

Cable wondered what financial arrangements had been made. It was likely that Cal-Pax wouldn't be charged any bill for the cleaning up. In return for this, Cal-Pax had donated its southern California equipment and personnel to the BOC. It didn't have much choice. The expense of cleaning up the oil would bankrupt even that financial colossus. It would, in fact, bankrupt the entire oil industry.

It also gave Cal-Pax a chance to look like a hero, a savior, instead of the devil incarnate, the company responsible for causing the Glory Hole to come into existence.

"I'm chief of operations here," Malone said, smiling as if he very much liked the idea. "I'm directly responsible to Renzel, the newly appointed chief of the BOC. You know Renzel, Jim. You and he were classmates at UCLA."

"More than that," Cable said, smiling. "We were roommates for a while. Look, things have gone too fast. I go to bed an employee of Cal-Pax, and a few hours later I find that there is no Cal-Pax. Not on the coast, anyway. So, what am I?"

Malone said, "For once they got off their asses in Washington. It took less than an hour to get the broad outlines of the reorganization settled. And you were made chief engineer of Project Glory Hole. There are others equally qualified, but you were Johnny-on-the-spot. And Renzel and I agreed that you should be in charge. Your salary will be raised about six thousand a year, and the fringe benefits will be proportionately increased. For the time being anyway. It'll take time for Cal-Pax to integrate as part of a government bureau. So congratulations."

"Thanks," Cable said. "I was afraid I'd be made the scapegoat since I was in charge of the operation."

"Not so far," Malone said hurriedly. "O.K. More rundown.

"Mr. Meisser, Mr. Tengel's liaison man here, will continue in that capacity.

"Ms. Gill here will film this project for posterity. She's on Cal-Pax's—I mean, the BOC's payroll—as of now. She's promised to get in the way as little as possible. But I expect full cooperation from everybody in regard to her."

"Just a minute," Meisser said. His hawkish face looked grave. "You neglected to mention an important item. I'm in charge of security of operations. From now on no statements for the public, no photographs or films or anything of that nature, will be issued from here until I've passed on them."

"Yeah, I forgot that," Malone said. "Sorry, Mr. Meisser."

"I'm directly responsible to the president, not the secretary of the DENR or the head of the BOC," Meisser said. "I was told there'd be no passing of the buck to anyone but him. So, you can expect a tight control. The president himself told me that he's very much concerned about a nationwide panic. There's a beginning of one right now, but it's strongest in this area. The Midwest and the east are apprehensive, but most people there don't think of themselves as being directly affected. The president wants to keep them thinking that . . ."

Cable said, "Look, Mr. Meisser. And the rest of you. All this political-legal activity is interesting. But couldn't we talk about it some other time? The only important thing is to cap the Hole. I do need to get squared away on my position, what I can and cannot do so I can know the limits of my work. But . . ."

"I don't like being interrupted," Meisser said.

Doctor Feesher, at the other side of the table, said, "Pardon me, Mr. Meisser, but the business of the world has been gravely interrupted. And if it's not resumed soon, if the Hole isn't capped or controlled, the interruption will be permanent."

"That's just the type of statement I don't want issued for the public," Meisser said, his voice rising. He looked up at Gill and Chang. She was standing by the cameraman, who was pointing the shoulder-supported camera at Meisser. "I want the film of this meeting, or any records you're making, handed over to me when we're through."

"I was expecting to do just that, Mr. Meisser," Dorothy Gill said. She sounded as if she hated the thought.

"Good. As for you, Doctor Feesher, I may as well tell you that we would just as soon you weren't assigned to this project."

Feesher rose, saying, "What?"

"Sit down, Doctor. There's nothing personal in this. It's a matter of security."

Feesher remained standing. "What are you talking about? I've been cleared by the company for top security, and I was also cleared for that when I worked on a government project on loan."

"I know all that," Meisser said. "That and much more about you. I know, for instance, that your parents were Testifiers! You were raised in that faith, and your younger brother is a member of the SOJ."

Feesher, his face red and twitching, sat down. He took out a handkerchief and began mopping his face. "What about it? I quit the church when I graduated from college. I was never a member of the SOJ. Aside from my brother, I don't know any of them. And I haven't seen him, heard from him, for years. He despises me."

"Or appears to," Meisser said.

The others around the table looked stunned. Malone opened his mouth several times as if to say something but each time closed it.

"If you think I'm not trustworthy, then get rid of me," Feesher said. "But I'll take this to the courts. I won't be blackballed when I'm innocent."

"That won't be necessary," Meisser said. "Though you would find that you couldn't get your case into court at this time. Nor get any publicity about it. The situation isn't quite what it was, Feesher. Yesterday, it was thought that the gusher was the result of an accident. But now, well, there's some suspicion that perhaps the SOJ might have been responsible. The blow-out preventers should have clamped off any pressure . . ."

"Not if it was over 30,000 psi," Cable said. "And it obviously was much more than that."

"I've been assured by other experts that such a pressure is unprecedented. It was even stated that it's impossible. We've been investigating the possibility that a bomb destroyed the BOPs. Also, that explosives might have been hidden at weak points on the platform. How else do you account for the gusher rising so high in its initial stage or for the platform, a massive construction with steel plates on its under parts, collapsing under the impact of what was, after all, only liquid?"

"Hell, man," Cable said. "You can drill a hole through steel with water if the pressure's strong enough and the jet is narrow enough."

"Hardly likely in this case, though," Meisser said. "What's more, explosives could have been placed on the pontoons, too."

"You saw the films," Feesher cried. "There was no evidence of explosives on the platform itself. You'd have seen the smoke."

"With all that oil spray flying around?" Meisser said.

"How would anybody get down to the BOPs at a depth of three hundred and fifty feet?" Cable said. "The surface is under observation at all times; the crews work around the clock. The approach would have to be made underwater by a sub. And I don't see anybody working at that depth unless he had a metal diving suit or a bell. There are very few of those, and I'll bet every one is accounted for."

"They are," Meisser said. "But do you remember reading about the theft of the Shell *Mobot* four months ago? From the offshore facilities in Oregon? Shell expected to get a ransom note, but they didn't."

Cable remembered reading about it. The *Mobot* was a self-propelled device, remotely controlled, used for both underwater exploration and specimen collecting. It had even been used to make underwater repairs.

"That pressure was natural," Cable said. "There's no known technology which could make the oil come out of a well at that pressure. None whatsoever."

"No known technology," Meisser said so smugly that Cable wanted to hit him. "Perhaps the SOJ stole plans or devices that some oil company was keeping a secret. And the theft wasn't reported. Or the scientist working on it might have passed on the information. His company would know nothing about it."

Cable restrained himself from calling Meisser a paranoiac.

"There's evidence that the SOJ might, I say might, be involved," Meisser said. "After all, there were three SOJ members working on the platform."

"Three?" Cable and Malone said at the same time.

Cable continued, "I knew about Baker. Who were the others?"

"I'm not authorized to tell their names, even here. But neither were down on the company records, or on any official record, as being SOJs. Baker was killed, you know, and so may not even have known about the others. They weren't present, they were off-duty. The . . . the authorities went to pick them up this morning, early, but they had disappeared. Looks pretty suspicious, doesn't it?"

"Not necessarily," Cable said. "Once the discovery of that bomb in the marina was announced, any SOJ with sense would make himself scarce."

"You seem to be making a lot of excuses for them," Meisser said.

"Hell, man, I'm an engineer. I try to be logical."

"We're wasting time," Malone said loudly. "Is it or isn't it O.K. for Feesher to continue working for us? He's a damn good man, Mr. Meisser, one of the best geophysicists in the world. I'd hate to lose him. Especially now."

"That's been taken into account," Meisser said. "I just want Feesher to be aware that we're aware of his past."

Then why didn't you tell him privately instead of humiliating him? Cable thought. Besides using up precious minutes.

"I may resign," Feesher said.

"Come on, doctor," Malone said. "Forget your personal feelings. The country needs you, you know that. The whole world needs you. Would you resign if we were at war?"

"If we were, Meisser'd have me in a concentration camp," Feesher said. "He's acting as if this were right after Pearl Harbor and I was a nisei."

"That's uncalled for," Meisser said. "And totally incorrect. I am not being hysterical."

"The first step is so obvious we've all agreed on it," Cable said. "We'll set up another platform, just north of the Hole, and drill a number of new holes. Hopefully, that'll relieve the pressure, and much oil can be drawn off from the deposit. We'll have to wait until the new lasers I ordered have arrived. That'll be three weeks, maybe more. So we'll use conventional means until then. Floating barges have been pulled out of the Santa Barbara Channel; they should be here in two days. Once they get going, they'll take about 90 days to drill 30,000 feet. So, the lasers will get here pretty late for that phase of the project.

"Last night, this morning, rather, we seemed to think that my floating pipeline idea was the best. But we didn't agree. I'm still in favor of it, and I think we should take a vote on it right now. And then get started immediately. I'll get started, anyway. The rest of you can talk over whatever there is to talk about. I want to take action within the next few minutes. Every second we talk, 850 gallons is added to that mess."

Doctor Georgeman, the EPA representative, spoke for the first time. "If you can build this pipe assembly, and if it works, how long will it take before you start pumping? And how much of the oil can you divert?"

"I don't know," Cable said. "It'd take about four months under ordinary conditions just to draw up the blueprints. That is, it would if we were going to build a floating pipeline from scratch. But I want to use parts and components that exist, if possible. Requisition them from anywhere and everywhere, and get top priority on their transportation, too. And engineers, draftsmen, labor, materials. Which means we can't use conventional means to get them. Hiring people, for instance, can't go at the usual pace. We need an overnight hiring program. Ads in the newspapers and on TV all over the country. Canada, too. The parts that we can't get second-hand will have to be made. Pressure should be, let me say, must be, put on the industries making the new parts.

"And then there's the space we'll need for the base. Someone suggested taking over the Will Rogers Beach and State Park. The state of California might be willing, even if it means wrecking it."

"That's what I was getting at!" Georgeman exploded. "You're going to ruin something that Nature took thousands of years to make! Ruin it in a few days!"

The others looked startled or disgusted. He said, "Just a minute! I know the urgency of this, I know that there's a much bigger issue at stake than a few square miles of forest and beach! But the ecology-minded are going to be out in full force! They'll be picketing you, bringing pressure to bear on Congress!"

"Let them," Meisser said grimly. "We'll roust them out so swiftly their heads'll swim! And their asses will cool off a long time in jail!"

Cable ignored him, saying, "Doctor Georgeman, what's all this concern about a small state park? You should be worrying about what the oil's doing to the ocean."

"I am!" Georgeman said. "Maybe I got off on the wrong foot. I was trying to save the Will Rogers area, and I feel justified in doing so. You need as short a pipeline as possible, don't you? You picked the park area as a base only because you couldn't get any closer. The optimum site for the base is a point directly opposite the Hole. On the shoreline of Santa Monica, say by the terminus of the Santa Monica Freeway. But you don't have room there because of the office buildings and hotels that front Ocean Park Drive. I say, use the right of public domain and let the federal government seize the area it needs. Tear the buildings down, level it off."

A few minutes of silence ticked off. The men looked at each other. Cable said slowly, "I thought I was thinking pretty big. But not big enough. That's exactly what should be done. The demolition could be done during the preliminary stages before the materials get there. I also recommend that the buildings along the leveled area be commandeered. They can house the office and field workers."

"You're crazy!" Warwick, the governor's representative, said. "Man, you got any idea of the uproar that'll cause, the money it'll cost! The lawsuits, and God knows what else?"

"The Glory Hole overrides everything!" Cable said. "I thought that everybody in this room completely understood that!"

"There's plenty of precedent!" Malone bellowed. "When Los Angeles wants space for a freeway, it takes over what it needs."

"Yes, but always through the houses in which the poor live," Dorothy Gill said. The others looked startled when she spoke, and she seemed surprised herself. "You never heard of a freeway going through Beverly Hills? Or Bel-Air, did you?"

"You forget yourself, Ms. Gill," Malone said. "You're here just to document the project. You weren't invited to participate actively."

He smiled as he said this. He was always conscious of public relations. Cable supposed he'd forgotten that Gill no longer worked for the network. Or perhaps he remembered but the habit was ruling him. Or maybe he had plans for getting Gill into his bed.

"I'm sorry," she said. "It won't happen again. But . . ."

"But nothing," Cable said. "Your remark was irrelevant to the situation. O.K.! Mr. Malone, can you get immediate action from Tengel? Or Renzel? From whoever has the final word? We need an area in Santa Monica for our base. Can you get this area condemned? By tomorrow, say?"

"Tomorrow!" Malone said.

"Today would be better."

"I'll see what can be done," Malone said. "But I can hear the screams now. We'll be accused of being Fascists or Communists. So, how much area do you need?"

"Including the space for the equipment and the workers' housing, I'd say a square of eight-tenths of a mile. The north side would be Santa Monica Boulevard; the south, Bicknell and Grant streets. It'll have to be off-limits to everybody except project workers, anyway. We can also use the municipal pier and the yacht club facilities for a while, though they'll have to go before the project is halfway through."

"Millions!" Malone said, and he leaned forward and put his face between his hands.

Cable rose. "Millions, billions, what's the difference? It's time that counts. I want to make a quick survey of the Santa Monica area. How soon can I get a chopper?"

"Right now," Malone said. "It's on standby on the roof. I got one for you this morning; it's for your personal use."

Georgeman said, "Could I go along with you?"

Cable nodded. Gill said, "Mr. Malone, is this conference to continue?"

"Yes. I don't know for how long."

"Well, I have another cameraman downstairs. I'd like to go with Mr. Cable. Chang can stay here and shoot you."

Malone grinned and said, "I feel like I'm half-shot already. Go ahead, Ms. Gill."

SIX

The Cal-Pax Building was about eight and a half miles northeast from the point at which the oil stream first touched Venice. Even so, standing on top of the building, Cable could smell oil. As the copter, flying at a thousand feet altitude, neared the beach, the odor seemed to become geometrically heavier. And arithmetically more sickening. The craft was headed for mid-Venice, since Cable wanted to get a view of the situation there first. The cameraman, Henry Grey, was not taking pictures yet. This area had been filmed yesterday and this morning. He was to shoot only when Gill thought there was something new.

The sky was unclouded. The late morning sun sparkled on the ocean except for the greenish-black triangle spreading out from the Glory Hole. Actually, it was a triangle by courtesy only. It was slowly becoming a lop-sided circle; the western side extended out beyond sight at a point opposite the Los Angeles International Airport. The beach south of Venice Boulevard formed the east border of the sinister-looking stream. North of it the oil had thinned enough to be emulsified by the seawater. Globules floated on it, and the beaches south of the city border of Santa Monica were blackish. A strong wind in this area would carry oil spray inland for blocks.

Cable located the section designated for clearing by the long municipal pier of Santa Monica and the freeway. If he could have his way, the bulldozers and the giant cranes with their battering balls and the dynamite squads would be marching on that area now. But, no matter what the urgency, the city authorities of Santa Monica and the federal and state authorities had to have a conference, and the legal obstacles had to be cleared away. The people in the hotels and the office buildings and the residences must be given notice. They had to determine where they were going and then arrange to have their possessions moved. Normally, this would take months or even a year. There wasn't time for this. If an atomic bomb warning had been given, they would have been forced to get out at a minute's notice. This crisis was just as deadly, or could be as deadly, as an attack. Getting the people to accept that was a different matter. They wouldn't, or couldn't, equate the two.

The chopper sped past the intersection of the San Diego and Santa Monica freeways. Cable, on the left-hand side, could see the enormous marina. Its broad base curved northward in from the sea, forming a figure that looked like a strangely shaped key. There were five huge teeth pointing Pacific-ward and three slanting northerly on the landward side. Ordinarily, the docks would have been jammed with thousands of craft from yachts to speedboats to sailing boats. But the blue waters were black now, and only about a dozen craft remained, coated with wind-blown oil spray. Their owners had not been available, and they would not be allowed to take them out now. Those that had gotten out had been forced to go south along the coast. But they wouldn't find safe harbor for long. Relentlessly, the oil was moving along the coasts, and the vessels would have to keep moving at least as far as the southern tip of the Mexican peninsula of Baja California. The small sailing craft, of course, could be put on trailers and carried inland. If trailers could be obtained. The demand for them exceeded the supply.

At Cable's orders, the pilot took the helicopter directly over the marina. At its mouth it turned northwest toward the Hole. George-man, leaning over to him, said, "There are thousands of dead seabirds so far. On the sea and on the beach. The seabird life along the entire coast will be killed before this is done. As for the fish . . ."

Cable nodded. The oil was cutting off both the sunlight and the oxygen over a constantly expanding area. Even if the oil flow could be cut off and a quick cleanup made, the fishing industry off Los Angeles was ruined for years to come. Maybe decades.

"The gray whales seemed to have just escaped the oil," Perune said. "But when they migrate north again, they'll get caught. Unless . . ."

He didn't seem to think that the *unless* would happen. Cable thought about the great gray whales, which migrated in winter from the Arctic to the Gulf of Baja California. Would they all perish when they ran into the oil stream in the spring? Probably. But if the Glory Hole was still going by then, whales would be the least of mankind's worries.

Over the Hole, at a thousand feet, Cable saw the tiny shapes of two floating platforms in the north. The tugs pulling them were almost indistinguishable. Others were following them and would be in position in a few days.

The Hole itself was still bubbling. According to a sonic probe, the well pressure was such that a gusher tore through the heavier seawater, dissipating only when it reached a height of three hundred feet above the bottom. Moreover, at distances of between a hundred and six hundred feet, oil was spurting from cracks in the sea floor. Their exact number had not been determined, but there were over a score.

Most of these flows were from fissures which Cable had cemented over after the earthquake. Evidently, the pressure from the deeper deposit had forced oil through the upper strata in vertical and horizontal movements. The upper deposits, pushed by the inflowing oil, were leaking out from the edges of the slurry caps. Possibly, they had even lifted the caps and carried them downstream.

North of the Hole, Coast Guard cutters and a large oceanographic survey ship were moving slowly. One cutter was heading for a large white yacht. Cable assumed that the yacht belonged to someone ignoring the warnings against private craft in this area. Rubbernecks were not confined to the land.

Georgeman gripped his arm and pointed to the west. "Clouds!" he said. "The weather reports say we'll have a storm along the coast by tonight."

Cable worked until two the next morning in the office assigned to him. It had begun raining heavily at eleven but it had stopped at one. During that time, thunder had boomed and lightning cracked. Each time a flash illumined the area, he jumped. He could not help visualizing all that electrical energy striking again and again the volatiles and the natural gas from the crude oil. He expected at any time to get a phone call telling him that the oil had been ignited. By the time he quit, the phone had rung at least thirty times. Each time, however, the caller was in Washington or Pittsburgh or Texas or Chicago, an industry executive telling him what he could or could not do to carry out his orders. The final call was from one of the platforms he had seen that afternoon. The storm had broken the tug cable, and the platform had been driven ashore. Though there was no loss of life, the platform would be out of action for at least a month.

With a long sigh of relief, he looked out the window. The night sky was heavy, but the rain seemed to be over. There was only a feeble flash in the northeast, a low defiant growl of thunder as the storm's fury died. The wind and the heavy downpour had combined to dissipate the vapors. If there had been any flames, they had been quenched immediately.

The wind had died, too, which meant that for a while the gases had been washed away and the Los Angelenos could breathe fresh air.

Next to his large office was a small one which had been equipped with a cot, a TV set, a refrigerator, and a camp stove. He entered it, locked the door, and was in bed and asleep in ten minutes. This would be his home for a long time; he did not want to waste time driving to and from his apartment.

SEVEN

Another advantage of the Cal-Pax residence was that Lee's calls had to go through a switchboard. Its operators had orders not to put her through to him. They would pass on her messages, allowing him to call her back if he had time or inclination. He seldom had either. However, he did want to talk to Katie. So, though he could not afford the time, he returned one out of about twenty of Lee's calls.

Except for one conversation, they were all the same. Two weeks after the Glory Hole had burst onto the world, he got lucky. Or at least he thought he was when Katie answered the phone.

"Hi, Katie," he said. "This is a pleasant surprise. The first time I've heard your voice in a month. Why haven't you talked to me the other times?"

Lee had always said that Katie wasn't home, but he had not believed it.

"Mother said you didn't want to talk to me," Katie said coldly. "She's not home; she went out shopping. I wouldn't go with her because I have too much homework."

"She lied then," he said. "I've asked for you every time. Haven't you heard her say you weren't home? And if you did, why'd you let her get away with it?"

"Because I didn't know she'd been talking to you. Mother had the phone moved into her bedroom. She keeps it on low, and since she spends most of her evenings in here, she's the only one that hears it."

"If you wouldn't play your records so high, you might hear it, too."

"Am I supposed to not listen to them so I can hear the phone? How *often* do you call?"

He paused, then said, "Not often. You know I'm very busy, Katie. If your mother didn't tell you that, the papers and the TV must have."

"You were *always* busy."

"That's true," he said slowly. "But we did have some good times now and then. I took you to the beach or the mountains whenever I could, and movies and museums, too. I can't now; you have to understand that."

"Mother says nobody could be that busy. You just don't love me. She says you probably spend all your free time with a woman."

"Damn it! I don't have any free time! And I haven't had a date for over a month now!"

"Mother says you don't have to have dates. You live in a swinger's commune. All you have to do is go next door."

One of the extension-line lights on his phone began flashing. He said, "I'm expecting a call from Washington. I have to hang up now. And I am sorry, Katie, really sorry, that things are going this way. One thing, though. Has your mother said anything to you about moving? Out of L.A., I mean?"

"No," she said. "Why should she?"

"I told her that you two should get out. As soon as possible. Why didn't she tell you?"

"I don't know," Katie said. "Maybe she thought you were trying to get rid of us entirely. Why should we move?"

"Doesn't that oil smell bother you?" he said.

"Sure it does. But why should we move just because of that. We can stand it. It's not too bad in Westwood. No worse than the smog, anyway. Well, not much worse. But why should we move, Daddy?"

"I can't tell you," he said. "But just take my word for it. You're better off somewhere else. Say, San Francisco, for instance. There's nothing to stop you. Your mother doesn't work. I'm supporting her."

He looked at the light again.

"Why should I leave all my friends and go to a strange place?"

"Because I love you. I don't want . . . Well, I must say goodbye, Katie."

"Go to hell," Katie said. The phone clicked.

Surprised, Cable held the receiver to his ear for a few seconds. Another click sounded just before he punched the flashing button.

The call was not from the Bureau of Crises. It was Doctor Georgeman.

"Hello, Jim. Just called to tell you that the Air Force will begin dropping the first load of Pseudomonas at seven sharp."

"Thanks," Cable said. "I won't be on hand to watch it. Too much paperwork here, plus another conference with the bigwigs. Listen, I'm expecting Renzel to call. Talk to you some other time. Sorry about that."

"I understand," Georgeman said. "I should have a report to you in about four days on how the bacteria is doing."

Cable wanted to discuss the Pseudomonas, but he said so long and hung up. Some years before, 1973, if he remembered correctly, Israeli scientists had announced development of an oil-eating bacterium. These could consume oleic substances but died in crude oil. Since then experiments in American universities and in some petroleum company laboratories had produced an improved mutation. The latest and most effective strain was said to eat crude oil like wildfire under certain conditions. This was an exaggeration, but it would increase a colony of 10,000 per milliliter to 20,000,000 within forty-eight hours. If conditions were optimum that is. The warmer the weather, the nearer it approached its maximum rate of growth. Since the vast black spot on the blue waters was itself a heat sink, the bacteria would be in a hospitable environment even if it was wintertime. They thrived especially during the hot noon hours.

A fleet of low flying bombers of all sizes had begun dropping thin-shelled cases filled with the oil-eating bacterium. These broke open on impact, scattering platelets of the bacteria. The airplanes returned to load up with more. Naval and Air Force planes at Hawaii also flew out, and two carriers cruised along the edge of the southern extension of the stream. Their craft dropped the "bombs" in around-the-clock warfare.

Meanwhile, more bacteria were ferried into bases near the California coast and to the islands. A horde of small planes were rented by the government to augment the attack, and these were engaged to drop the OEB in the area of the Hole itself. The Mexican Air Force, using bacteria flown by airliners to Ensenada, joined in. Mexico was in a panic, though the North Equatorial Current off the tip of the peninsula was carrying the oil westward across the Pacific. However, a certain amount was bound to get caught in currents taking it up the Gulf of California and then along the western shores of Mexico. As of the moment, the stream had reached a point about 125 miles down the west coast of Baja California.

The heat-sink action was causing all sorts of "crazy weather." The deserts of the Mexican peninsula, which had not had a drop of rain for years, were twice deluged in six days. Meteorologists estimated that more rain had fallen on that area than in the last two hundred years. Los Angeles, on the other hand, was treated to a week of unseasonable Santa Anas, dry hot winds blowing in from the inland deserts.

Mexico was, by now, not the only country in a panic.

"Here's why," Doctor Steans, the BOC oceanographer said during the conference held on the third week. "The North Equatorial Current will take the oil in a broad stream hundreds of miles wide to Hawaii. It'll keep going and when it gets to the Caroline Islands area, a good part of it will be carried into the Micronesian Islands seas. Eventually, some of it will be washing up against the shores of New Guinea. Another part will curve northward and surround the Philippine Islands. It'll keep going, carried by the current, and eventually will be in the China Sea, the Yellow Sea, and then the Japan Sea. There are countercurrents off the eastern shores of the Japanese Islands, but in time the oil will surround Japan. It'll keep going, be taken eastward, drift across the North Pacific. Then part will be taken westward along the south coast of Alaska; the other will be caught by the California Current. You'll have a complete circle formed, then, oil flowing from the north joining its source at the Glory Hole.

"It'll take some time to get up the Bering Sea because of strong south-flowing currents from the polar seas. But it will do so eventually.

When that happens, the ice there is going to melt very fast. There won't be as much ice to melt when the oil gets there because the heat sink is already raising the global temperature. Not by much, by only two-tenths of a degree Fahrenheit. But on a worldwide basis that's a lot. You can imagine what the temperature will be when the oil has girdled the Pacific. By then there may be no ice in the Arctic and not much left in the Antarctic."

Feesher said, "How much will the sea level rise?"

"Anywhere from two to three hundred feet. Or maybe more."

"Well, at least we don't have to worry about an ice age," Malone said. His smile was slight, and nobody laughed.

"How long before the circuit is completed?" Cable said.

"I really can't say. You see, the presence of the oil itself is going to affect the ocean currents and the winds. Just how they'll be changed is beyond my present knowledge. The problem is being worked on at Harvard. They're using computers, of course. But the situation changes so much from day to day, the flow is so uneven in different areas, and we can't predict, extrapolate I should say, can't extrapolate well under the shifting conditions."

"Yes, but given present conditions, say, at the known rate of speed of currents as they are, how long?" Cable said.

"Perhaps three years. Maybe four. I don't like to say. By then, of course, the fish life in the entire North Pacific, and much of it in the South Seas, will be dead. You know what that will mean to those nations that depend to a large extent on sea fish for their diet. However, that means little compared to another, and much quicker, form of starvation.

"I refer to oxygen starvation. The world's supply is mainly dependent upon plants, converters of carbon dioxide to oxygen. Apparently, a certain amount is manufactured by still mysterious processes in the stratosphere. But not enough. At least seventy percent of our oxygen comes from plants in the ocean. I refer to the phytoplankton, microscopic plants which exist in all the oceans.

"With the Pacific largely covered, about one-fifth of our oxygen factory, if I may call it that, shuts down. How long do you think you could survive with a fifth less oxygen? However, before that event occurs, you'll be choking to death on the oil fumes. You can't retreat to the high mountains because the oxygen content of the air will be much less there. Besides . . . need I go on?"

Malone jumped up, saying, "Jesus Christ, man! That well can't flow forever! It has to run dry sometime! Soon! The flow has been slowing; it's down to eight hundred gallons a second now! If we get lucky, it may slow down so much we won't have much trouble, not an unsurpassable amount of trouble, anyway, capping it!"

"I devoutly hope so," Steans said.

Cable rose, wondering if he looked as pale and as drawn as the others. He felt as if he did.

"I don't mind being summoned to discuss technical problems directly connected with my job," he said. "But I don't want to attend any more meetings to discuss those which are irrelevant to my job. They waste my time. So, unless you have something relevant to tell or ask me, I'll get back to work."

"Jim's an engineer, not a scientist, a philosopher, or a politician," Malone said to the others. "He may take a narrow view, but in his case it's the only one to take. He's got enough to do without talking about the end of the world. As far as he's concerned, that's idle chatter. Right, Jim?"

"Right," Cable said. "Now can I go? No, one more thing. I suggest, insist in fact, that when these meetings are held, anything relevant to my job be brought up first. I'll leave as soon as my part of the conference is over."

"Sure thing," Malone said. "You can take off now. But I want to talk to you for just a minute. Outside."

Malone called a halt when they were far enough away from the office personnel not to be heard.

"Jim," Malone said. "You look like hell. You need a rest."

"I could use one," Cable said. "So could you. So what? We don't have time, and you know it."

"Never mind me," Malone said. "I know my limits. I work hard but I get my rest by playing hard. A little bonded bourbon and a good piece of ass refreshes me more than twelve hours' sleep. But you don't play, you just work until you fall into bed like a punch-drunk boxer down for the count. What good are you to anybody if you get a heart attack or an ulcer? Why don't you take at least a day off, drink some booze, get laid. Jacobs can fill in for you; he's a damned good man."

"Wouldn't do any good," Cable said. "I couldn't stop thinking about the job."

"Yeah? Well, Jim, you're going to get a thorough checkup by a doctor. Right now. I got the company quack, Doctor Williamson, waiting in his office for you."

"I don't want to waste my time."

"Your needle's stuck in the groove. You don't have a choice. I'm ordering you, Jim."

"And if I refuse?"

"Don't bristle at me. I'm your boss. I'll lay you off for a week if you don't obey. I can do it, Jim."

"Eight hundred gallons a second!"

"You know where the doc's office is. Get moving."

"Son of a bitch," Cable said, but he moved.

EIGHT

Do you get dizzy or light-headed at times?" Doctor Williamson said. "Feel your heart beating hard when it shouldn't be?"

"No to the first and yes to the second," Cable said.

"When was the last time you had eight hours' sleep?"

"I don't know," Cable said. "A few years ago, I think."

"Malone tells me you haven't taken a vacation for the last two years."

Williamson sat down behind the desk and church-steepled his fingers. He was about fifty, a short slightly built man with a long ascetic face. His brown hair was brushed over his forehead à la Hitler, but his mustache was as thick and long as a British brigadier general's. The eyes behind the rimless spectacles were pale blue.

"You were in Alaska," he said. "Up near Prudhoe Bay. You asked to be assigned there right after your divorce. Twice you refused to take the three weeks off that was your rightful due. You pleaded that you were too vital for the job. In other words, indispensable. I find you an extremely interesting phenomenon. Unique, I might say. I never met an indispensable man before."

Cable felt himself flushing.

"I could do without the sarcasm."

"Do you have any plans for getting married again? Are you engaged?"

"That's none of your business," Cable said. "What the hell is this? Are you a psychiatrist?"

"I went through two years of analysis," Williamson said. "I was on the receiving end, and I don't have a degree in psychotherapy. But I know a hell of a lot about the human psyche. Any doctor who doesn't isn't worth his salt. Unfortunately, many of my colleagues don't. Tell me, are you a homosexual?"

Cable was startled. He said, "That wouldn't be any of your business either. No, I'm not. What does that have to do with this?"

Williamson chuckled and said, "Just trying to figure out why you drive yourself so hard you don't have time or energy for getting into bed with a woman. A lot of executives are in overdrive because they're suppressed homosexuals. They don't know it, of course. They'd be horrified if they were told that."

"Knock it off," Cable said. "You're barking up the wrong tree."

"No, I'm just shaking a few branches so I can find out what kind of fruit the tree bears. No pun intended."

Cable decided that under different circumstances he might like Williamson. He'd make a good companion.

"Sex isn't everything."

"No, but it's a big part of everything. Listen, did you know that there was an article in the recent *Journal of Psychotherapy and Psychology* about a man who had an orgasm when he saw the Glory Hole blowing while watching TV?"

"What's that got to do with me?"

"Nothing, directly, though it has a lot to do with all of us indirectly. The journal also recorded some years ago the case of a woman who had to read chemical formulae before she could get sexually excited. When the husband wanted to go to bed with her, she'd first go through a half-page of her dead father's reference book. He was a chemist, of course. What really turned her on was the formula for testosterone. Strangely, the simplified diagram of it showing the molecular structure did nothing for her."

"Well?" Cable said.

"Chemical formulae was, for her, a stimulus. Drilling for oil is for you a sublimation. That long hard pipe screwing into Mother Earth."

Cable laughed long and uproariously. Williamson waited for him to finish, and he said, "How long since you had a good hard laugh?"

"It seems like a long time."

"Feel better?"

"Much."

"Good. Now for a note of seriousness, unfortunately. Your father died when he was about your age. In a hospital for the insane. Of syphilis of the brain. Your mother divorced him shortly before he went into the hospital."

"Did you get this from the company files?" Cable said.

"There is no such thing as privacy anymore. Never mind where I got the data. You didn't tell the company about your father, so how could they know? And when you went to work in Alaska, you did take a weekend off, flew down to Anchorage, and came back to your base with a case of gonorrhea."

Cable felt his face getting red again.

"You didn't get the clap off a whore," Williamson said. "You got it from a state senator's daughter you met when you were invited to dinner at the senator's house. Nice clean girl, Phi Beta Kappa, and all that. Since then you've probably, I'm only surmising, since no one but you knows, you've probably only had occasional sexual intercourse. You haven't thought about why you haven't, but I'll bet that you have a deep unconscious worry about venereal disease. And a fear of going mad from it."

Cable stared for a moment, then said, "Do you really think that's why I work so hard? Really?"

"I don't know. It could be. Ask yourself. Did you divorce your wife for adultery? Was it not so much for unfaithfulness, your generation is pretty broad-minded about that, but because you were afraid she might catch something and pass it on to you?"

Cable stood up. He felt heated but it was from anger, not embarrassment.

"If you're as wrong about your previous diagnoses as you were about my wife, then you're full of shit."

"Aren't we all?" Williamson said calmly. "Well, it doesn't matter. I am right about your physical condition. Even a first-year medical student could tell you're close to collapse from exhaustion. Malone says he'll enforce any recommendation I make for you. I'd like to give you a month off, but neither he nor you would accept that. But I am going to recommend three days off. And don't say no. Malone won't let you into the building until the three days are up."

"O.K." Cable said. "But only because it's logical. If I did fall apart, I'd be off the job a lot longer than three days, right?"

"Correct. Don't forget I have to give you a clean bill of health before you can return. I'll be here at seven in the morning three days from now."

Cable stepped out of the office. Dorothy Gill was coming down the hall toward him, Chang and his camera behind her. She was wearing a tight-fitting blouse and short skirt, both white, gold yellow pantyhose, and high heels. Her breasts looked fuller than they did in the loose jumper suit.

Cable thought, what am I doing, trying to prove something to myself and Williamson?

Perhaps he was. But she was very attractive, and though she had been standoffish, she might be as a matter of policy. No mixing of business with pleasure for her.

There was only one way to find out. He said hello to her hello, and seeing she was not going to stop, said, "Just a minute, Dorothy."

She stopped. "Dorothy?"

"We've been together too long to be formal," he said, smiling. "Especially since I'm asking you if you'd care to have dinner with me tonight."

"You won't be working?" she said. Then, "Stupid of me to say that. But you shook me up. Yes, I'd like that very much. If we won't talk shop, I'm sick of that. And if you'll promise not to fall asleep. You look as if you're about to pass out right now."

He smiled and said, "I'm going to get some shuteye this afternoon. What about seven-thirty? At the Scandia? Or wherever you prefer?"

"There's a French restaurant on Sunset, rather a small place but with delicious food and wines."

"Should I pick you up?"

"Why not? I'm a women's libber, but I'm also a woman."

"What's your address and phone number?"

"I live in an apartment building on 8th," she said. "Only a few blocks from here. Here. I'll write it out for you. Did you want the phone number in case you changed your mind?"

"I won't be changing my mind. I've been given three days' sick leave—sort of."

"I haven't had a date with an invalid in a long time," she said. She finished scribbling on a piece of notepaper she had removed from her handbag. "Here. See you at the stipulated time."

She walked away. He watched the slim hips and long legs and felt happy for the first time in a long time.

NINE

Y ou still have dark circles under your eyes," Williamson said. "Did you get much of the stuff that knits up the raveled sleeve?"

"Enough."

"Close-mouthed, aren't you?" He removed the light he'd been shining in Cable's eyes. "I hope you relaxed in your awake time with feminine or perhaps I should say, female, companions?"

"It's none of your business, Mr. Parker, but I had two dates."

"Parker? Oh, I see. You think I'm nosey, huh? Who isn't? Anyway, as your doctor, I'm interested in your nervous system."

Cable said nothing. Williamson said, "How was *L'Auberge*?"

Cable looked startled. "How'd you know?"

Williamson chuckled and said, "A Cal-Pax employee saw you and Gill go in there. I won't tell you her name, but she certainly isn't reticent. It's all over the building. *L'Auberge* surprises me, though. I'd say you were a strictly meat and potatoes man."

"I didn't get much of a chance to talk to her. It seems that half of the TV industry was there, and they all knew her."

"Not in the biblical sense, I trust," the doctor said.

"There's not much chance of that," Cable said. He regretted the remark as soon as it came out.

"I've heard that Ms. Gill is rather chaste," Williamson said. "Or at least very discreet. No first night stands for her, heh? How about the second night? After you two dined at *La Villa Basque*?"

"That's in Vernon! Now how in hell . . . ?"

"Sorry, I can't reveal the source of that information."

Williamson sat down behind his desk. "You can go back to work any time now."

"Listen," Cable said. "Am I being shadowed by the company? The BOC? Somebody else?"

"How would I know? Would anybody tell me if they were trailing you? It's possible they are, since you are very valuable. Maybe the Secret Service is. Who knows? No, I'll tell you. Gill left her monogrammed handkerchief in the women's room. The restaurant called up her apartment, her cleaning lady gave it Cal-Pax's number, and an employee in Malone's office answered the phone. I happened to have lunch with the lady."

"That sounds like too much of a coincidence to me."

"Don't get paranoiac," Williamson said. "You have too many neuroses as it is. Only take on a neurosis if you need it to survive."

Cable rose and said, "I hope I won't be seeing you for a long time."

"Not in my professional capacity, anyway. I'd like to buy you a drink some time. Meanwhile, may your relationship with Ms. Gill flourish and build to a proper climax."

"Go to hell," Cable said.

TEN

Near-miracles had been produced on order. Ruthlessly, the White House and Congress had cut red tape, overridden legislation, ignored protests from industries, businesses, civil rights organizations, and, in fact, anybody or anything standing in the way of the project. In the beginning, though the seriousness of the situation had been explained to Congress, a number of senators and representatives had attached riders to various project bills. The president had called in the congressmen responsible for these and demanded that they be eliminated. Now was no time to play politics. So back went the proposed legislation, stripped of the barnacles, to the House.

Among the protestors were the petroleum industries. They acknowledged the intense gravity of the crisis. But pulling off floating rigs from their drilling to relocate them at the Hole meant less fuel for the nation's vehicles and industries. There was a shortage as it was. So be it, said the authorities, and strict fuel rationing was imposed.

None of this was done without trouble. The taxpayer cried out, too, because an additional ten percent was added to the income tax. The government informed the public just why this was necessary, but only the southern Californians accepted the additional burden. It was difficult to get most Americans, remote from the coast, to fully comprehend that they were as endangered as those living next to the oil stream. They had by now been told again and again, via mass media, that starvation from lack of food and of oxygen might result. But this was too vast a concept for most Americans to visualize.

Curiously, the nations across the Pacific were much more panicked. Perhaps it was because they had much more experience with catastrophes. They were intimate with suffering and death on a large scale.

The official protests were strong; the action by crowds was violent. Anti-American demonstrations got out of hand even in those countries where riots occurred only if the government gave its tacit consent. U.S. embassies were stormed, sacked, and burned down. A number of embassy personnel were seriously injured. The U.S. ambassador in Tokyo was thrown out of a fifth story window and killed. Several American tourists in Manila were beaten to death. The Saigon police opened fire on a crowd, killing thirty and wounding eighty. Nevertheless, the embassy was reduced to ashes.

At the same time, the peoples of China, Japan, the Philippine Republic, and, later, Australia, demanded that the U.S. pay for any damages, sufferings, or deaths caused by the oil. Though the stream would not reach the shores of these countries for many months, its citizens required assurance now that reparations would be made. They wanted to establish legal grounds for claims to come. North Viet Nam was the first to appeal to the International Court of Justice. The others filed suit shortly after.

The leaders of these nations knew, however, that the U.S. did not have the money to pay for the claims. The American governments, federal, state, and municipal, could not handle the millions of lawsuits being brought by its own citizens. The courts were drowned in these, and in the end the state and federal supreme courts threw them out. The situation was not a matter of justice but of desperate expediency.

Moreover, as the president of the U.S. pointed out in a speech transmitted worldwide, this was a global problem. Every country was going to have to pitch in to help, give its utmost. And they must do it without being paid by America.

As the president left the United Nations building, he was shot at by a sniper. The bullets narrowly missed him, killing one Secret Service operative, wounding another, and blowing the head off of a baby in its mother's arms. A search was immediately made in the buildings of the Dag Hammarskjöld Plaza. The sniper, cornered in a corridor, shot it out and died from a hail of bullets. He was easily identified as a Soldier of Jehovah. He carried a letter clearly meant to establish his membership in the SOJ and its aims.

"The Lord Jehovah, as is written in His Book, intends to destroy the world, to bring about His justice, His wrath, on the Servants of Satan. The Lord Jehovah intends to bring about the Last Days swiftly, and any who help Him do this are His Loyal Soldiers, any who attempt to prevent this are His Godless Enemies. Wickedness and sodomy must be crushed to hasten the Last Glorious Day, the Trumpet Call of Gabriel. The Soldiers who die in hastening His Heavenly Labors will be among the elect, those who stand on His Right Side when the Children, evil or good, goats or sheep, are judged and given their just rewards. Satan has ruled this dark planet too long! The Lord Jehovah is impatient! Repent now, those of you who still have a spark of Godliness. Repent now and enlist with His True Soldiers!

"Hellalujah! Glod and Gory forever!"

Evidently the letter had been penned hurriedly, supposedly while the sniper had been waiting at his station for the president to emerge from the U.N. building. The last two lines had been scribbled just before he took up his rifle.

In the reaction following the publication of this letter, several SOJs, and at least five innocent people, were lynched by mobs or vigilante groups. A child of five was among the victims.

These events were remote from Cable. He worked from eighteen to twenty hours a day, snatching catnaps now and then, falling asleep after midnight while watching the news channel.

Once, he had a date with Dorothy Gill. It did not turn out as he had hoped for, though he might have expected it. She entered his living quarters at midnight, and though she was not working nearly as hard as he, she looked as tired as he felt. After looking with raised eyebrows at the Army cot, she sat down in a big easy chair. They had a drink and talked while the voice of the newscaster, barely audible, interwove with theirs.

"This isn't very romantic," Dorothy said. "Where's the soft music, the champagne, the huge bed with the scarlet spread?"

"You haven't even let me kiss you good night," he said. "I know you said you only do that when you know a man well and are fond of him. Pretty old-fashioned, but I respect that. Now, you sound disappointed because you're not in a seduction trap."

"I didn't *sound* disappointed," she said. "It's just that, oh, well, I was making a little joke. I'm so used to the seduction trap, as you call it. I like it here; I wasn't putting you down. I don't feel like fighting you off . . . I mean, I'm glad I don't have to bat off passes. Not that I ever stay long when that starts."

"You're not exactly the emancipated brave new woman."

"Who is? That's a mythical image. A stereotype."

They fell silent for a moment. Cable was thinking of a short conversation he'd had with Chang.

"She had two bad short marriages, though they were two years apart," Chang had said. "I don't really know what was wrong. Dorothy is a nice person to work with, though she's a slave driver. But she has to be to get where she is. She's a perfectionist, and even in this day and age a woman has to be better than a man to get an equivalent position. Or keep it, anyway.

"She may be cold, though she's friendly and warm enough with me and her colleagues. Maybe I shouldn't say this, but, what the hell, she's made no secret of it herself. After each divorce, for a short while, she was sort of promiscuous. Then she'd freeze up. Hands off, everything off after that. Not even many dates. I don't know what went wrong between her and her husbands. Her mother died when she was very young, and she was raised by five stepmothers. Five. The old man couldn't hang on to a woman for long, though his present wife has lasted four years. He's in his late sixties now, so maybe he's settled down. And maybe her father has nothing to do with it."

"Everybody's his own Freud nowadays," Cable said.

"Yeah, I know. Whatever causes her hang-ups, she's afraid to get emotionally involved. A lot of women are that way, but that doesn't keep them from going to bed with men. It's bam-bam, thank you Sam, and off into the sunset. I was kind of surprised when she said she'd go out with you. It was her first date in two months, and, frankly, you don't seem her type. But what is her type? All I know is that her husbands were easy-going guys, not very ambitious. But they did bitch a lot because her job kept her away from home so much."

Now, thinking of this, he asked her about her parents. She hesitated a minute before replying. But once she got going, she concentrated on telling him of the few memories she had of her mother. He awoke at six A.M. slumped in his chair and covered with a blanket. There was a note on his desk.

"You're some lover. Your only passion is for Morpheus. But I forgive you. You looked so tired and yet so boyish. So I'm going to give you a good night kiss. It's safe to do that, and I wish, I think, that it wasn't. But please let me bring up the subject, not you."

When he saw her later that morning, he was unable to talk privately to her. Malone called the conference to order at once, and Cable left after he had given a short report. She smiled at him, and when he walked toward her she put a finger on her lips and shook her head. He walked on out, wondering what kind of a kook he was beginning to fall in love with. Or, at least, becoming fond of.

After that, there was no more time for even short tête-à-têtes, out of his quarters or in. The scheduled date for installation of the pipe-pump complex was rapidly approaching, and everything seemed to be going wrong.

ELEVEN

It was almost March. Two months had passed since the deeps of the earth had burst into the ocean. The flow was undiminished, staying at an estimated eight hundred and fifty gallons a second.

It was thought that about a sixteenth of the flow came from the half dozen or so fissures within a quarter-mile radius of the Hole. The news media and Congress had asked why these, at least, could not be capped. The BOC's reply was simple. It was too dangerous to attempt it before the Hole itself was plugged.

The air around the gusher was too explosive. Natural gas and petroleum volatiles could be set off by one spark. Though the gases were dissipated by the winds to some extent just north of the Hole, they were still too thick. The fissures couldn't be dealt with until Operation Flying Lid was completed.

One of the first things Cable had done, however, was to order erection of a slant rig in Santa Monica. This had started drilling a month after the birth of the Hole. It had been given one of the few laser drills available and was proceeding much faster than with conventional means. The shaft was directed at the shaft of the Hole. If it hit true it would penetrate the casing of the Hole shaft at 25,000 feet.

In effect, its operators were trying to hit the eye of a needle from the end of a wire thread over five miles long. If, however, the eye was missed, the shaft would still—it was hoped—tap the deposit. It had to be a widespread "lake" to exert such pressure, and so hitting the bull's eye was not a necessity.

It would be another month before the drilling reached its goal. This was just as well, since the pipeline to siphon off the oil was missing. The pipes were being laid as fast as possible, but the line would not be finished for three months. Even so, its rate of speed was a miracle of steel production and of installation.

Another pump-pipeline-storage tank complex had been constructed, terminating in the project's Santa Monica base. This was an even greater miracle, possible only because it was relatively short. The oil from this would flow into existing pipelines.

To do this, it was necessary to cut off the operation of most of the oil wells in southern California. Their storage and pipeline facilities had to be used to take in the output from Cable's Flying Lid. This inevitability had brought forth a storm of protest from the companies owning the wells to be shut down. Nor were their stockholders less voluble. The White House, Congress, and state legislatures had been deluged with letters, telegrams, and phone calls. The oil lobbyists—except for Cal-Pax's—had applied tremendous pressure.

Who was going to pay for the loss of profits?

The federal government was in an awkward situation. It had always—with a few exceptions—cooperated fully with the petroleum industries. Indeed, it was a poorly concealed secret that the federal government—and most state governments—*was* the oil industry. The most powerful factor in American politics, in the management of the country, was oil. It might lose a few battles here and there, but even these were temporary setbacks. When the public attended mass meetings to protest oil pollution or the jacking up of oil prices, they rode to the meetings in vehicles powered by gas, lubricated by oil. Protesting telegrams could not be sent without the oil powering electrical generators. Protesting letters were carried by trains and aircraft which could not move without petroleum fuels. The mailmen delivering the letters drove gas-powered trucks and jeeps. If a well or a drilling rig was shut down, or an operation forbidden to start, the loss had to be balanced by new operations elsewhere.

The president and the legislators proposed a solution they hoped would satisfy everybody. The profits from the Hole petroleum would be used to reimburse the losses. This would, hopefully, be a short-term situation. New facilities and pipelines would eventually handle the Hole's output. Then the "borrowed" facilities would be handed back to the owners.

The question was: who would own the Hole oil after the Hole was well under control? Was the federal government going into the petroleum business itself? Or did Cal-Pax get the oil after the crisis was over?

The other companies resented both possibilities, fought them viciously. In no way could the federal government be allowed to continue its proprietorship. It could set its prices lower and thus unfairly compete. Moreover, this might be the first step to nationalization of the industry. What next? Would the federal government then eye the electrical power industry? The insurance companies? Everything?

No. Admittedly, the U.S. government had to handle the Glory Hole at present. But once its flow was safely channeled, its output would have to be the property of Cal-Pax.

But—and it was a big but—Cal-Pax would have to buy the new facilities back from the government. It would have to pay a certain amount for the oil piped and stored in these. And it would have to foot some of the bill for the cleanup. Otherwise, Cal-Pax would dominate the industry. And that would be against the principles of free competition. Cal-Pax had to pay enough so that it would not make such enormous profits that it would have a great edge over the other companies.

As of the moment, no legislation had been introduced concerning these matters. Nothing would be done until the Hole was capped.

TWELVE

Under the vast dark cover, the sea life died. Deprived of sunlight and oxygen, they perished, the fish and crustacea by billions, the microscopic oxygen-making plankton by sextillions. Seabirds by the hundreds of thousands landed on the sinister green-black. Their feathers stuck, buoyancy lost, they sank and died. Those who struggled to shore, and the beach-dwelling birds, picked off the oil from their feathers. They died with a bellyful of poisonous hydrocarbons. Whales and porpoises, their blowholes caked, died.

South of Santa Monica to the tip of the Baja California peninsula, over ten thousand miles of coastline, the beaches were black. Winds picked up the emulsified oil and tarred the sands, rocks, cars, and houses. The black sticky belt varied from a hundred yards to a half-mile wide.

The harbors were empty except where a few craft had not moved out for some reason or other. The naval bases at San Piedro, Long Beach, and San Diego were abandoned. Freighters and tankers no longer moved a ceaseless supply of goods and oil into Los Angeles and San Diego. Everything had to be brought in by truck, train, or plane.

The freighting industries were unable to cope. They had been under a severe strain for some years, and this sudden great increase was too much. The government stepped in to provide Army trucks and personnel to haul the excess. Even though the freighting-trucking industry acknowledged its helplessness, and admitted that people would starve if this step had not been taken, it objected. This expedient might become permanent. It could be the first move by the federal government toward nationalization. The West Coast unions even threatened a strike. They quickly backed off when the president said that he would use the military to run the trucks, trains, and aircraft. If the pickets used violence, they would be met with violence. He would see to it that martial law was applied to southern California.

There was an uproar about violation of civil rights.

The president made a speech in which he said that "life-rights" superseded civil rights in this crisis. The life of the whole earth was at stake; the general good overrode that of the individual.

His logic was unanswerable, but many worried that the U.S. was swiftly advancing toward a totalitarian government. It was true that this seemed to be the only type that could adequately deal with the situation. But when would the crisis be over? After the Hole was capped? Or after the Pacific was cleaned up? The latter would take a long time, perhaps ten years or more. Would the government then return to a constitutional normalcy? They had good reason to be concerned. It was seldom that any government, having gotten control, gave it up. Moreover, there was a large minority in the U.S. that thought that a totalitarian government, as long as it operated on their principles, was the best thing that could happen.

The liberals warned that conditions were getting to the point where the Constitution would be suspended.

The Americans had another large problem to handle. A strip at least half a mile broad from Santa Monica down to San Diego had been evacuated. The city of San Diego itself was emptied of three-fourths of its people. The odor of gas and threat of fire had driven them out. But there was no place to go. The unemployment rate was at six percent before the crisis. Even if the dispossessed had been able to get jobs, there were few houses to be purchased. At least a million had left the coast and had to be taken care of. Again, the federal government stepped in. In a situation somewhat reminiscent of the period immediately after Pearl Harbor, huge camps were thrown up in the Mohave desert, Arizona, and Nevada. The Army did the building and the administrating until a bureaucracy could be created to take its place. The government carefully avoided the use of "internment camps," in its references, but it wasn't long before the mass media was calling them just that. But in a short while the popular term was "Hole camps." There was a great amount of hardship and the inevitable injustice. Blacks and Chicanos complained that their housing and food wasn't as good as those of the whites. The whites complained that their food and housing was as bad as the blacks' and Chicanos'. Both inmates and Army personnel were engaged in a black market; those who had no money suffered.

What made the situation worse was the sense of hopelessness among the "holers." It would be several years before the coast could be cleaned up enough to permit their return home. That is, it would be if the hole was capped at once. But what if it couldn't be controlled? They'd be in the same position as the Palestine refugees.

Within a month the situation looked brighter. The winds, which usually came off the sea, had shifted to an inland source. The black surface of the vast blotch on the ocean absorbed heat by day and gave it out at night. The overall effect was to make air above the stream hotter than that of the land alongside it. As a result, its low air pressure pulled in the surrounding surface air. And this kept southern California from getting the full effect of the gases.

Life was endurable in the Los Angeles-Orange County area, though just barely. The beach cities would have to be kept empty, since they did not extend far inland. But plans were made to return a good part of San Diego's population. Unfortunately for this, a sizeable portion relied upon the naval base and trade connected with the sea for their living. If they went back, they would have to live off welfare. Almost one hundred percent said they would. Anything was better than the camps.

The evil-smelling Black Sea of California, as it was sometimes called, covered an estimated 2,754,561 square miles. This was more than half of the area of Europe. Every three seconds, the Hole poured out enough oil to spread over a square mile. In one hour, its output could cover an area equal to that of the state of Rhode Island. If the oil were spread out over the fifty states of the U.S., it would blanket all but Texas and Alaska and a small part of Oklahoma. In approximately 27 days, the sinister splotch shown via satellite could equal the U.S. in area.

However, man was temporarily holding his own. The oil-eating bacteria were devouring every hour an area somewhat more than that of Rhode Island. The mouth of the dark river was not moving westward. The bacteria were doing their best work at its terminus, eating up the enemy as fast as it advanced.

The Hawaiian Islands and the western Pacific states were, for the time being, safe.

In addition, an international fleet of three hundred ships was being equipped with huge scooping mechanisms. These could, theoretically, scoop up 720,000 gallons a minute. Close behind them would come tankers which would take in the mixed oil and sea water from hoses connected to the scoopers. On board the tankers were separation chambers which sent the oil into the holds and piped the water back into the sea.

Due to the time taken by disconnection procedures, mechanical breakdowns, and storms, the maximum input would be reduced to about 300,000 gallons a minute. Moreover, there just were not enough tankers to maintain a continuous flow. Once filled, the tankers had to leave on a long journey to the homeport.

The scoopers and tankers operated on the western terminus and along the central western edge of the stream. Here, the gases had dissipated enough so that the danger from fire was absent.

But they had to deal with the oil-eating bacteria. It would do no good to load up a tanker with twenty million gallons and find them disappeared when the ship pulled into port. A chemical to kill the bacteria was injected into the tanks. This chemical had to be removed before the oil went to the refineries, which upped the cost of the oil.

Also, pulling the tankers off their regular routes meant that the oil-producing countries were seriously deprived of their shipping. Their revenues were suddenly gone, along with their political clout. Of course, they raised a howl and threatened all sorts of reprisals.

It was pointed out to them, again and again, that they would die with the rest of the world if the oceans died. No matter. Incredible as it seemed, the idea was not accepted. Or, if it were, it was pushed deep under where the light of consciousness could not penetrate. Business as usual.

Finding that they were not going to get the tankers put back into their services, the oil-producing nations tried another tactic. They asked that they be paid for the loss of revenues during the crisis. No one could afford this, of course, and so the demand was rejected.

Meanwhile, the Hole spurted like blood from the wound of a dying beast.

THIRTEEN

The night before the final phase, Cable took a sleeping pill. It was at Doctor Williamson's orders, which Cable was glad to obey. There was little he could do himself; the final preparations were in good hands; he needed to be alert and vigorous for the task tomorrow. To make sure he would have quiet, he stayed in his office. A cot had been brought in for him by the maintenance man.

Despite the sedative, he had some trouble getting to sleep. His mind kept switching from the job tomorrow to Dorothy and back again. He felt a keen desire for her, a desire that had been working on him for weeks but had been easily suppressed because of his fatigue.

At eight, he stepped out onto the roof of the Cal-Pax building. George Shattuck, a stocky brown-haired, blue-eyed man of thirty-five, was with him. He had taken the place of Banks, Cable's old foreman, when Banks had been killed in a freeway accident six weeks ago. Shattuck was also the "pilot" of the Flying Lid or the "Hoover," as it was popularly called. He was a taciturn man, a widower, and needed fourteen more hours to get his mechanical engineer's degree. His wife and two children had been drowned while fishing in a Minnesota lake five years earlier. Cable had at first thought that Shattuck's grave bearing and silence had been caused by the death of his family. He seemed to be carrying deep within him a slowly bleeding wound, a half-frozen grief. But Shattuck's employment profile, which Cable had seen, indicated that he had always behaved thus.

The sky was an unbroken blue. Only a slight breeze stirred. It stank of oil, as usual, though today the odor was less. From the streets below came a bedlam of horns. Cable didn't know the reason for it, but he would find out. The helicopter was waiting for them, though the pilot had not started its engines yet. Dorothy Gill, Chang, Grey, and Meisser were standing by the craft. Meisser stood apart from the others, seeming to watch them with disapproval.

Cable greeted them, then said, "Where's Malone?"

Dorothy smiled. Meisser said, grimly, "He got caught in the traffic. He'll try to get out later. But if he's late, he won't be allowed to land on the platform. Once the operation's started, no aircraft can come close."

"I'll tell you all about it when we're on our way," Dorothy said. She grinned again, and Chang and Grey grinned back at her.

The copter took off. Cable said, "What's so funny now?"

"I just happened to be standing by Keppler, you know, Mrs. Adkins' new secretary, when Malone called in. He was furious, said he couldn't get through the traffic. No wonder, look, the streets are jammed. Everybody and his brother is trying to get down to Santa Monica to see the Hoover leave."

Cable looked down. Wilshire, Beverly Boulevard, Olympic, the side streets, as far as he could see were clogged with vehicles. And they were not moving.

"What's the matter with them?" he said. "They can see the whole thing on TV. The Hole's too far away to be seen from shore."

"You tell them that," she said. "They were warned to stay away from the beach. But they're going anyway. They think they can at least watch the Hoover take off from the pier."

"They're nuts," he said. "Anyway, what about Malone?"

"And Adkins," she said. "Malone said he'd stopped at her apartment to pick her up on his way in. He was calling from there. They started out in his car, got a block, couldn't get any further. So they walked back to her place."

She stopped, smiled, and said, "But he wasn't telling it as it was—not exactly. He'd no sooner hung up than his wife called. She asked to speak to him. Keppler doesn't know much about Malone's private life, she's only been working for Adkins a week. Keppler told her what had happened. Mrs. Malone blistered her ears. It seemed Malone hadn't been home all night. He'd told her he was working at the office until dawn, and he'd get a little sleep on the couch. Obviously he had been with Adkins in her apartment. Keppler felt terrible, but how was she to know what she was supposed to say? What's worse, she gave Mrs. Malone Adkins' phone number."

"So he got caught in more ways than one?" Cable said. "Well, he's also going to have a bad time when he tries to explain to the board why he didn't get to the platform. He's supposed to make a speech there."

"It's all out now," she said. "I imagine Mrs. Malone would be on her way to Adkins' place now if it wasn't for the traffic jam."

They passed over the junctions of the Santa Monica and San Diego freeways. The on-off ramps, the streets leading to them, were clotted with vehicles. Not one was moving. Moreover, here and there, some impatient driver had used the lane reserved for the police, ambulances, and tow trucks. There were black and white cars with flashing red lights behind them. But even though the drivers would be ticketed, there was no way, at present, to get them back into the legal lanes.

"They can't all be trying to get to the beach," Cable said. "Most of them, surely, must have been on their way to work. They aren't going to make it today."

Ahead lay the shore of Santa Monica. To the north on the highway, cars were backed up for miles. The same situation existed to the south. The Army, and the police, were holding them back from driving into the forbidden area. Cable shook his head. The news media had been telling the populace for a week that the project strip along the shore was off-limits. Moreover, south of the project, the streets leading in to the black strip had been blocked off. Yet, a number of the reckless, the uncaring, those who were everywhere chiefly responsible for traffic accidents, those who drove to witness fires and accidents, had thronged into the area. Their tires must be sticky with the oil blown inland; they must be suffocating from the gases.

Among them were the flashing red lights of the local police and the state patrol. They'd be arresting drivers and hauling them off. But he imagined that most of the fools had found that they were suffocating, or sickened, by the odor and had tried to get out. Unable to move their cars, they had fled on foot inland. And that had made the jam worse.

No wonder humanity was in such a mess. Out of every hundred beings, there were at least ten fools. No, make that at least twenty.

Out there, the green-black stain lay heavily over the ocean. North of it, just visible, were the towers of the giant platform and smaller platforms northwest of the Hole. Normally, the winds carried the gases away from them, though a certain amount still reached them. Today, the quiet air allowed the gases to spread northward. But the "sniffers" on the platform indicated that the density had not reached a danger level. As long as that situation remained, it was perfect for the operation. Strong winds and heavy seas would have delayed the final phase.

Even so, the only surface craft permitted within a mile of the Hole were vessels specially designed to operate in the potentially explosive atmosphere. Aircraft had to keep at least three-quarters of a mile north of the gusher. The only planes that had flown over were those that had dropped the Pseudomonas. These had to stay at a minimum sixty thousand foot altitude and parachute their containers in.

Near the shore, a building the size and shape of a zeppelin hangar dominated the area. Its open western end received a complex of round pipes each of which was fifteen feet in diameter. These were arranged in twelve units, three in a row and three high. The other ends of the pipes came out of the sea, passed across the land and under an iron bridge crossing the highway. The oil from the Hole would pass into the building, where giant pumps and separation chambers would work. The seawater, mixed with the oil, would be removed and passed back to the sea. The oil would pass through the pipes from the building's eastern end. These dipped into the ground and went their subterranean routes to different pumps inland. From there they went to storage tanks rented from other companies or recently built.

Under the water, near the shore, Cable knew, were other pumps. From their west side the pipes were triangular-shaped to resist rolling by the currents. Their covering of cement, thick paper, and thick plastic prevented corrosion and kept the oil from cooling too rapidly.

The pipes followed along the sea bottom to a point about a hundred feet just northeast of the Hole. They had been carried out from land by barges specially fitted to prevent sparks. The workers had worn rubber suits and breathed through oxygen masks. The pipes were let down to the bottom by cranes, where divers and two submarine cranes placed the pipes correctly. All welding of the pipe sections had been done on the bottom. The divers wore heated dry suits and breathed a hyperoxygenated saline solution heated to body temperature. This was pumped to and from the lungs, enabling the diver to work under high pressures for many hours. In effect, the divers were fish, breathing a liquid element. Their internal body pressure was kept equal to the water pressure and so there were no decompression problems.

The divers and submersibles had completed their phase of work yesterday. Until the Hoover was situated over the Hole on the bottom, they could do nothing more. Once that was done, they would bring in a hundred foot length of pipe complex. This would join the terminus of the big pipeline and the outlet pipes of the Hoover. And the pumping could begin.

Five miles to the north, three and a half miles offshore, a strange flotilla moved steadily southward. Its spearhead was the colossal Hoover, a steel object shaped like a candy heart. It had left the Project's docks at Santa Barbara two days before. Now the tip was almost directly at the Hole, its course determined by two laser beam projectors on the giant platform, the *Sea Ichneumon*. One was aimed at the precise center of the Hole. The other was fixed on an antenna on top of the curving shell of the Hoover.

Seen at surface level from the side, the Hoover looked like the shell of an unbelievably large turtle. Its size and shape had caused one TV commentator to compare it with one of those monsters that appeared so frequently in Japanese science-fiction movies. From the apex of the heart-shape to its stern, it measured thirty-five hundred feet. A half a mile plus eight hundred and sixty feet. At its widest, it was three thousand feet, a hundred feet over half a mile. Its hull was steel, two inches thick. Along its sides, from the tip to the curve of the lobes, were twelve pontoons. These were gray, dirigible-shaped, each six hundred feet long.

The pontoons—called hindenburgs—helped provide buoyancy for the shell and the machines inside it. They were filled with helium as were the huge buoyancy chambers under the shell. In addition, air trapped under the hull gave the immensely heavy structure more buoyancy. Even so, the Hoover displaced as much as six battleships.

Along each side, by the pontoons, two nuclear-powered submarines helped steer the Hoover. Twenty large Navy tugs pushed it from the rear, their prows fitting snugly into V-shaped indentations. These were lined with heavy plastic bumpers to prevent damage to the tugs.

Behind the tugs, at three-eighths of a mile, were two nuclear-powered cruisers. They were on a course which kept them exactly on a line with the outer edges of the Hoover's stern. Their prows were fitted with specially designed attachments and releasing mechanisms for the ends of the enormous twin cables each carried. The other ends were attached to similar mechanisms on the Hoover's hull. Though the tugs were within the line of the cables, their propellers were inside cages to prevent any fouling.

There had been time enough to test the Hoover only twice. It had been pushed to a point opposite Santa Barbara where the depth was three hundred and fifty feet. Cable and Shattuck had been present to run through the simulated operations, and both runs had gone perfectly. But there was one thing lacking. There had not been time enough to build a simulation of the gusher. Scale models in the laboratory had indicated that the Hoover would function as hoped for. It should descend upon the Hole and cover it. But not until the actual operation was carried out could anybody be sure that the extrapolations were accurate.

It was a go-for-broke launch in more ways than one. The Hoover and all activities connected with it had cost three billion dollars. If this phase failed, another Hoover would not be built. At least, Congress said it wouldn't, and the secretary of the DENR had passed on this word to Cable.

Cable had answered simply, "Either build another one or let the Glory Hole destroy the world."

"But Congress won't authorize another one!"

"They'll have to!"

"But they won't. Cable, the cost of just cleaning up will be equal to the military budget for the past two years. Over one hundred and seventy-two billion dollars. Do you realize what the taxpayers are going to say, what they'll do? They'll vote the present Congress right out of office. And Congress knows that. They won't appropriate the money. And let me tell you, Cable, if this Hoover doesn't work, it'll be your ass! They have to have a scapegoat. Guess who?"

"As if I didn't have enough on my mind," Cable had said. "But I should worry. If the Hole isn't capped, I won't be living more than two years, and the disgrace will be over then. But there won't be anybody around to blame me, either. Can't people get that into their heads? Money doesn't mean anything now. Politics shouldn't mean anything either."

"But you have to deal with reality," Tengel had said.

"There's only one reality, and that's the Hole. O.K. Anything else to discuss? I have work to do."

Cable's concept of the Hoover had been both simple and grand. Too simple, too grand to be accepted at once. But nobody had come up with a better idea, and so, after two days of bitter wrangling, of dozens of phone calls between the Cal-Pax building, Tengel, the White House, the Congress, the Army, the Navy, the project had been given the go-ahead.

The tugs were dropping back now, beginning to turn, ten going to the left, ten to the right, getting out of the way. The cruisers would get the word from Shattuck to begin slowing down, to slowly pick up the slack of the cables. The Hoover had been traveling at four knots under the push of the tugs. It would lose its impetus, but slowly. By the time it reached the Hole, it would be going at two knots. That is, it would if it were not restrained by the cruisers. These would have taken up the cables gently, delicately. A sudden strain would snap even these four sixteen-inch thick monsters. But the commanders of the *New Orleans* and the *Syracuse* were being aided by their own laser beams and by strain gauges. They would know exactly what power to order applied by their reversing engines.

The chopper angled down toward the white circle on the *Sea Ichneumon*. The drill of the giant floating platform and the other rigs would be silent now, stopped so that there would be no electrical interference with radio communication. This helicopter would be the last permitted to land. All other aircraft were to stay at a minimum thousand feet altitude a mile north of the Hole. Malone and Adkins would not make it; they might be in a craft circling up there now, Malone cursing.

The chopper landed, and Cable got out with the others. He ducked beneath the whirling blades as they whined to a stop. Cable pushed through the crowd of reporters thrusting microphones at him. "No comment now!" he roared. "No time now!"

Beyond was a line of Marines and inside them a number of Secret Service agents. The Marines carried rifles, and the Secret Service men would be packing automatic pistols. Yet it was forbidden to shoot firearms on the platform, and if Cable had had his way they would have been left on shore. The odor of the volatiles was strong enough to make a person almost sick. Medics stood by with oxygen masks for those who needed them. But the platform was three-quarters of a mile northwest of the Hole. Under normal circumstances, the winds beat against the gas. Today, the gases had expanded northward through the still air. They were not, however, heavy enough to be set off by a flame. Not at the moment. If they became more dense, they might. And the situation might change swiftly. Hence, there was no smoking. And under no conditions could a gun be fired.

There was little chance some maniac might smuggle a gun aboard. Two Marines were frisking him now, though his identity was not in doubt. Every person who'd landed, including the secretary of the DENR, the diplomats, and the White House representative, was frisked.

The Marine sergeant nodded, said, "Sorry, Mr. Cable. Orders. You can go now."

Cable passed through the crowd, noting the five TV sets brought in for the benefit of the dignitaries. He shook hands with Tengel and Connor, chief of the White House staff. They exchanged a few meaningless pleasantries. Cable saw Doctor Feesher and Meisser by the control panel shack. Feesher smiled. Meisser's face was stony, as usual.

Cable walked over to the shack. Its two sides had been removed so that the dignitaries and the newsmen could see it. The control panel, with its multitude of dials, gauges, CRT screens, switches, and buttons, exposed to the TV cameras. All over the world, wherever a set existed, this scene was on. Well, he supposed that there must be some who were cursing because their favorite program had been cancelled.

Shattuck sat on a revolvable chair before the panel. He was wearing a radiophone headset and saying something inaudible. Probably reporting the input from the two laser projectors on the southwest corner of the platform. This was unnecessary, since the cruisers were receiving the data on their screens in the bridges. But redundancy was safety and accuracy, and this operation had to be both.

Scott Jacobs came out of the crowd from somewhere. "Hello Jim. You had me worried. What if the chopper'd had a malfunction and couldn't take off?"

Jacobs had not understood why Cable had not spent the night on the platform. Cable had explained that there was nothing for him to do until the launch was in its final stage. And there wasn't much to do then. He wanted to get away from the place, take a sedative, and so be refreshed in the morning. If he'd stayed here, he would have been too tense to sleep.

"There's plenty of time left," Cable said, looking at the hour chronometer on the panel. "It'll take the Hoover half an hour to drift onto the Hole."

"Twenty-nine minutes," Jacobs said. He gestured at the TV sets. "The president's about finished with his speech. He won't be allowed to run over; nobody's going to go a second past their allotted time. Then he'll speak briefly over TV with Tengel and you. Then Tengel will make a short speech—three minutes only. Then you'll give . . ."

"I know all that," Cable said. "I haven't forgotten. Calm down, Scott. You look like you have a bad case of the jitters."

"You look kind of strung up yourself," Jacobs said. "Geeze! If this doesn't work . . ."

"Yes, the whole world's watching, and that's no exaggeration," Cable said. "That's what makes the tension worse. But everything's figured out, the weather's ideal . . ."

"Yeah, but I can't help thinking what might happen if there's an electrical or mechanical malfunction. You know . . . Finnegan's law . . ."

Cable nodded and said, "If anything can go wrong, it will. Give us a smile, Scott. You don't want to make a billion TV watchers nervous, too."

"To hell with them," Jacobs said. But he managed a quick smile before looking around as if he suddenly realized something was wrong.

"Where's Malone?"

Cable didn't want to indulge in irrelevant conversation. Actually, he was just as nervous as Jacobs, and he wanted to get to the job immediately. But he told him curtly what had happened.

Jacobs broke into a laugh. Cable managed a grin. Telling him Malone's predicament hadn't been pointless; it had loosened them up a little.

"Malone must be blowing his top," Jacobs said. "Caught with his pants down, mud on his face. I thought he was laying Adkins, not to mention a dozen others. But I didn't think he'd have nerve enough to stay at her place all night. Maybe his wife doesn't give a damn, though. She might be playing around too. But this is going to kill him, missing this. Who's going to introduce Tengel? Wasn't Malone supposed to . . . oh, oh!"

"What's the matter?" Cable said. He looked around, his heart suddenly thumping. Had something gone wrong with the Hoover?

"I forgot about lip readers," Jacobs said, his hand over his mouth. "There're cameras on us! There must be any number of people watching this who read what we said!"

"Maybe not," Cable said. He looked at the cameras pointing at them and turned his back on them. "Well, what if some people did read us?"

Jacobs turned too. "There's always some crackpots that write in to the networks. Jesus, it'll be all over the media by tonight! Malone'll fire us if he gets in trouble!"

"I doubt it," Cable said. "Anyway, we have something a hell of a lot bigger than that to worry about!"

Jacobs walked off, shaking his head.

A minute, later, the ceremony started.

Cable could hear the president's speech on the news channel. He walked to a position behind Shattuck, close enough to hear him.

"L-Tracker-Two reports the Hoover is right on schedule. Three point four two seven knots velocity at checkpoint twenty. What's the reading on the strain?"

Cable couldn't hear the reply from Admiral Byrnes of the *Syracuse*. He could read the strain on a CRT. It was slowly increasing, but there was a lot of slack left yet.

The Hoover was nearer, immense even at this distance. He couldn't keep from thinking about what would happen if it went off course. Should those million and a quarter tons head for the platform, they would rip through the platform as if it were paper. But it wasn't going to get off course. Everything was accounted for, velocity of the Hoover, the rate of the wind, of current. The meteorologists and oceanographers had said that this was the ideal weather. There were dozens of them now, in planes and ships in the area and hundreds of miles to the west. They were checking atmospheric and pelagic currents, monitoring pressures, trying to anticipate any change that might affect the course of the Hoover.

He looked at the crowd. The dignitaries sat in wooden chairs, some of them looking as if they needed a smoke. But maybe that was a projection of his own desire. Beyond them were some shacks where the network commentators reported to the world. Chang was sitting on top of a wooden stepladder, pointing his camera in his direction. Dorothy stood by the ladder, holding an oxygen mask. She looked pale, though whether from sickness from the odor or tension, he could not know.

Jacobs said, "Hey, Jim, you'll be on in ten seconds!"

Cable turned. A small worried-looking man stood behind him. The coordinator, or whatever he was called, of the program.

He glanced at his wristwatch. Nine. Right on schedule. Cable walked to Tengel, stood by him while a man handed him a microphone. Tengel turned, smiling as if he were at a ribbon-cutting ceremony.

"And now, may I introduce a man who needs no introduction . . . ?"

Where's the chicken and the mashed potatoes and candied carrots? Cable thought.

". . . James Cable, chief engineer of Project Glory Hole."

Tengel glanced at his watch and mopped his forehead with a handkerchief.

The cameramen moved a little closer, their directional mikes pointing at Cable.

"Thank you," Cable said in a suddenly dry voice. He was keenly aware of the cameras and of the microphone shaking in his hand. He could almost feel the cameras rubbing against him. The world was watching him as if its fate depended on him. In a sense, it did. But he had done all he could. Except reassure them.

For a second, a gap appeared in the crowd, and he saw Dorothy. She lifted a hand and closed thumb and finger in a circle.

"Thank you," he said. "I've been described as the person who built the Hoover. That's not true. I did originate the idea, the concept of it. But it was no inspiration of genius on my part. The concept was crude, brutal, almost. The Hoover is a sort of flattened diving bell. It had to be built on a grand scale to handle a monster, a sort of robot St. George constructed to battle a dragon. It had to be simple because we, the world, didn't have time to construct a complicated sophisticated device. As it was, completing it in two months was a miracle. A miracle of cooperation, self-sacrifice, and ruthless efficiency."

Despite all the obstacles thrown in our path by unthinking and selfish people, he thought.

The coordinator, standing near the control panel, put his hand out and extended four fingers. Four minutes more.

"You all must have heard and read the details of the Hoover's electromechanical operation and of just how it is going to be settled over the Hole. But I've been ordered to make a final summary.

So . . . the two cruisers"—he saw on a set an aerial pan of the two ships—"are gently taking up the strain of the cables attached to the Hoover. By the time the Hoover gets within a quarter mile of the target, the Hole, the cruisers will be keeping the Hoover down to a half a knot speed.

"Meanwhile, a radio signal has been sent to a device in the Hoover. This has caused the winches to lower cables attached to enormously heavy steel blocks. Anchors, in effect. When the Hoover is over target, the anchors will be within ten feet of the sea bottom. Each anchor is equipped with a sonar device which enables the winch mechanism to know just how far the anchor is from the bottom.

"As the Hoover stops, another radio signal will cause the anchors to drop the rest of the way.

"The second the Hoover is firmly anchored, it will flash a signal to Mr. Shattuck, the operator of the control panel. He will send a signal back. Release mechanisms will drop the cables from the Hoover and from the cruisers.

"At the same time, release mechanisms will unlock the pontoons, and they will float away.

"Immediately thereafter, the winches will start to draw the Hoover below the surface toward the anchors.

"At the same time, hatches will open in the top of the Hoover, and the trapped helium will escape. The buoyancy chambers inside the hull will expel their helium and start taking in the oil. This will make the structure even heavier.

"Inclinometers on the circumference of the Hoover will be transmitting by sonar to a transponder on a pontoon of this platform. The electrical signals from it will go through a computer. If there is any tilting of the Hoover, the computer will send back rectifying signals. These control the individual winch mechanisms. If a cable must be extended or shortened to restore the horizontal attitude of the Hoover, it will be properly adjusted.

"At fifty feet down, the Hoover will hit the top of the gusher. This force is enormous and could easily move the Hoover along or displace it. But the open hatches will permit dissipation of the force of the gusher. The Hoover will settle down, under its own enormous weight and the action of the winches. Once settled, the pump-pipe-line in the Hoover will be connected to the pipeline on the bottom. This will start pumping out the oil-seawater mixture to facilities on the land.

"The pressure of the oil flow is such that a certain amount of oil will force its way from under the edges of the shell even if it has sunk deeply into the mud.

"We won't be able to pump out more than about four hundred and fifty gallons a second at first. But there are other pumps inside the shell and their pipes only have to have their ports opened to be connected to another pipeline. Even now, two more pipelines as large as the first, are being constructed. Eventually, eight hundred and fifty gallons, the output of the well itself and the flow from the fissures nearby, will be sucked out from the shell. Meanwhile, a quick-drying slurry will be placed around the edge of the shell to help seal in the oil seeping from the edges."

He paused. The coordinator held up one finger.

"Then, the hard part begins. The cleanup. I thank you."

He handed the microphone to a technician and walked over to a position behind Shattuck. Jacobs handed him a headset connected by a long cord to the control panel.

"An informative speech," Jacobs said in a low voice. "But I think they were expecting something poetic, something quotable. You know, like 'We are here, Lafayette,' or 'This is one giant step for mankind.'"

"Tough," Cable said. He put on the headset and began to listen.

By then the cruisers had put near-maximum strain on the cables.

"Hoover traveling at one point four zero one knots, Twin-C. Reverse until velocity is zero point nine nine zero knots."

"Received, L-Tracker-Two."

The nose, the apex of the heart-shape, slid by the platform. The ridge of the arching back was on a level with Cable's head. And he stood fifty feet above the surface of the sea.

The antenna on its top was sliding upward. As the structure sank, the antenna would be driven upward. When the Hoover hit bottom, twenty feet of the antenna would be sticking above the surface. It would receive the radio signals which would cause activation of the giant pumps inside it. If, however, there was a malfunction in the telescoping mechanism, if the antenna got stuck below the surface, a sonar transceiver could take over.

A voice: "Monitor GC reporting. Stand by. Gas count three hundred parts per million. Stand by. Oxygen masks ready!"

Another voice: "Received, Monitor GC. Warden One reads you. Will act. Roger."

The wardens, men wearing orange armbands, began to move through the crowd, quietly passing the word to check the oxygen masks.

Jacobs handed Cable a nose mask-earphone set connected to the panel. Cable removed his headset and slipped the mask over the lower part of his face and its phones over his ears. He adjusted the band behind his head.

The proportion of volatiles in the air hadn't reached the danger point, but all precautions were being taken. He should have put the mask on before, he realized. A dull headache had sneaked up on him, and he was beginning to feel sick in his stomach. The queasiness, however, could have been caused by the tension of making a speech.

"L-Tracker-One here. Hoover nose within one thousand three hundred feet of target."

"L-Tracker-Two here. Hoover velocity at zero point three five seven knots. On course. Increase scheduled strain, Twin-C."

"Twin-C here. We read you, L-Tracker-Two."

Cable was breathing fresh air, so the oil odor wasn't responsible for the upset stomach. And his heart was beating hard. Yet, he told himself, he had no reason to feel such anxiety. Everything was going as planned. Everything would go as planned.

"L-Tracker-Two. Hoover velocity at scheduled zero point two nine nine knots. On course. Hoover nose within six hundred seventy-two feet of target."

"Shattuck here. Anchors at scheduled depth, ten feet from sea bottom."

The green-black boiled out, the apex of a triangle. The sea north of it moved in gentle slow rollers. The black stream moved across a flat plain, as smooth as a soot-covered salt lake. The tiny breeze had died down. For a few seconds the voices were still in the phones. There might be some sounds outside, mutters from the crowd, the drone of distant circling aircraft. The earphones barred these. All was silent, as if the world was holding its breath.

The silence was suddenly jarred.

"L-Tracker-Two here. Hoover at scheduled zero point zero nine two knots. Get ready . . . GOD!"

Cable jumped as the scream filled his ear. At the same time, he saw why the operator had yelled, was still yelling.

The lead pontoon had been released, was floating away from the hull.

"Twin-C here! Port pontoon No. 1 released . . ."

The lead pontoon on the other side was loose, too, Cable numbly realized. But what, how, no, it couldn't happen!

Cable restrained himself from shouting orders at Shattuck. The man had been trained, he was cool and steady. He would make the necessary adjustments. The Hoover had lost a certain amount of buoyancy. It would sink somewhat; the anchors would drag on the bottom, slowing it. But . . .

Shattuck pressed the computer override button, pressed the winch master button and rotated a dial. The indicator showed that the anchors were being pulled up.

"Twin-C!" Shattuck said. "Release strain a little. The front will dip too much if you don't!"

"Received, Shattuck!" the admiral's voice said.

Cable watched the vast curving shell move a trifle faster. The pontoon in his field of vision was still near to the hull, like a baby whale cruising by its mother's side. It didn't matter what happened to it now.

The laser operator had cut off his yelling within a few seconds. His voice shook, but the hysteria was gone.

"L-Tracker-Two here. Hoover nose within forty feet of target. Proceeding at zero point zero eight four knots. Off schedule. Proper velocity should be . . ."

"I'll take over, L-Tracker-Two," Shattuck said. "L-Tracker-One. Ready to report bull's eye."

"Received, Shattuck."

"Twin-C. Increase strain. Gently, gently."

"Received, Shattuck."

The cruisers were increasing the rate of rotation of their reversed screws slowly, the eyes of their commanders fastened on the strain indicators.

"L-Tracker-One here. Twenty feet past bull's eyes. One thousand seven hundred and thirty feet to zero."

"Come on, Shattuck," Cable murmured. "Check the depth of the anchors. Let them down again. They have to establish contact as quickly as possible."

The oil boiling out at sixteen knots on the surface would have caught the interior of the front edge. It would be pressing against it, and the cruisers would have to increase their reverse speed. No, they must be doing it now, must have done it. But the dip of the front edge would mean an uncalculated force against it, and the commanders of the cruisers would have to guess the proper strain.

Cable could see both pontoons now. They had been caught in the black stream and were moving along like two downed zeppelins. Or two submarines.

"L-Tracker-One here. One thousand six hundred and seventy feet from zero. Ready for zero signal, Shattuck? Ready, Twin-C?"

"Shattuck here. Ready."

"Twin-C here. Ready."

Cable looked up from the control panel just as it happened.

The two pontoons became orange flames, swallowed immediately in the heavy red of oil fumes exploding.

The blast deafened him, knocked him down.

The heat sped in on the heels of the explosion.

The wave of flame seemed to race across the Hole toward him, to sweep over him. Of course, as he later figured out, it had not. Otherwise, he and everybody on the platform would have been fried.

But the fire had burned up the gases a quarter of mile north of the Hole. Past that point, the concentration was too diluted.

If anybody was screaming, he couldn't hear them.

He tore off his earphones, only later thinking how lucky he

was to have worn them. Those without protection had been totally deafened.

A quick glance around him. Nobody had gotten to their feet yet. They stared at him with wide eyes and gaping mouths. Their skins would have been gray if they had not been slightly reddened by the heat.

The first front of the blast had passed over them. But thunder came from the south as the fire raced southward.

The flames in the area of the hole were leaping at least fifty feet.

Black greasy looking smoke was rising, pillar-like, and slowly forming a mushroom cloud.

Cable could see nothing of the hull of the Hoover. Red fire enveloped the area.

He whirled and jumped toward Shattuck. The man had been knocked sidewise on his chair. He was sitting up now, leaning on one hand, shaking his head.

Cable stared at the control panel. The winch indicator showed that the anchors were being drawn up!

Shattuck, in falling, must have inadvertently hit the master dial and somehow twisted it.

He stepped forward and hit the master down button and set the dial for SE BOT. The winches would start lowering the anchors now, and when their sonars reported that they had struck bottom, they would cease operation. But he must be too late. The cables pulled by the two cruisers must have snapped. Yet, that didn't seem likely unless something had caused the cruisers to reverse too swiftly. The explosion had startled the commanders into ordering such a speed? It didn't seem likely.

Or had the explosion shaken the electromechanical releasing mechanism of the cables attached to the Hoover? Had the terrific jar caused a switch to open or close? Or ripped off a wire?

He picked up Shattuck's headset, which had been torn off when he had fallen. He placed the phones over his ears and spoke into the nose-mask.

"Twin-C! Twin-C! This is Cable, filling in for Shattuck! Come in, Twin-C!"

"Twin-C here."

"What happened to the cables, Twin-C?"

"God damn it, I don't know," the admiral said. "Whoever activated the release of the pontoons, then set off the bombs in them, could just as well have blown up the cable locks!"

Cable was silent for a moment. Then he said, "I'm still sort of stunned, admiral. I should have guessed that. All right. Our laser trackers seem to be stunned, too. The control panel indicator for the lasers indicates nothing. The Hoover's gone on past them. What does your radar read?"

There was a pause. Then: "It's fifty feet past the target area, and still going. Seven knots but slowing down fast. It's lost. There's no way to go after it! Not in that hell!"

Cable felt an increase of heat on his back. He turned. The fire must be at least fifty miles to the south, still racing along. The total effect of the fire was raising the temperature around the edges of the stream.

He turned again. The helicopter had not been knocked over. Its pilot was standing by now. A crowd of people was crossing the platform, going up the steps toward the landing platform. But the Marines were coming out of their shock. A captain was sending some men to the chopper, barking orders to hold the craft for priority passengers. Cable wasn't going to be on the first load. The statesmen would get first choice. And by the time the copter got back, it would find an empty platform. The heat would have driven the others off. In any event, Cable felt that he must be the last one off—just like the captain of a ship.

Fortunately, the landing platform was at the northeast corner, the furthest point from the heat. He helped Shattuck get up, and said, "You stick with me."

Shattuck gestured at the panel. Cable said, "There's nothing you can do now. On the way in, you'd better recall exactly what happened, what you did. We'll be facing a board of inquiry."

Meisser, his hat blown off, staggered up to them. "Give me the headset," he said. "I want to call the admiral of the *Syracuse*."

"What for?" Cable said, but Meisser took the set without

answering. He looked so desperate that Cable decided he could spare a minute to listen in. But the heat was increasing swiftly. A wind from the north had begun, however, helping to keep some of the heat away. The intense temperature was creating a low-pressure area, pulling in the air from around the stream.

Cable put on the maskless set.

". . . demand that you place everybody under arrest! It's obviously sabotage, and someone on this platform is responsible."

"I can't arrest the foreigners. Or Connor," the admiral said coldly. "In fact, I can't arrest anybody. I don't have the authority."

"By God, you'll have to explain this lack of action later!" Meisser said. "Put me into contact with the FBI office in Los Angeles then."

He looked up and saw Cable. He snatched off the mask, and snarled something. Cable lifted one earphone. "What?"

"Eavesdropping, Cable? You aren't above suspicion, you know. You were present twice at the disasters!"

"You're a goddam spy, aren't you, Meisser? I thought somebody was tapping my phone."

"It was legal," Meisser said, and put the mask back on.

Cable walked away. Chang was nearby, filming the fire. Cable said, "Where's Dorothy?"

Chang stopped the camera, grinned, and said, "She's in the women's room. It shocked the piss out of her!"

Cable looked at the landing platform. The chopper was taking off. The Marine captain was talking on a walkie-talkie. He was probably calling in other choppers to lift the passengers. Maybe he'd called the cruisers, too. They were turning toward the platform now in a wide circle. Probably going to stand by and take on the refugees.

Dorothy appeared from a hatch. The front of her jumpsuit was wet. She walked to Cable and said, in a firm voice, "My God, Jim, it's the end of the world!"

"Not yet," he said.

"But there's no way to put out a fire like that!"

"Yes, there is. If the Hole can be plugged, the oil will burn itself out. Eventually."

She looked surprised. "You mean—another Hoover? But that'll

take at least two months to build! And think of what all that heat, all that smoke, is going to do!"

"I know. But it can be done. Come on. You can't stay here."

"You're so cool, so self-controlled. But, there's something that's given you away."

She pointed at him. He looked downward and for the first time was aware of the coolness around his crotch. A big dark wet area stained his pants.

FOURTEEN

Jim Cable sat on the right side of the Navy helicopter. The *Sea Ichneumon* dwindled, as did the two cruisers standing by. Dorothy had elected to stay on the platform, which had taken a new position a half a mile to the north of its former site. The drilling equipment had been quickly disconnected, the anchors drawn up, and the structure moved away. During this operation, a swarm of helicopters had landed and taken off from it. Cable had decided not to wait for the BOC chopper to return. He'd asked permission from the admiral to be a passenger on a chopper from the *Syracuse*.

Dorothy had handed him the films she'd shot just before he boarded the craft. "I'll stay here a while," she said. "Then I'll be coming in to film the fire along the shore."

"Be careful," he said, and kissed her lightly on her lips.

"So far I have been," she said.

He wanted to ask her what she meant by that, but the pilot was waving at him to get in.

Most of the other passengers were foreign diplomats and scientist-observers. They were silent, speaking only now and then in murmurs. Like him, they were half-numb with shock. But his mind, a hot core in a lump of ice, was leaping ahead of the flames. He could see them as if he were a satellite photographing the coast of California.

It would be a few seconds before the pontoons exploded. From Santa Cruz in the north to Ensenada in Baja California, no cloud barred the camera's view. The sea was blue except for that black vaguely dragon-shaped stream. Then, the tiniest brightness at the top of the dragon's crest, as if the beast was growing a halo. The spark would seem very small to the camera, though by then the fire would have covered five square miles. The camera's eye would see the smoke cover the initial brightness. But the red front would travel faster than the smoke as it ate up the volatiles. The flames would speed past Manhattan Beach, Hermosa Beach, Redondo Beach, around the jut holding the Palos Verdes estates, then southeastward, past the marine land of the Pacific, and up into Los Angeles Harbor. They would fill San Pedro Bay, and then flash past Long Beach, Seal Beach, along the U.S. Naval Weapons Station, Huntington Beach, Newport Beach, Laguna Beach, down, down to Capistrano Beach, past San Clemente, along the thirty-odd mile stretch occupied by the U.S. Marines on the other side of Route 1, Oceanside, Carlsbad, Leucadia, Cardiff-by-the-Sea, Solana Beach, La Jolla, Mission Beach, Ocean Beach, San Diego, Imperial Beach, and the Mexican coast.

And then, just below Ensenada, the flames should die. Clouds covered the area there, according to the weather reports and heavy winds should be sweeping the volatile gases inland, and the flames would not have enough to feed on.

The smoke was soaring straight up, carried by the winds rushing in to the roaring monolith. Probably, little of it would fall on Los Angeles. The high global winds would catch the smoke and carry it eastward over the mountains. As the winds traveled east, the smoke would drop. Enough would fall to blanket Nevada and Arizona. Most of it would be borne on, however, parts falling on New Mexico, Colorado, Oklahoma, Texas, Missouri, Arkansas.

The sun would be hidden in all the southwestern states, then in the midwest states. It would shine palely for miles in the states just east of the Mississippi. Then the clouds would get blacker as the flaming ocean poured unceasing greasy black clouds into the atmosphere.

Later, the smoke would girdle the earth. The satellite would see a black globe. Here and there, winds would part the veil, but these rents would be closed again.

He looked out the window toward the coast. As far as he could see along the beach, buildings were burning. They had been covered with layer on layer of wind-blown oil spray for two months, and these had caught fire quickly from the furnace heat of the sea. The Marina del Rey was aflame, and the buildings between it and the ocean were leaping rednesses, vomiting smoke.

The streets and the San Diego and Santa Monica freeways were still jammed with vehicles, still unmoving. The thousands of dots alongside them were their drivers, gotten out to look the situation over. On an entrance ramp into San Diego freeway, a jackknifed semitrailer burned. And a little to the north another semi was jack-knifed across the northbound lanes.

The chopper passed over the city while he gazed down at the worst traffic jam in history. Every avenue he could see was packed with motionless vehicles.

It was then that Cable had an impulse to tell the pilot to take him on to the Ontario International Airport. He said nothing, however, and a minute later he got out of the chopper. It swung away, taking its distinguished passengers to safety.

The two security guards who always stood at the entrance on the roof were gone. Cable wondered what had happened. Had they been so excited about the eruption at the Glory Hole that they had gone downstairs to see the pictures on TV? It didn't seem likely.

He walked toward the little house which enclosed the elevator. He stopped. There were plumes of smoke arising from the north. From the vicinity of Mulholland Drive, the ridge beyond which was the San Fernando Valley. What the hell was going on? He turned to his right. Clouds were rising from the vicinity of Griffith Park. And there, to the east and the southeast, were more columns of smoke.

He entered the house, and shouted for the guards. There was no reply even when he stuck his head into the tiny washroom. He shrugged and went into the elevator. Stepping out after a one-story descent, he was surprised to find that the corridor was empty. So were the offices he passed on his way to Malone's executive suite.

A man stepped out of the door to Malone's office. He was Jenkyns, second assistant vice-president. He held a transistor radio from which a near-hysterical voice chattered.

"Cable! What're you . . . ? We thought maybe something had happened to you! We expected to hear from you right away, and . . ."

"I couldn't get through," Cable said. "I didn't have enough priority. Too many big shots there. I'm here, that's what matters. Where is everybody?"

"You don't know?"

"Would I ask if I did?"

"It's a panic, a real panic. Just about everybody took off when the news came. But Malone and Adkins, and Doctor Williamson are still here. And there are some maintenance workers and office girls packing up the secret files. There were up to a minute ago, anyway. We decided we'd wait for the chopper. Malone can't get through the lines. They're jammed, but he's sure the chopper'll be back."

"Yes, but what is this all about?" Cable said.

"Hey!" Jenkyns said. "The chopper must've brought you here. Thank God for that! There's no way . . ."

"It was a Navy chopper," Cable said. "It dropped me off. Our chopper's probably been commandeered by the Navy. Now, for God's sake, will you tell me what's going on?"

"Oh, my God! Oh, my God! They can't do that!" Jenkyns said.

Two young women came out of the door. They half-ran to the elevator, and one punched the down button. Their sweat-soaked hair hung limply, their makeup was running, and their armpits and the backs of their blouses were stained with sweat. One was talking away, though the other didn't seem to be listening. Her eyes were fastened on the floor indicator lights.

". . . and he said there are about twenty big buildings on fire in Downey, Montebello, Rosemead, Hollywood, Lynwood, Boyle Heights, oh, I don't know, many places. The fire engines can't get to them because of the traffic. It has to be arson . . ."

"Jack said it must be the SOJ," the other girl said. "He said they're the ones blew up the Glory Hole. They ought to be shot on sight!"

Cable looked sideways at Jenkyns. Jenkyns nodded.

"Yeah, and there's lots of brush fires in the hills suddenly sprung up," the first girl said. "I tell you, they're trying to burn down Los Angeles!"

"Where'd you hear all this?" Cable said.

The girl looked at him strangely.

"Why, it's all over the TV! Oh, you're Mr. Cable! What's going to happen, Mr. Cable?"

"A hell of a fire until we put it out. Did they say who's behind the fires here?"

"Why, you know! It's the SOJ! They sabotaged the Hoover, and now they're trying to burn down all of Los Angeles! Trap us like rats!"

"Aren't you girls supposed to be helping pack the files?" Jenkyns said.

"Fuck the files!" the girl said. "I'm not going to be burned to death just to save your lousy records! Come on, Lois! That elevator's never going to get here! We'll walk down!"

"Forty stories?" the other said weakly. But she followed.

Jenkyns said, "They'll never work for us again. I can't really blame them, though. And how in hell can we carry all that crap if the chopper doesn't show? We're loading up trucks in the rear of the building with the most expensive equipment and confidential files. And the trucks can't even get out of the lot!"

Cable entered the outer office. There were about fifteen people there, secretaries, maintenance men, and two security guards. MacDonald, the first assistant vice-president, was supervising them. They were placing file folders and documents in cardboard boxes and cartons or piling the containers on hand trucks.

Cable, closely followed by Jenkyns, went into Malone's office. A TV set in a corner was on, and the newsman was saying, ". . . blocked the junctions of the San Diego and Ventura freeways. Two of the drivers were shot by police as they attempted to escape. They have been identified as members of the Soldiers of Jehovah. Furthermore . . ."

Mrs. Adkins was placing file folders in a large cardboard box. Malone was standing by the opened drawer of a tall file case, throwing some papers on the floor, piling others on a table. Doctor Williamson was by the window, looking down at Wilshire Boulevard. He turned as Cable said, "Hello, everybody!" Malone and Adkins looked startled.

Malone said, "So! You got here! Good! Will you go back up and tell the pilot . . ."

"There isn't any chopper," Jenkyns said.

Malone dropped a folder, scattering its papers.

"What? Jim, why didn't you hold it? I told the guards to nab the chopper as soon as it touched . . ."

Cable explained. Malone said, "Well, the pilot has his instructions."

"He's probably been snatched by the military or the navy," Cable said. "They'll be using him to help them out in this mess."

"Mess is right," Williamson said. He gestured toward the window. "The reports aren't just hysterical rumors. The brush is burning in a dozen places along Mulholland Drive and in the canyons. Somebody scattered incendiary bombs from a private plane over Griffith Park. And somebody else blew up a building off the edge of the park."

"Those sons of bitches!" Malone said. "They ought to be shot down like mad dogs! And where was the FBI? They said the SOJ wouldn't dare show its face again! They'd be nabbed at once!"

Williamson went to a table on which sat his black bag. He removed a stethoscope, a thermometer, and a blood-pressure tester.

"I'll check you out, Jim," he said. "You must be in a state of shock. Pneumonia can follow shock, you know."

"Forget it," Cable said. "I'm all right. Anyway, if I did have pneumonia, how would you get me to a hospital? The streets are blocked."

"You could go to bed here," Williamson said. "There's an oxygen tent in the medical suite, you know."

"Doc," Cable said. "Don't you understand? This city has to be evacuated. We have all the ingredients for a firestorm."

Adkins said, "Oh, my god!"

Malone dropped another folder. "You can't mean that?"

"I just ran across two of your girls who seem to understand the situation better than you," Cable said. "Forget the files. Tell those people in the next office to take off, start walking. As for us, we can do two things. We can wait for the chopper, but I don't think it's going to show. Or we can start walking. I'm walking."

"Are you nuts?" Malone said. "Myrna and I walked ten blocks from her apartment, and we're pooped! Where the hell we supposed to hoof it to? The Valley? You any idea how far that is? Of course you do! It must be seventeen miles from here—as the crow flies. And we aren't crows!"

"You look as if you're going to have a stroke," Cable said. "Get hold of yourself and do some straight thinking. The brush in the canyons is unusually dry for this season, since we've had this crazy weather. It's apparently been started in a number of widely scattered places. The fire fighters can't get to it, not easily, anyway. The fire'll sweep down damned fast, and it's going to cut off anybody trying to get up on the freeways or Laurel Canyon or any other route to the Valley.

"The best way is west, on Wilshire or Olympic or the other parallel streets nearby. When we get to the ocean, we'll go north up the Pacific West Coast Highway."

"Right into the fire?" Malone said. "Jesus, by the time we get there, Santa Monica'll be one big fire, Jim! The newsman said the fire'd crossed Venice Boulevard!"

"That's our only chance," Cable said. "We can't go east. It's about seventeen miles from here to Rosemead, and the fires the SOJ set out there will be sweeping in from Rosemead and the other places around it long before we get there.

"Every minute counts. So let's go!"

Malone waved at the file cases and the cartons and the boxes. "But—the records! We can't just leave them here! They're classified secret, and I'm responsible for them!"

"Nobody's going to bother with them," Cable said impatiently. "They'll burn, and that's that."

"But there are a lot of documents not duplicated in Washington! They'll be lost!"

Jenkyns, who had been listening to his radio, said, "Hold it, everybody! The announcer said we should take the streets, stay off the freeways. They're trying to get the freeways cleared."

"They must have plans for evacuation," Adkins said.

"Not for this situation," Cable said. "They didn't expect a jam this size before the fire even started. Nor did they expect fires set by saboteurs. This is happening too fast for them, I'll bet."

"I can't leave the secret files behind," Malone said. "I'll have to destroy them first. That's the procedure!"

"Don't be so stupid," Cable said.

Malone's face became purple. "*You* calling *me* stupid?"

"Yes. Look. I'll try to get what's happening in your head. Draw you a picture."

He strode to the large detailed map of the Los Angeles area on the wall.

"Venice is burning. That's our immediate concern, because Santa Monica is just north of it. But the overall situation is this. The whole coast is burning from Venice to a point just short of Ensenada, Mexico. The heat is terrific, cataclysmic, I should say. As far as I know, it's the greatest fire since the earth cooled off after formation. The heat output per square inch is low, just enough to boil a panful of eggs or to cook bacon. But the accumulated heat . . ."

"God damn it, I'm not still in diapers!" Malone said. But he had sat down, and the purple was cooling off to a bright red.

"No," Cable said, "but I think that you've shut out all this elementary stuff. You don't want to face it. I want you to face it. Besides, there are some factors that weren't considered, couldn't have been.

"The SOJ have started fires in various strategic places and may start more. In any event, there would be plenty of accidental fires, and these plus those started by the SOJ are going to make the situation worse.

"The winds are being pulled into the fire on the ocean, and this in a way is a blessing. The fires won't spread eastward as fast as if the winds were coming from the ocean. This is only a temporary advantage, however. The winds will carry the flames of the fires in inland L.A. westward. The winds are going to get stronger as the temperature of the oil fire builds up. The stronger the winds, the faster the fires spread. Meanwhile, the hot air over the oil fires rises, cools, and sinks. A convection current is set up. Much of the cooling air, which is still hot by human standards, is drawn downward. It joins the hotter ground air and adds its heat to the ground air. This air rushes into the area over the oil fire and rises even faster because it's hotter.

"A vast cycle of air, a fiery wheel, rotates over southern California. It gets hotter with every cycle. Eventually, it gets so hot that the temperature in the air above the buildings—and refineries, and vehicles, and so on—causes the buildings to burn. Long before this happens, any people on the ground under this immense heat will have died. And all this time, people are in a panic and there is no way of enforcing an orderly evacuation. The areas in the east should be cleared first, and then evacuation should proceed progressively westward. But . . ."

Malone stood up. "O.K.! O.K.! I know all that! But I don't think it's going to happen that fast! It takes time for the heat to build up! Things are in a mess right now because of the initial panic! But all service forces, federal, state, municipal, local are mobilized, and . . ."

"Mobilized isn't the right word," Cable said. "To be mobile you have to be able to move . . ."

Jenkyns, Cable noticed, had moved away from him when he had accused Malone of stupidity. Apparently, he hadn't wanted to be close to Cable when the fireworks started. He was afraid of guilt by association. Adkins had a peculiar expression. She looked as if she had not heard Cable's description, as if she was still thinking of Malone's reaction to his insult. She seemed almost pleased.

There was silence for a moment, broken by Malone. "O.K., Cable, I lost my cool for a moment. But the records have to be gotten out! We, Cal-Pax, the BOC, can't function without them. We wouldn't know who or which was what without our files!"

"You're going to lose them anyway," Cable said. "The people carrying them aren't going to hang on to them when they'll die if they do!"

"Who's getting hysterical now?" Malone said.

Jenkyns said, "I don't know how a pessimist like you ever got to be a chief engineer."

"Shut up!" Malone said. "There's been too much gabbing. We have to move! Mrs. Adkins! Phone the loading dock! Tell the foreman to forget the equipment. Send his men up here to hand carry the files. But only those with security clearances!"

"Yes, sir," Mrs. Adkins said, her voice quavering slightly. She went into the outer office. Malone said, "Poor woman! She's about to shit in her drawers, but she's hanging on. Worth every cent of her salary!"

He pointed at two boxes on the table by him. "You can carry those, Jim. Guard them well, or it'll be your ass!"

"You can shove them," Cable said.

Malone, his face even more purple, shouted, "You do as I say or you're fired!"

"So I'm fired."

Malone glared, then picked up the boxes, one on top of each other, in his arms. Adkins came back in. Looking distressed, she said, "Nobody answers at the loading dock."

"What?" Malone said.

"Not only that," she said. "Everybody's gone from the office. Even MacDonald!"

"The rats!" Malone said. "Without a word to me!"

"They're not so dumb," Cable said.

Malone scowled at Cable. "You really mean what you said about quitting?"

"I didn't quit. I was fired."

"Well then, get out!" Malone yelled. "You've no business being here. You're unauthorized!"

"I'll leave," Cable said. "But as a friend, or an ex-friend, listen to me. Don't burden yourself with that stuff. You'll throw it away before you get two blocks. You'll have to if you want to survive."

And at that moment he thought of Lee and Katie. He'd completely forgotten them. He'd been too numb and too concerned with the overall picture. And things had gone too fast. Should he try to walk to Westwood? That would mean heading into the fire, and they were probably, no, undoubtedly, gone by now. They'd be lost among the millions on the streets. That is, they would be if Lee could get herself going. No doubt, she'd tried to get through to him on the phone to ask him what she should do. But Katie would force her to leave.

He hoped that Dorothy was still on the platform. But when she heard about the fires set by the SOJ, she would get to the shore.

He looked at his wristwatch. 10:47. Had it really only been an hour and forty-seven minutes since the ceremony on the *Sea Ichneumon* had started?

"What do you think, Jenkyns?" Malone said suddenly.

Jenkyns started, turned pale, and said, "Whatever you think, Mr. Malone."

"I don't want any Yes-Master crap from you," Malone said. "What's your honest opinion?"

Jenkyns' face looked as if he were undergoing some deep agony. "Well, I . . . I . . ."

"Speak up!"

"I think we ought to get the hell out of here!"

"What about you, Myrna?" Malone said.

Mrs. Adkins said, "I'm of the same opinion. But maybe we ought to see if the helicopter's coming. It might even be on the roof now."

"You get up there and see," Malone said. "But don't take long."

Adkins left hurriedly. Cable said, "I'm going up, too."

"You're not going with us," Malone said. "You don't work for me."

"Try and stop me," Cable said. "I'm not going to burn to death if I can help it."

Jenkyns made a strangled sound. Malone's mouth worked but nothing came out of it. Cable walked out. He found the woman standing by the waist-high rampart, her hand shading her eyes even though there was no sun. He looked over the rampart.

The streets were still clogged with unmoving cars and trucks. Moreover, the sidewalks were filled with vehicles. People had taken their cars onto them—to hell with the law and the pedestrians—only to be stopped there. The hooting of horns even at this altitude was loud. No wonder. The great majority of horns in the L.A. area must be clamoring. Sound expelled by machines operated by furious idiots. Signifying nothing but panic, frustration, and desperation.

His nostrils expanded to the odor of exhaust fumes and a faint underlying burning. The streets were filling with gases from idling motors and the first intimations of the atmospheric recycling of heat and smoke.

In the east, the sky was clear but turning a milky blue-white. Plumes of smoke rose from a dozen scattered places, too distant to define their origins. Over Santa Monica and Venice, as far south as he could see, and east to downtown Los Angeles, the sky was black.

Here and there he could see redness flickering. To the north, the smoke was thicker, and he saw pale orange flames at its base.

The wind had increased to about seventeen miles an hour, 4 on the Beaufort scale. It was warm, laden with a diffused heat from the fires over the ocean. He could see between two tall buildings the Crenshaw entrances to the Santa Monica freeway. They were jammed with vehicles that had been stopped. The cars on the off ramps were pointed the wrong way, filled with cars whose drivers had decided that if they couldn't get onto the freeway in the lawful manner they would take the unlawful. But they'd been halted by the frozen traffic, too.

Adkins, pale and shivering, turned to him. "It's awful! I'm so *scared*!"

"So am I," he said. "I wish Malone would get scared, too. More scared for his life than of losing the secret papers."

"He always did go by the book," she said.

He looked around once more. There were five helicopters in the north, two in the east. But none were coming this way.

"Listen, Myrna," he said, "you're not going to carry those files, are you? You'll never make it if you do."

"I don't know. I've worked twenty years for him."

"And you're in love with him. Your affair's an open secret. Well, come on. There's no use waiting any more."

He took her by the hand and led her down the steps. He didn't trust the elevator. The power might be cut off at any moment.

FIFTEEN

Williamson met them in the hall. "It's here?"

Cable shook his head.

"How's it look to you? Overall?"

"As bad as it can be. Even if the junctions of the freeways are cleared, it'll be impossible to get the traffic moving. You can bet that any number of cars have broken down, radiators must have boiled over—not everybody uses coolants—and what's worse, there must be a hell of a lot of people who've abandoned their cars and started walking. They'll have taken their keys, some of them will have locked their cars, though God knows there's no rational reason for that, and plenty of the locked cars will be left in gear. It's a real mess. A general fatal mess."

Adkins had gone into the office. The two men entered a minute later. She was holding the bars of a pushcart. Malone was just placing the last box on the pile. While the two watched him, he strode to his desk and grabbed his dispatch case. "I got to get hold of myself. I almost forgot this, and it contains the most important papers!"

"Forget it," Cable said. "Forget about taking anything but food and water. Especially water. Do you have anything we can carry water in?"

"What's the matter with you?" Malone said. "I told you you were through! Kaputt!"

Adkins walked to the far wall and pressed a button on it. A section slid open to reveal a bar and shelves of bottles of liquor. Cable went around behind the bar and turned on a faucet.

131

"Good. The water supply's still coming through."

He opened two fifths of whiskey and started to pour them down the sink. Malone said, "My god, man, that's Schenley's best blend! You have to get on a waiting list to get that, and it isn't easy to get on the list!"

Cable did not reply. Malone said, "What the hell you looking so disgusted . . . ?" He stopped and said, "O.K. I'm an idiot. It'll burn anyway."

Cable rinsed the bottles out and filled them with water, recapping them and sticking them in the pockets of his jumpsuit. Williamson filled three bottles and jammed them in his black bag along with a sack of potato chips. Cable put a big bag of beer nuts in a pocket. Mrs. Adkins emptied her handbag of everything except her purse, a photograph, and her credit cards. She jammed a fifth filled with water into it. Cable handed Malone two more capped fifths of water and then drank two large glasses of water. He popped an ice cube into his mouth and said, "I'm going. Anybody coming along?"

"Didn't you hear me, Cable?" Malone yelled. Cable said nothing. Malone said, "What about you, Doc? You could carry those boxes there."

"I'm carrying water and food and the tools of my trade," Williamson said. "And if it comes to a choice, out go the tools."

"Damn it!" Malone said, looking as if he were going to weep.

"By now, everybody should have left," Cable said. "I'm joining them." He walked out of the office without looking back.

Williamson, carrying only his bag, joined him. A moment later, Adkins was in the hall, holding her handbag. Malone, snarling, holding his dispatch case, charged out after her.

"Myrna! You can't do this!"

Jenkyns stepped out into the hall, then stepped back into the office. He's afraid to be in the line of fire, Cable thought.

"I'm sorry," she said. Then, "No, I'm not. Fuck you, Britt. Who the hell are you to ask me to haul this bunch of shit when I'll be lucky to get out alive if I could run sixty miles an hour? You asshole!"

Malone's eyes widened, showing the expanse of red veins in the eyeballs, and his mouth dropped. Finally he said, "Myrna! After all we meant to each other!"

"After all we meant to each other!" she said in a high-pitched tone. "After all we meant to each other! What the shit did I ever mean to you but a mother substitute who'd suck you off when you couldn't get enough kick out of fucking your eighteen-year-old typists from the pool. You dumbass! You think I didn't know you were conning me when you said you needed a mature woman? After all we meant to each other! After all we meant to each other! Bullshit! Bullshit! What the shit do I mean to you but a pack animal and a blowjob! Fuck you! Fuck you!"

Malone struck her across the cheek. Perhaps he did it because he thought, having seen so many TV shows and movies, that that was the medically accepted manner to quiet down hysterics. Or perhaps he did it because he felt betrayed. Or because he himself was hysterical. Or for all of these reasons.

Whatever the reason, he failed. She screamed, "After all we meant to each other! After all . . . ! God damn it, we're going to die, Britt! Die! And all you can think about are your lousy meaningless wipe-ass records! You don't care about me, you don't care about your wife in Beverly Hills, you don't care about your drunken son in Westwood, you don't care about anything but your dumbass records! Where the fuck is your soul, Britt, where the fuck is it?"

Weeping, she staggered toward Cable. He folded his arms around her, feeling sorry for both her and Malone, gray-skinned with a purple overlay. His eyes and mouth looked as if he were undergoing, or about to undergo, a stroke or a heart attack.

Mrs. Adkins' shoulders shook, and she sobbed as if a lifetime of anger and frustration had broken through. He patted her shoulder and said, "Listen, that was good for you. And for him. But you don't have enough tears to put out the fires."

"I need the job! And the pension!" she wailed.

"He isn't going to fire you," Cable said. He was beginning to feel uncomfortable and ridiculous. "He wouldn't dare."

"After that!" she said, looking up at him.

"After that," he said and pushed her away from him. But not too violently. She was ready to break completely, and anything she could interpret as rejection would do it.

The elevator doors opened, and Williamson started in, but Cable said, "Hold it, Doc! What if the electricity should be cut off while we're on the way down?"

Williamson's eyes widened, and he stepped back. Malone said, "You *are* nuts, Cable!" and he went into the cage, Jenkyns on his heels. The doors started to close, Malone dropped the case, leaped forward, grabbed the edges of the doors, pushed them open, and almost sprang through. Jenkyns followed him. "Damn it, you've got me spooked!"

"No," Cable said, "you've been spooking yourself all along. Anyway, you can pick that case up downstairs if the elevator's working. If you still want to."

"Fuck it!" Malone said. "I don't owe my life to the company."

Cable didn't ask him what had changed his attitude. He pointed to the butt of the automatic pistol sticking out of the front of Malone's belt. "Got any more of those?"

Mrs. Adkins said, "Oh, my God!" and stared at the weapon. Perhaps she was thinking that she might have angered Malone enough to cause him to shoot her.

Malone, grinning, shook his head and said, "Let's get on the road."

He seemed to have shucked an invisible weight when he had abandoned the case. His expression and a hitherto missing spring in his legs made him look almost happy. He was no longer responsible for the great organization of Cal-Pax; he was on his own now. His only responsibility was himself and the small company with him. Evidently, he still thought of himself as their leader. That was fine with Cable as long as Malone showed himself capable. There was no reason why he shouldn't be, now that he had accepted this unprecedented situation. He'd captained a destroyer during the Viet Nam conflict and had won several medals for distinguished conduct and bravery.

They went in Indian file down the steps, emerging after forty floors into the lobby. They did not see or hear anyone else, and the lobby was deserted. Wilshire, however, was still jammed with cars and the sidewalks were filled with people going westward or eastward. The horns had ceased bleating, and the people, when they did speak, did so in low tones. The loudest sound was the crying of a baby half a block away.

Cable stopped for a minute while the pedestrians flowed around him as if he were a rock in the sea. The sky was black now, and the air was at least several degrees hotter. The wind seemed to be a little stronger. Two huge helicopters, Sikorsky S-61s buzzed overhead at an altitude of a thousand feet. Probably, they were on the way to the Hollywood Freeway. There they would use their 9000-pound lifting powers in conjunction to pick up stalled or abandoned cars and deposit them off the freeway. But the supply of such copters was limited, and there might be thousands of cars to lift out.

Moreover, as space was made, more cars would come onto the freeways. A number of these were bound to become inoperative from boiled over radiators, empty gas tanks, or batteries suddenly gone dead. There was a certain amount of these on the freeways every day, but their incidence would rise enormously because of the abnormal number of cars present.

There were men and women coming from the Los Angeles County Art Museum, paintings, statuettes, and other artifacts in their arms. The glass doors had been shattered by some vandal, and the museum itself was being looted. It was inevitable, though Jenkyns had said that the governor had declared that looters and vandals caught in the act would be arrested. There was no way of enforcing this, however, since the militia and police could not get through to any reported scene of a crime. What difference did it make, anyway? The museum treasures would be burned up if left there. And the chances were that they would be burned up if carried off. In time, as the looters realized the desperation of their situation, they would abandon their burdens.

The fountains in front of the museum were still jetting up high streams of water. If the looters had any sense they'd choose the vital water instead of the valuable but useless artifacts.

Malone said, "The quickest way to get to the Valley is to go up Fairfax and down Sunset to Laurel Canyon Road."

"That's true," Cable said. "But you'll run right into the fire. It's moving down from Mulholland Drive. Look, you can see the smoke from here," and he pointed north at the Hollywood Hills.

"I have eyes!" Malone said. "What are you proposing, Cable? That we walk east? You know how many miles we'd have to hoof it to get out of this area?"

"About fifty miles or three days," Cable said. "The authorities should be concentrating on getting rid of traffic obstacles at the extremes of the main roads out of Los Angeles. North of Santa Monica on the Pacific Highway. North at the conjunction of the San Diego and Ventura Freeways. East in North Hollywood where the Ventura and Hollywood freeways meet. Still further east where the Golden Gate and Ventura freeways meet. Far east in Pomona or West Covina through which the San Bernardino freeway runs. And in the southeast, near Downey, I suppose, on the Santa Ana freeway. But the cars that can be hauled away by chopper or pushed off the freeway—they'll have to cut the wire fences along them—must be staggering. And you can bet that the freeways will be clogged with pedestrians, people just taking the main arteries or begging others to take them in their cars.

"The SOJ planned hellishly well. The fires in Rosemund and South El Monte will spread and join and cut off the San Bernardino freeway. The fire in Downey will cut off the Santa Ana freeway. The fires in Griffith Park, Mulholland Drive, and the canyons will cut off the northward-going freeways. Maybe the traffic can be started on the eastern freeways before the fires really get going. Maybe the choppers are dropping foam on the fires and putting them out. I hope so.

"But the fires in the north are too big to smother now, and no way am I going to go that way. The shortest distance is the best. That's west, southwest for a while, to the ocean. By the time we get there, I suspect the fire from Venice will have spread to Santa Monica. But we'll cut along its north side, on or along San Vicente Boulevard."

He pointed at Mrs. Adkins' feet. "Better take off those high heels."

"I can't walk all that distance with bare feet!" she said. But she removed them.

Jenkyns said, "What about it, Mr. Malone? Cable makes sense."

Malone had looked angry when Cable had spoken to Mrs. Adkins. Evidently he felt that he should have made the suggestion, that he had somehow lost the initiative. Or perhaps he had never had it.

"It's the shortest way out," Malone said. "But . . . I don't know. The fire from Venice will be coming into Santa Monica from the south, and the hills just north of Santa Monica may also be on fire for all we know. We could find the whole town on fire by the time we got there, and then we would be trapped. It'd be too late to try to go back east. Besides, we'll be pooped by the time we get to Santa Monica. That's a hell of a long walk!"

"You do what you want to," Cable said. "I'm going my way."

He looked at Williamson, and the doctor said, "I'm going with you, Cable."

"No!" Malone said. "You're working for me, Williamson, and . . ."

By then Cable had stepped into the flow of people. Malone's voice, though still audible, was no longer intelligible. Cable was among an aged white-haired man and woman, a tall woman of about thirty-five, and a girl of about eleven. The woman did not look at all like Lee, but the child reminded him of Katie. For a moment he almost gave in to the impulse to go to Westwood and look for them. However, it was, he told himself, stupid and totally useless to even think about it. They would long ago have been in that stream of refugees going oceanward—he hoped.

Directly ahead of him were two women. One was six feet tall, fat, and sweating profusely. Her short black hair was plastered to her skull with sweat. The other was short and fat and evidently in need of comforting. The big one had an arm about her and was speaking softly in her ear. Once, the short one turned her head, and Cable could see the tears running down her blotched cheeks. Just as she turned her head away, the big one stopped and gasped. There was some confusion before her, people stopping, being jostled, and then going on. The big woman said, "Oh, my God!" and stepped over the man on the sidewalk, pulling her companion along.

A man had collapsed face down on the sidewalk. His skin was blue gray, and he did not seem to be breathing. There was some blood on both sides of his face and on the cement. The impact of his nose against the ground may have caused a nosebleed, but his heart had stopped altogether shortly after his fall.

Williamson's voice came from behind Cable. "There'll be a lot of those today. Stand to one side, Cable." Cable moved but bumped into a large man wearing a yellow hardhat. The man said, "Watch it, you bastard!"

Cable turned but the man was already gone, his place taken by a youth with long greasy hair, a guitar strapped to his back.

Williamson knelt down by the body, felt the pulse at the neck, stood up, bent over, and rolled the body over. A look at the opened eyes satisfied him. He straightened up and said, "Even if he was still living, what could I do for him?"

"Then quit wasting time," Cable said. "Your services are going to be very much needed but not until you get to the end of the line. And you won't unless you think of nothing but getting there."

He looked past Williamson and saw Malone's red face and Adkins' and Jenkyns' pale faces. "So they decided to come this way after all."

"Yes, Mrs. Adkins told him she had to go the shortest way because of her bare feet. He cursed her out and fired her, and she walked away, but they seem to be together again."

Cable turned without speaking and moved into the crowd again. Bodies pressed him on all sides, the pressure was momentarily relieved, then he was enfolded in the mass again. The stink of sweat shot with fear filled his nostrils, but after a while he was no longer aware of it. When he got to Orange he left Wilshire and cut across Orange. Williamson, now several people behind him, called out, "Where you going?"

"To Olympic," Cable said. A half a block later, the doctor had caught up with him. The three others were about a dozen people behind the doctor. "Why Olympic? It'll cut southward and bring you closer to Venice."

Cable pointed westward between two tall buildings. "See that mass of smoke there? I can't tell exactly where it's coming from, but it looks like it might be originating from the hills north of the Brentwood heights. With this wind, the fire'll be racing through the canyons and it might not be long before it gets to Brentwood Heights. That'll cut off San Vicente Boulevard, and then the fire'll be in the north part of Santa Monica. Olympic's the best compromise route, an alleyway between the northern and southern fires. I hope."

"Maybe Malone was right," Williamson muttered.

Cable did not reply. He wished that the people in front of him would walk more swiftly. If he could have an unimpeded path, he could walk at least a third faster. But there was no organization, no police to direct the strong walkers into one channel, the medium walkers into another, and the weak into a third. As a result, the weak ones were slowing down everybody else. So far, there had been little impatience shown. He'd seen no shoving or shouting to go faster or get out of the way. But, except for the clouds of smoke, there was nothing to spook them. The orders over Jenkyn's radio had stressed that all should evacuate. At the same time, they had insisted that everybody should remain calm, that there was no reason to panic.

Getting across Orange Street wasn't easy. Cars three abreast and bumper to bumper filled the street, many of them with one set of wheels over the curb. The more agile pedestrians were climbing onto the hoods and stepping across to the other side. The older people and the crippled were holding up those behind them. Cable waited, unable to get through the press at first, then urged forward by those piling up behind him. Just ahead of him, on the bumpers between a small Ford and a large Oldsmobile, were two men and a St. Bernard dog. The dog was on a leash, and the man in front of him was pulling on it while urging the giant to follow him. The man behind was pushing on the massive shaggy rear and swearing loudly. But the dog was sitting down, its tail lying along the bumpers, and he would go no further.

Both men were wearing the headgear affected by some Californians this year, pink berets on top of which were tiny plastic bananas, grapes, apples, oranges, and plums. Their sleeveless openwork lace shirts with Elizabethan neck ruffs were soaked with sweat.

"God damn it, you fruits!" a man beside Cable said. "Get that monstrosity out of the way or let a man at him!"

The youth on the leash quit pulling and straightened up. He wiped the sweat off his forehead and snarled, "Up yours! Nobody's touching Charlus!"

The man was tall, beefy, large-paunched, and red-faced. He said, "Yeah?" and his hand went into his hip pocket and came out with a knife handle. There was a snick, and a blade shot out. He pushed Cable to one side, leaned forward, and thrust the knife between the legs of the youth pushing on the dog. The St. Bernard yelped, sprang up, knocked the youth before him flat on his back, and, still yelping, scrambled over him. He leaped from the ends of the bumpers onto the hood of a Plymouth, his paws skidded, and he fell between the Plymouth and a Mazda. Wedged between, he struggled and howled.

The man with the knife got onto the bumper. He looked down at the two sprawled before him. "Get out of the way, you queers! Or I'll stick you too!"

The man facing forward rose and helped the other to his feet. The latter, his face twisted, said, "God damn you, you made me hurt my back!"

"Too bad," the man with the knife said. "You stupid fruits, the city's burning down and you're worrying about a worthless dog. I hate those big stinking sons of bitches anyway!"

The man nearest him suddenly whirled. There was a sharp explosion, and the man with the knife fell backward, striking Cable on his shoulder. Cable went down while people screamed and yelled around him and those nearest tried to press back.

Cable looked. The youth was holding a short-barreled .22 revolver in one hand and staring wild-eyed down at the man on the sidewalk. "You dumbass!" he said. "You *made* me do it!"

Cable got to his feet. The man was lying on his back, holding his paunch. Blood was streaming from between his fingers, and his skin was turning from red to gray. His mouth hung open; his eyes were large. Cable bent down and picked up the knife, folded the blade back into the handle, and put the knife in his pants pocket. He stepped over the man and onto the end of the bumper. The youth, still holding the gun, said, "What are you going to do?"

"Take it easy," Cable said. "Put the gun away and get going. If there's a panic, you'll get trampled to death."

"What about him?" the youth said, pointing with the gun at the wounded man. The gesture brought more cries from the crowd below him; they thought that he was going to shoot at them.

"He'll die," Cable said. "Nobody can help him."

The youth burst into tears. Cable said, "Do your crying elsewhere. These people have to get through. What's the matter, you want us all to burn to death?"

The other youth, standing on the hood above the dog, said, "Come on, Al, help me get Charlus out of here!"

Cable thought they'd be better advised to shoot the dog and go on, but he did not say so. The hysterical youth might shoot him instead. He walked along the bumpers, stepped onto the hood of a car before him, and crossing on another hood and the roof of a Vega, came to the other side of Orange.

He couldn't pause to take his bearings or decide which way to go. Behind him came a horde of men and women and some children. There were cries for help from some of the old people who were having difficulty and some yelling and shoving from people who found their passage blocked by the oldsters.

He walked south on the west side of Orange until he came to an alleyway between two apartment buildings. He went down that, feeling easier somewhat because there were only a few people in it. But, on emerging onto Fairfax, he was again in the crowd. And he had to climb over cars again to get to the west side of the street.

The juncture of Fairfax, San Vicente, and Olympic was a mass of babbling, cursing, struggling people. He passed a number of old men and women who were sitting or lying on the yards or sidewalks. Several of them were dead or looked as if they were dead. Heart failure, he supposed. The others had walked too far and climbed over too many automobiles to go another step. And now they waited, silent, moaning, weeping, a few begging for help from passersby. One old woman sat in a wheelchair and stared straight ahead, her lips moving silently. He supposed that she had been pushed from an apartment building, or possibly the home for retired Jews located on Beverly near Fairfax. Someone or someones had gotten her through the crowds, carried the wheelchair over cars at a number of intersections, gone back, carried her over the cars, put her back into the vehicle, and then had decided that he, she, or they could do it no longer. Or the pusher had collapsed, unable to get even himself on the way.

Stepping from one hood to the next on San Vicente, Cable saw below him a man of about eighty. He was lying face upward, stuck between the two car bodies. Cable looked down at the open blue eyes, cursed himself, and got down on his knees.

"Are you hurt?" he said.

The old man, in a thin quavering voice, said, "I lost my hearing aid. Get me out of here, for God's sake!"

Cable leaned down and got one arm, and the old man grabbed his arm with the other. Cable pulled him out and they sat down side by side. Looking directly at him, hoping he could lip-read, Cable said, "Can you walk?"

The old man's face was twisted with pain. He shook his head and said, "I hurt my ankle. Go on, son. I'd just hold you back. No use both of us dying. But I thank you. I was just about to start screaming. I didn't want to do that."

Cable stood up and pulled the old man up. He put the old man's arms around his shoulder and began the lengthy and tiring effort of getting him across the peaks and valleys of the jammed cars. By the time he succeeded in easing him down the car on the edge, he was drenched in sweat and feeling even more tired.

He raised him again and supporting him while he hobbled on one leg, got him to a yard before a small bungalow. The old man sat with his back against a tree, eyes closed for a moment. When he opened his eyes, he said, "If you could get me a drink of water. That's all I ask."

Cable licked his dry lips and said, huskily, "I'll see what I can do."

He walked to the house while he told himself that he had to stick to his original resolution. Once he got started giving his water away, he was done for.

The front door was locked. He went to the back, found it locked, picked up a large stone frog by a tiny pool, and smashed the glass in the door. Reaching in, he turned the lock and shot two bolts and entered a small kitchen. He grinned when the faucet gave water. He had not been sure that the supply had not been cut off. He drank two large glasses and then returned on his original route to the old man. Once he had seated him on the sofa in the front room, he filled a bucket with water. The refrigerator was empty except for a bowl of potato salad. He took it and a spoon and a large glass in for the old man, setting them on the coffee table in front of him.

"That's all I can do," he said.

"God bless you," the old man said. He closed his eyes, and he died.

SIXTEEN

Cable was angry at the old man. This was an irrational reaction. He was angry at himself, which was rational. He'd wasted time and energy, neither of which he could afford, because of a temporary softness. No more of that.

He heard noises at the back door and walked down the short hall to the kitchen. Several of the old people who had been sitting in the front yard were at the sink filling glasses with water. They looked at him but said nothing. He said, "There's a dead man in the front room. But there's also some potato salad." He turned and went through the house to the front door. A fly was on the lower lip of the old man's open mouth.

Malone, Williamson, Jenkyns, and Adkins were standing by the gate. They didn't seem surprised to see him, so they must have observed him going into the house. Evidently, they did not want to proceed without him. For some reason that was beyond him, they had decided to rely on him. Even Malone was watching him with expectancy. Somewhere during the brief passage from the Cal-Pax building to this house, he had lost his drive to be the leader.

But if he should survive, he would never be able to forgive Cable for having become the dominant member of the group.

He looked at their sweating drawn faces and cracked lips. Heat and fear were pumps driving the water from them. Of the two, fear was the strongest.

Malone took a bottle from his pocket and started to uncap it.

Cable said, "You'd better save all of that you can. There's water inside the house. Go in there and fill up your bellies."

Malone put the bottle back. Adkins said, "You won't leave us while we're in there?"

"Don't dawdle," Cable said, though he knew the advice was superfluous. It was better to say something, though, and he had no intention of making any promises.

Malone, Jenkyns and Adkins hastened up the walk. Williamson said, "I'll stay. I drank enough at the office for two camels. In fact, I got a bellyache from it. You'd think a doctor would know better, wouldn't you?"

Cable, watching Adkins, said, "She's limping already. She'll never make it with bare feet, especially on hot pavement."

"Yeah, I know," Williamson said. "Maybe she should have left her high heels on."

"Either way, she's screwed."

"That's a hard-hearted way to look at it," the doctor said. But he didn't seem shocked.

"I should have told her to look for shoes that might fit her in the house," Cable said. He hesitated a moment and then went after her. Just as he got to the front door, he saw her through the screen. She was sitting in a chair across from the sofa with the dead man. She had one of the old man's flat-heeled shoes on and was putting on another. She tied them while he waited. "They fit," she called.

"Maybe you'll make it after all," Cable murmured. A moment later, Malone came out of the kitchen, followed by three white-haired and wrinkled women. Adkins did not wait for him but went through the door ahead of him.

Malone turned at the door and shouted something at one of the old women. He slammed the door in her face and ran after Adkins and Cable, who had not stopped walking but had been watching over their shoulders.

"Jesus Christ!" he said. "You won't believe it, but that old woman offered me a thousand dollars cash, and all her jewelry, if I'd help her! I told her I'd dropped more than that in ten minutes at Las Vegas, and she began cursing me. You never heard such language from an old lady!"

"You'd have done the same if it'd been your grandmother," Adkins said.

Malone looked startled. "What? What the hell's the matter with you, Myrna?"

"What did you expect from her?" Williamson said. "She's letting loose twenty years of frustration and resentment."

Cable said, "Save your breath. Where's Jenkyns?"

Malone looked around and said, "I don't know. He went into the crapper, that's the last I saw of him."

"He looked awful pale, gray, in fact," Adkins said. "Do you suppose he's sick?"

"Let's go," Cable said. He turned away and began walking. Adkins ran after him and took hold of his arm. "Are you going to leave Jenkyns there?"

Cable shook her hand off and said, "Look! I tried to get into your head that we can't be burdened. If you try to help somebody else, you're going to get caught along with him. It may seem heartless, but it's stupid to throw away your life trying to help somebody that can't be helped. Get that now, because I'm not going to say another word about it!"

"And what if you get sick or hurt?"

"Then you go on without me if you have any sense."

Nevertheless, he could not help wondering if he might cut back north to Wilshire to get to Westwood. He had already rejected the idea that he could find Lee and his daughter there. And going north would bring him that much closer to the fires sweeping down the hills. Yet . . . what if they could not for some reason walk? What if Lee or Katie were sick? What if? What if? There were a thousand what ifs and to think about them would drain him of strength and resolution. And there was Dorothy. Where was she? If she'd come ashore, she doubtless was with her crew, filming the exodus. Recording the fire and the people fleeing from it when she and the crew should be running with the rest. But she was tough, she could take care of herself. Nevertheless . . .

The crowd ahead, relatively a loose assemblage, suddenly became packed. He stopped, and Adkins bumped into him. "What is it?" she said breathlessly.

"Just another barricade of cars," he said. "The people climbing over the cars where Sloat meets Olympic are holding up those behind. It's going to be this way at every corner."

Williamson joined them, and a few seconds later Malone had caught up with them. "Jesus!" Malone said. "It'll take us three times as long. Isn't there any other way? What about the smaller streets, the side streets?"

"They'll be just as jammed with cars and people," Cable said.

Cable stepped forward as those ahead moved about a foot. The sky everywhere was black, and the air had become a little darker during the half a block passage. He sniffed and thought he could smell a trace of smoke, though that could be his imagination. It would, however, only be a matter of time, and then the smoke would be on them. As the fires got closer the smoke would get thicker. How many hundreds of thousands of bushes and trees, how many thousands of houses, were burning up there?

And how long before this parade became a stampede?

He moved another step forward. Adkins plucked the sleeve of his shirt. He looked back, and she said, "That child?"

He had been aware of an infant's crying nearby but had made no attempt to locate its source. Nor did he want to do so. Now, at Adkins' insistence, he looked to his right. The bodies of those between him and the building blocked his view for a moment. Then he glimpsed the huge black woman sitting on the sidewalk with her back against the building. By her side stood a black girl of about three years of age. She was crying loudly and at the same time tugging on the woman's shoulder. The crowd closed up again, and he could no longer see the two.

"What about it," he said.

"The woman looks like she's passed out. Maybe she's dead."

Cable said nothing. Adkins left him, pushing through people who gave way reluctantly before her determination. Cable caught sight briefly of Williamson, kneeling down by the woman. He was looking into her eyes and feeling her pulse.

Cable gained another foot toward the intersection. He looked to his left and saw several young men and women on top of the cars on Olympic. They were going westward, walking on the roofs, stepping down to the hoods, leaping up onto the roof of the next. There were not enough of them to slow down their passage; the only thing limiting their speed was their degree of agility and endurance.

Cable had thought of that route, but he had decided that it was far too exhausting. It would take a mountain goat to travel on that up-and-down hazardous route. Maybe a fresh youth in good shape could make it to the coast, but he was thirty-four and had been wrung out emotionally and physically this morning.

Yet, it would take him all day and maybe part of the night to get to the other end of Olympic at this rate. This was a race, and yet he was forced to travel not much faster than a tortoise, and to survive he had to be a hare.

He pushed through the crowd in a zigzag, caused by the hard resistance of some and the nonaggressiveness of others. A man snarled at him, "Watch it, you son of a bitch!" but most of the stand fasts just glared at him or leaned their bodies against him.

Reaching the edge of the sidewalk, he climbed on his hands and knees onto the hood of the nearest car. It was a light-green Impala Chevrolet. The car just ahead was a tiny convertible 1958 Volkswagen, its top down. He stepped down on the sloping rear and from it into the back seat. It was another step over the back of the right front seat and over the windshield and onto its hood. In front of it was a car seen only in some numbers in Beverly Hills and Bel Air. It was a Silver Cloud Rolls Royce, which had a rear that did not slope gently. Instead of trying its steep back, he jumped onto the hood of the Dodge Demon beside the Volkswagen. And he told himself that his wits must be getting dull. He should have avoided the convertible because it took too much energy to get across a low open vehicle. He should have stepped across the Buick from the Impala.

He paused for a moment, looking ahead and then behind. Six cars directly ahead loomed the rear of an Onondaga motor home. He'd have to go around that. Also ahead were a number of people climbing up from the sidewalk. Like him, they had finally understood that there was only one fast escape route. And like him, they must have been dulled by the mass mentality, the sluggish overbrain of the crowd.

Behind him came some young people who had taken this rough highway some time before. And along the edges of the jam, on both sides of the street, others were leaving the sidewalk and its jam.

If this continued, the tops of the cars would also soon be crowded. But not, however, as thickly as the sidewalks. There were too many, the old, the sick, those hampered with small children, who could not or would not get up onto the vehicles.

Malone's and Adkins' faces appeared over the top of a Mercury MX station wagon. Williamson joined them several seconds later. Adkins disappeared, reappeared with the small black face of the little girl he'd seen crying by her collapsed mother. She was boosted, still weeping and bawling, onto the roof of the wagon. A moment later, the two men and the woman were on the hood. Adkins took the child's hand and helped her onto the next vehicle, an Oldsmobile Toronado.

Cable did not intend to wait for them. He knew without asking what had happened. The black woman was either dead or too sick to go on, and Adkins had been unable to abandon the child. He hoped that she would have no cause to regret her decision, but he doubted it.

He turned away and stepped down from the roof onto the hood and sprang across to the trunk cover of a Plymouth Duster Custom. He went over its roof and onto its hood and sprang again. After passing over about twelve cars, he was forced to step across to the Ford Gran Torino beside him. Six youths sat jammed on the roof of the car ahead, a Lincoln Continental. From their loud gaspings, they had evidently been going too swiftly. That was a mistake. The time they'd made in racing was being lost in resting. Moreover, running would eat up energy out of all proportion to the distance gained. This wasn't going to be a dash.

As Cable passed the group, one of them, a plump huge-breasted blonde in scarlet halter and blue shorts, said, "Hey, he's got a bottle! How about a drink, mister?"

Cable did not reply. He jumped to the next car, but when he was seven cars away from the youths, stopped to look back. The three males had stepped onto the roof of the Oldsmobile Delta 88 Royale next to them and were waiting for Malone. They had spotted the bottle sticking out of his coat pocket. Malone crossed to the roof of a Mercury Montego to avoid them, but they leaped across to face him. They pulled long switchblade knives out of the back pockets of their Levis.

Malone, his face red, shouted something at them. They started toward him, but he pulled the .45 automatic out of his belt and pointed it at them. He yelled again and waved the gun, and they jumped back to the roof with the girls. Malone waited until the doctor and Adkins and the child had passed him. He jumped to the Mercury Cougar ahead, whirled to make sure the youths weren't about to jump him from behind, saw they weren't, and proceeded. The youths were shouting obscenities at him and gesturing with their extended middle fingers. But it was obvious they were afraid to tackle him.

At least, they were not going to do it at once. When Malone had crossed four cars, they stepped onto the next one and started after him at a walk. Maybe they were just going on after resting. Or maybe they intended to wait until they could catch Malone off-guard. Whichever the case, it was no business of his, Cable told himself.

He stepped onto the trunk lid of a Dodge Monaco. Ten cars ahead, the towering rear of another trailer blocked his path. Between Fairfax and La Cienega was a stretch of ten blocks. Approximately three-quarters of a mile. He looked at his wristwatch. It had taken him twenty minutes since he had climbed onto the first car.

A man carrying a knapsack on his back, a canteen on his belt, and holding a transistor radio went by in the next lane. Cable called to him. "Say anything about the fires in the north?"

The man, without slowing, shouted, "It's about two miles south from Mulholland Drive! All along the Santa Monica range!"

"How far has it gotten into Santa Monica City from Venice?"

Cable had shouted, but the man increased his pace without replying. Cable caught up with him and said, "Do you know how much of the Santa Monica is on fire?"

The man looked annoyed, but he said, "It's almost to Ocean Park Boulevard!"

That would mean that the flames were very close to Olympic, Cable thought. He felt a shock, almost a blow, pass through him. At the rate he was traveling, all of Santa Monica would be burning before he even got close to it. The flames were sweeping along far more swiftly than he had expected, both from the north and the south. He wasn't quite sure how far the city of Beverly Hills extended to the north. He did know that it flung out a pseudopod from its northwest side, one that covered many houses in the canyons. If the fire hadn't reached that area, it soon would. As the flames raced down the canyons and jumped the ridges, it would spill into the heavily populated northern part. And the same thing would happen to Bel Air. Everywhere south of the hills.

From his slight elevation, he could see a bright flicker among the hills. The smoke was heavier, oily looking now. He turned to look southwestward. The smoke from the Venice area was just visible. The winds were, however, rushing it off toward the ocean. Eventually, and not soon, he prayed, the recirculation of heated air would start a firestorm. Then the winds would become strong, would hit the people with ever hotter air, would make houses untouched by the fire begin to send up curls of smoke, would . . . he couldn't bear to think any more about that. He had to go on, keep the panic down so he wouldn't start running, think of nothing but the end of his road.

The end of the road. It could no longer be on Olympic. He'd have to cut north. But not yet. He'd wait until he got to Spalding, which cut across Olympic to go north. Until then, Olympic went straight west. He should have stayed on Wilshire.

SEVENTEEN

Something had spooked the crowd at the same time it spooked him. Either the news had traveled from people with radios or the sight of the advancing flames had done it. Or both. Many more were shouting now or screaming. Most of the people on top of the cars were running. Those on the ground were suddenly struggling, pushing, knocking others down or being knocked down.

At the intersection of Olympic and Le Doux, the people on the east sides had piled up by the cars blocking them. Cable saw a huge hairy man, clad only in Levis cut off at the knees, step on a head, put the other foot on the back of a woman trying to stand up on the pile, take another step, and then fall backward as a man behind him grabbed him by his hair. The grabber fell with him onto the body of an old woman.

The pile must have been at least five bodies deep and about seven wide, though it was difficult to tell. Those deep under must have been crushed, and those alive had little chance to get out. For a minute, there was a space before the pile, and then those in the front, fighting to keep from being carried forward onto the pile, went down. The long line stretching from street to street, at least ten abreast, maybe, seemed to flow like lava. But some fell here and there and others fell over them, creating eddies, whirlpools.

Those who got to the hoods and the roofs of the cars ran if they were able. If they weren't, they got knocked down. A number fell into the very narrow spaces between the cars and added their cries to the others.

Despite the roars and shrieks, he heard the pounding of feet on the metal roofs behind him. He looked back to see the six youths running toward him. One, the tallest, held a whiskey bottle in his hand. Ten cars behind them, on the roof of a long limousine-type car, were the doctor and Adkins. They were looking down between a pickup truck and a semi. Cable did not need to go back to find out what had happened. The youth with the bottle must have snatched it out of Malone's pocket. Then either he or one of his group had slugged Malone and tumbled him into the space between the vehicles. The child had got caught in the action and gone over also.

They weren't the only victims. The tops of the cars were filling up with men, women, and some children. Part of these had come running up Olympic, having gotten onto the roofs further down the street. Others were climbing up from the sidewalks. The faster ones, angered by being held up, shoved the slow ones to one side. These stumbled and caught themselves or fell shrieking. Some went to their knees or on their faces, and those behind them sometimes sprawled over them. Then still others would fall over them.

Adkins and Williamson, on their knees to help Malone and the child, were shoved into the gap on top of them. No doubt they were screaming, but Cable could not hear them above the cries of the multitude.

He thought it better to get out of the way for a minute or two. Maybe the panic would subside. He stepped down onto the fender of a station wagon and then sat down on it. The fender shook as feet pounded by; a horde thundered by, gasping, cursing, sobbing. Some looked wild-eyed at him, though he doubted that they saw him as anything but a nonobstacle. At this moment the refugees were classifying all people into two groups: those who were not in the way and those who were. The former were nothing but lumps of flesh, inanimate objects that did not threaten. The latter were also objects, not human beings, dangerous objects.

Cable waited while his breathing became normal or as normal as it could get under the circumstances. The sky was darker, and the flames to the north were brighter and higher. The wind had increased in the last ten minutes, but it did not cool. The cloud of smoke from

Venice and Santa Monica seemed to be a trifle nearer, but this was only his imagination. Or he hoped it was.

His mouth felt dry. He licked his lips and then slid down from the fender into the crevasse of the hood and the trunk of the Ford Granada ahead. Wedged in the narrow space, lying on his back, he took the bottle from his coat pocket and drank from it. People leaped over him, shaking the cars. But they did not notice that he had a bottle of water. Or else they were blind with panic.

A girl screamed above, a shadow fell on him, and a foot kicked him on top of the head. He bit down hard on the neck of the bottle, but he felt no pain in his mouth at the moment. The foot had knocked him half-senseless; streaks of light shot through darkness. His sight cleared. His teeth and tongue hurt, he tasted blood, his head hurt, and his neck hurt. The foot had knocked his head back so sharply that he had wrenched his neck. And the bottle was gone from his hand.

He struggled up, groaning a little, and managed to raise himself up. The bottle was nowhere in sight. He gripped the edge of the station wagon's hood, and pulled himself up. A shoe came down within an inch of his fingers and was gone. Other shoes followed it. He clung on and twisted around slowly. A girl was sprawled face down on the fender. She was breathing but showed no signs of consciousness.

He ran his tongue around his teeth. There was a chip at the corner of a front tooth and a gouge in his palate. That seemed to be all the damage there. He swallowed some blood and removed the other bottle from the other coat pocket. He drank swiftly, washing out his mouth and swallowing the mingled blood and water. It was too precious to spit out. Quickly, he screwed the cap back on and stuck the bottle into his pocket.

The traffic was slowing down above. Both cars bobbed as the weight of passersby varied on front and back, but the feet no longer pounded. The running had worn them out quickly, and their progress was now relatively sedate.

Getting back up wasn't easy. It was painful—both his neck and his left shoulder hurt—but he got up. About a dozen passed on both sides of him as he stood on the bumpers. The girl lying between the hoods stirred, raised her head, and tried to push herself up with her arms. Blood streaked the side of her jaw and matted a part of her long yellow hair.

Something roared overhead. He looked up, sending sharp pains through his neck as he did so. A four-motored propellor airplane, big-bellied, shot above him at a height of about five hundred feet. It disappeared beyond the buildings in the direction of Venice. It was probably loaded with foam to be dropped on the fire there. Maybe, and he hoped he was right, it was the forerunner of a fleet sent to keep the lane open between the fires. But how many loads would have to be dumped to do any good? Were there enough planes available? It didn't seem likely.

He heard a shot behind him, and he hurt his neck again as he jerked it to look around. He saw Malone's head rise above the roof of a car. Williamson and Adkins were helping him up. There was no sign of the little girl. Nor was there anybody holding a gun, though the shooter could easily be behind any number of people. Many people had stopped at the report and some had thrown themselves down. But now they moved forward, assured that there was no immediate danger to themselves.

Cable went on, felt pain again in his neck as he jumped from a Volkswagen trunk cover onto the rear of a Cadillac Fleetwood Brougham, crossed that, crossed an Audi Fox, was blocked by the high vertical rear of a Winnebago motor home, crossed onto another Volkswagen, and waited until there was a momentary gap in the traffic on the roof of the Malibu Chevelle beside the German vehicle. Then he got onto that and continued onto the small Fiat in front of the Chevelle.

About every ten minutes by his wristwatch, he sat down on the edge of a roof and rested until his wind returned. Twice he was forced to step aside, straddling the hoods of two cars to keep from being knocked down.

However, the people were not progressing as swiftly as they had. Going over the cars was like climbing a rough mountain, tiring even to juveniles. The number of those sitting on the roof edges was increasing. There were few voices heard now, though much heavy breathing. The loudest were the babies and small children, and there were only a few here and there.

Ten minutes passed too swiftly, and he forced himself to get up. His legs quickly stiffened when he sat down.

From La Cienega to Spalding, where he intended to go north, was about thirty-two blocks. Almost two miles. And from Spalding up to Wilshire and down Wilshire to the ocean would be nearly eight miles. Ten miles all told—if he were walking on ground level. But the up-and-down and sidewise obstacle course of the cars must add at least two more miles. Add to that one and a half miles, more or less, from the Cal-Pax building to La Cienega, and he would have to walk-leap-climb fourteen and a half miles.

He shook his head as if he were trying to dislodge the thought— hurting his neck in doing so—and decided to keep his mind on a short-term goal. He would think only of getting from the end of one block to the next. One block at a time.

Before he had reached Spalding, long before, it had become one step, one jump at a time.

At least twenty times he was completely blocked by groups sitting on roof and hood, jammed together and forcing him to cross over. Several times he had to zigzag back and forth to get to a comparatively unoccupied space. At least half of the resters were youths. They were as exhausted as their elders and much more vociferous with their complaints. They were soft, many of them overweight. Too little walking, too much food, cigarettes, soft drinks, and beer had done them in. Now they sat breathing hard, their clothes and hair soaked in sweat, cursing their charley horses, their sore feet, their tired muscles. Most of all, they talked of their thirst.

Cable had longed for another drink before he reached Spalding, but he didn't want to be robbed of the bottle. He got down from a Buick Regal at the west side of the street and headed for an office building. Inside it, away from the sight of others, he would drink at least a quarter of the bottle. And if he could find a faucet quickly, and the water was still running, he'd refill the bottle. This would take time, and from the height of the flames in the north, he didn't have time to waste. But he couldn't help that. If he didn't get more water he wasn't going to make it anyway.

Why didn't the others go into the buildings and houses in search of water? He didn't know—unless it was a numbness of thought, a reluctance to make an extra effort, that made them do nothing but sit and complain.

After a while, though, when they became maddened with thirst, they would go into the buildings. By then, there probably would be no water. The fire would have burned out the pumping stations or the power stations that provided the electricity for the pumps. Or both.

The building was forty stories, constructed the year before. Inside was a large lobby with several large counters along the walls. A candy and tobacco and newspaper stand, according to a sign, was operated by a blind man. He had left, of course, and must now be feeling his way along the sidewalk or groping as he climbed over the vehicles at the junctions.

The lobby was unlit. The big clock on the wall near the elevators had stopped. Cable checked his wristwatch. The electricity had been cut off an hour ago.

He went into the men's room and turned a washbowl faucet on. Water gushed into his palms, became a trickle, and the pipes rattled. He drank water from his palms and went down the line of washbowls until he had emptied them all. He went into the women's rooms and repeated the procedure. The toilet bowls were still full, but he wasn't desperate enough to drink from them. Though he had sweated heavily, his bladder was full. He relieved himself against the wall. There was no reason to spoil the water in a toilet bowl. Someone would be drinking from it, someone maddened by thirst.

Leaving the women's room, he went down the hall and entered the first office he came to. Some offices used water coolers, and he could spare a few minutes to look for one.

The third one had a water cooler. It was of no use. Somebody, no doubt out of malice, a senseless desire to destroy, had pushed it over onto the floor. It had shattered, of course, and the water had soaked into the thick carpet. He turned to leave. A groan from somewhere stopped him. He looked around at the four rows of desks covered by typewriters and plastic trays full of paper. He could see nobody. Then the groan came again, and he went between a row of desks into an inner office.

A young woman lay on her back on the floor. Her skirt had been pulled up around her waist, and her pantyhose taken off and thrown in a heap by her head. Her blouse and bra had been torn off. Large bruises covered her breasts; one nipple had bled heavily for some time; it had been half-bitten off. Her face and neck were covered with black marks and bloody scratches. Drying blood streaked her lips and chin and the front part of her neck. The blood had gushed out of a broken nose and from smashed lips. Beaten and raped and left to die.

She had also been robbed. Her purse lay open by a desk, most of its contents spilled on the floor.

Cable told himself that there was nothing he could do for her except put her out of her pain. And he could not do that.

It was the hardest thing he had done so far, but he left the office. He closed the door, then opened it. Maybe somebody might come along and be foolish enough to try to help her. He or she would be committing suicide, but if he or she wanted to do that, he would make it easy for them. And who knew? Maybe the fire would be stopped . . . he shook his head, sending pain through his neck again, and told himself not to think like that. The girl would lie there until she burned to death. Or, if she were lucky, she'd be suffocated by smoke first. Or die of her injuries first.

He went into four more suites of offices. Only one had a cooler, and that had also been broken. Two rest rooms, however, contained washbowls. He emptied their pipes, but still was unsatisfied. There might be offices in the upper floors which had unbroken coolers. He did not have the time to walk up the stairs and look. Besides, though it did not seem likely, the rapists might still be roaming through the building. If they had any sense they wouldn't be. But if they had any sense they wouldn't have delayed to vandalize and rape. He didn't want to run into them if they were still here.

He left, wishing fiercely that he had a gun and had encountered them. He would have shot them without a qualm of conscience.

In the lobby he found about twenty people with more crowding through the door. Somebody had seen him go in and figured that he was looking for water. And others, sheeplike, had followed that person. He couldn't even get out because of the crowd. He turned and walked down a hall which led to a side exit. Instead of climbing back onto the cars, he walked northward on the sidewalk. The pedestrians had thinned out here enough for him to walk comparatively unimpeded. Instead of walking straight to Santa Monica Boulevard on Spalding, he turned left onto Moreno and followed it up. It curved northwestward and saved him time and distance. He went over the railroad tracks that ran along the south side of Santa Monica Boulevard, crossed the boulevard, and stopped before a wire fence. Beyond lay the broad grounds of the Los Angeles Country Club.

He climbed over the fence and continued across the greens. There were many people who had the same idea. But they were not by any means a crowd. He walked over the turf, grateful for its softness. The flags of the poles stuck in the holes whipped with the wind from the north, a wind which was getting hotter. Bushes and small trees were beginning to sway, and a sheet of newspaper rolled and flapped before him like wings without a bird. It was moving at about 24 miles an hour, he estimated. About 5 on the Beaufort scale. It wouldn't be long before it was 6. The greater the fire became, the greater the wind. And the more the wind, the faster the fire would spread.

On the other hand, though the vast flames on the Pacific were pulling in the air from the land, the smaller but still large fires on the range were sucking in the air along their edges. This counterattraction would slow down the spread around the edges. Just so, the fires along the edge of the Venice-Santa Monica would be checked somewhat by the southward wind.

He began walking faster. He had a long way to go.

EIGHTEEN

North, on the other side of Wilshire, the links were beginning to be jammed with people. These, he supposed, had left Sunset Boulevard. He hoped it wasn't because the fires were so close that they had driven the refugees to the south. It didn't look like it to him. There were no smoke plumes drifting upward from nearby.

Wilshire was as jammed with cars and with people as Olympic. The same comparative quiet lay along the avenue, punctuated only by the cries of some infants and a few here and there calling for help.

He walked along the edge of the crowd for a while. Then, seeing a momentary break, he angled in toward the road. It was slow work because of their closeness, and he did not want to shove if he could help it. There were too many obviously on the edge, ready to shove back or even swing at him. He couldn't afford to waste his depleted energy in a fistfight. But by moving in whenever there was the slightest break, by ignoring curses or insults, he got to the cars. By then he had reached Beverly Glen, which crossed Wilshire in a north-south direction. He had trouble getting onto a Caprice because of the pressure of bodies against him. He allowed himself to be carried along slowly by the crowd and just before the passage came to a standstill, blocked by the cars across Beverly Glen, he rolled into an open MG convertible. He got up and climbed up onto the hood of a Toyota Corona and from there went onto the rear of a Ford.

When he reached the first car on the junction, he made the transition easily. It consisted of stepping across six roofs and then returning to the westward-pointed cars on Wilshire. The traffic here was not as heavy as it had been on Olympic. Most of the people looked as if they had been on it for a long time. At least half were resting, and the others lacked spring in their legs. They shambled along, slowly, made their little jumps as if they thought each would be the last. And they spoke mainly, not of their exhaustion but of their thirst. Cable told himself that he must, he must, push away the impulse to give his water to the crying children. It would in the end do them no good, and he would perish without it. Fortunately, there were very few children on the tops of the cars, and the further away they were, the weaker was his impulse.

He tried not to think of how far he still had to go. One block at a time, one block at a time. And then he was at the juncture of Wilshire and the San Diego freeway. Here he gained some time by leaving the road and cutting across the Veterans Cemetery. There were many people on the green grass, but there was also more space for them. He felt a renewal of strength then, as if the closeness of others had been draining him.

There was row on row of little headstones with their brief inscriptions. He remembered having been here once when he first came to Los Angeles. Like so many, he had come just to look upon one memorial, that of the fabled mountain man, "Liver Eating" Johnston. And he remembered thinking, as he looked at the stone, how jammed together all the graves were, how Johnston, who couldn't breathe freely unless his nearest neighbor was fifty miles away, would resent being so crowded. There wasn't room for him to turn over.

He climbed up the steep slope to the freeway, slipping, going down on all fours and staying there. It was easier to stay down than to get up, and he came over the top on his hands and knees. The fence, however, had been collapsed under the weight of many bodies climbing it or else a group had made a concerted effort to bring it down. There was a gap of about twenty feet here and up and down its length were other openings. He got up and walked across the wire, climbed onto the first car he came to, a Ford LTD, and stepped across. There was no need for him to climb over the center fence. Cars filled the lanes on both sides of the fence, the lanes that were supposed to be left open for police cars, ambulances, tow trucks, and broken-down vehicles.

Cable had gone north to avoid the ramps. When he came down the other side of the freeway, he was on Pepper Street. This was one of the few streets in the grounds of the National Home for Veterans. It was almost deserted now, though a few faces were at the windows of the hospitals and four men sat in wheelchairs on a lawn. They were passing a bottle of whiskey back and forth and jeering at the passersby.

Whatever efforts had been made to evacuate all the sick and crippled had obviously failed. But someone had given these men liquor to sustain them. Or else, they had brought out from their hiding place the liquor they'd smuggled in.

Cable looked at his wristwatch. It was 4:28 P.M. The entire north was a mass of flames. The flames to the south were not visible, but above them, on the black smoke, a dull red glowered.

He could not be sure, but it looked to him as if the southern fire might have reached, or was close to, Olympic Boulevard in the city of Santa Monica. The northern fire could have reached Santa Monica Boulevard along its straight east-west extent. And if a line were drawn straight west from it at the point where it began to curve south, that line would go through the northern part of Beverly Hills and Bel Air. And straight out to the ocean.

The hot wind was whipping at him from the north. About forty miles an hour now. Maybe more. It sucked the sweat off him as fast as it poured from his body. And the odor of smoke, which had been steadily increasing, was strong now. It would not be long before he'd be coughing. Along with millions of others.

He decided to take San Vicente Boulevard. Wilshire dropped too far south, too close to the flames creeping northward from the lower part of Santa Monica city. He tried to think through the numbness and heaviness settling, like smoke, on his brain and body. The adrenalin that had driven him this far was gone. He was exhausted, breathing hard, his legs and his lower back muscles like rusted metal. His mouth was powdered metal, and his lips were cracked. He took the bottle from his pocket. To hell with anyone noticing it, he had to have water. His hands shook as he held the bottle and unscrewed the cap. He lifted it to his lips and drank until it was half-empty. He wanted to take it all in, but he would need more later on. If he remembered correctly, he had over four miles to go before reaching the Pacific. And that would not be the end of the road. By then the heat might be so terrific that he would have to get into the water up to his neck. And that might not be enough. His skin, his hair, might start smoking, the ocean might boil. Of pigs and sealing wax and boiling seas, how'd that go? Never mind. He must go.

The jam along San Vicente Boulevard slowed him. It was impossible to thread through the crowd. There were no openings. The jam on top of the cars seemed almost as thick. But he got up onto a Dodge pickup truck and fell in between two groups of youths. When the group ahead of him stopped to sit down and rub their calves, their faces twisted with the pain of cramped muscles, he walked among them, the sides of his legs brushing their backs. His own calves were tightening up, but he did not want to spend any more time sitting. He had to go on, on.

When he came to Montana, which ran southwestward from San Vicente at an oblique angle, he switched to it. The traffic was somewhat thinner on its cartops, though the sidewalks were as heavily peopled as the boulevards.

Suddenly, the pressure of the bodies eased. They were leaving the walks and spreading out on the links of the Brentwood Country Club. He climbed down off the cars and walked north until he could step along more freely. It felt good to be on soft ground again, not to have to jump, climb, step down, leap, wait for those ahead of him to move slowly or be shoved now and then by those impatient behind him.

He crossed Burlingame and Moreno, which, miraculously, were free of cars and then proceeded on Alta. This ran parallel with Montana and was crowded with cars. But there were not quite as many people on top of them.

It was brighter now. The black skies were throwing back the glare even more harshly. The wind had increased during his passage from San Vicente to this point. Forty-five miles an hour. The smoke was thicker, too; the more sensitive were beginning to cough.

A middle-aged man in front of him suddenly staggered, clutching his throat, and fell down on the roof of a Ford Mustang. Cable went to step over him, but the man rolled over on his back, and his foot struck the side of Cable's leg. Cable caught sight of a red agonized face as he sprawled over him and fell on his side beside the man. He heard the bottle break and felt the water gush down his arm. For a moment he lay face down breathing hard, cursing weakly, feeling tears run down his nose. Then he struggled up to a sitting position and pulled the broken bottle from his pocket. There was still some water, a few inches, in it. He held the jagged end above his mouth so he wouldn't cut it, his neck paining him as he tilted his head far back, and he drained it. A piece of glass fell on his tongue, but instead of spitting out along with the precious water, he reached in with a finger and extracted it.

Above him, a woman passed. He stared, not believing it for a moment. She was carrying a reel of film under one arm, and behind her came Chang, carrying the camera, and Grey with two reels.

He croaked, "Dorothy!" but she had gone down onto the hood and stepped onto the trunk of the car ahead.

The men, either not hearing him or not caring if they heard, went on, too. But even if he had his full voice, he probably wouldn't have been heard. The cries and babble from dry throats and swollen tongues and cracked lips was an unintelligible muted roar everywhere. He'd have had to be next to her for her to hear him.

He scrambled up the fender and onto the hood. He had to wait a moment while a dozen young men and women staggered by, and then he was able to stand up. The roof was free of the man's body now; somebody had rolled it into the narrow space between roofs. Or the man had rolled himself off in his contortions.

There was no way for him to catch up with Dorothy. He would just have to hope that those between him and her would stop to rest. This didn't seem likely now. The flames, even though they were quite a distance away, seemed to be close, and fear would allow no one who was capable of going on to stop.

The wind whipped at his clothes and brought a heaviness of smoke. He coughed, and he had to slow down while he tried to stop the racking. Somebody shoved him from behind, almost sending him off the hood. He was too tired and numb to snarl at the person, almost too tired to feel angry. He stopped, took out his handkerchief, and tied it around the lower part of his face. That helped him breathe somewhat easier, though it would have been more efficient if he could soak it in water.

Others were covering their noses, too. Those who didn't have handkerchiefs were stripping off their shirts and blouses to use as smoke screens. The crowd was beginning to look like masked bandits fleeing an unsuccessful bank robbery. He giggled at the thought. He was close to hysteria. But he felt a little better. The giggles had relieved some tension.

He went on. Up and down and across. Up and down and across. And the wind was slowing him down. He had to lean a little to his right and a little back to keep from being pushed off. It blew the long hair of the youths ahead of him, wrapping the strands around their faces so they had to keep brushing it away. A boy on the edge of a roof was blinded for a moment and with a scream fell between a car and a semi. His companions went on, perhaps not seeing or hearing him. Cable did not even look down to see what condition the youth was in. He did not want to know.

Now and then, he could see Dorothy's back. She was stumbling. Why didn't she throw the heavy reel away? The two men with her were also hanging on to their equipment. No, they weren't. Chang had dropped the camera between a radiator and the rear of a car. Now Grey was abandoning his film. But she was ahead of them, had not seen them, and was clinging to hers.

"Damn it!" he muttered. "Get rid of it, Dorothy!"

How many blocks had he covered since he'd gotten onto Alta? Six? How many to go? He didn't know. Now it was one step at a time, one little jump at a time.

More and more were staggering, stumbling, falling. Those behind stepped around or over the collapsed people. Sometimes a person tripped, and there would be a sudden stop. If the lanes opposite were blocked, the body would be rolled over to one side. Or simply be stepped on.

UP FROM THE BOTTOMLESS PIT

The junction of Alta and 19th Street lay before him. He'd gone seven blocks. And many to go, many to go, the lines from the song Harry Belafonte used to sing about the fox carrying the stolen chicken circling through his mind, many a mile to go, many a mile to go.

It was then that he saw Dorothy, almost lost in the redly flickering darkness. She had fallen to her knees on the roof of a Corvette. The reel dropped from under her arm and disappeared into the gap between the Corvette and the cab of a huge semi. The man behind her pushed her, and she fell sideways between the vehicles.

NINETEEN

Dorothy was lying on her right side on the pavement. Her back was against the lower part of the Corvette's door. Her face was a few inches from the wheel of the semi. Cable slipped down from the trunk cover of the car and squeezed between the two vehicles. He pulled her back by her legs into the more open space, though the effort sent agony through his neck and back muscles. He rolled her over. Her face was streaked with makeup, sweat, and smoke. One eye was blackened, and she had a bloody lump just above the cheekbone. Her lips were cracked and bleeding.

He lifted her to a sitting position. She stared at him as if she didn't recognize him.

"It's Jim, Dorothy!" he croaked. She opened her mouth, exposing a swollen tongue. She said, "Jim," and closed her eyes. But she opened them again a few seconds later.

"We have to get back up!" he said.

She shook her head, though he did not know if that meant that she couldn't hear him clearly or if she just could not move.

He brought his face close to hers. She stank of smoke and fear. "Water!" she mumbled.

For a moment he thought of urinating into his cupped palms. Urine could be drunk twice before it became too poisonous with salts. But would she accept it? Or, if she did, would she get sick when she thought about it and vomit it back up?

"There isn't any," he said. "I thought of drawing off water from a radiator. But almost all cars use coolants. They . . ."

169

She interrupted, speaking a little more strongly. "I saw an old car back a little way. Three lanes over. Maybe . . ."

He got her to her feet, and they managed to struggle into the cab of the semi. He opened the door on the left side, and looked back. About twenty cars back was the tall square top of a 1929 Stearns-Knight. A real collector's item.

He moved back on the seat and reached across Dorothy to open the glove compartment. There were several pairs of different-sized pliers. He took a small pair and also a long screwdriver. The screwdriver might come in handy as a weapon. He got down onto the edge of the roof of a Pontiac Grand Le Mans and helped Dorothy down onto it. A group of about twelve people passed him. There was a break then; the nearest person in this lane was twenty feet away.

They stepped across two lanes of cars between more breaks and made their way to the Stearns-Knight against the flow of traffic. By straddling between two cars, they allowed people to pass them.

The old car was in front of a Ventura and behind a Mercury Monarch. But there was enough space on its left side between it and a Ford Elite for them to get between. It wasn't easy to slide down into the gap and wriggle under the Stearns-Knight on their backs. It would have been easy to just lie there and let the world go by above. But thirst was driving Dorothy, and the knowledge of how fast the fires were advancing drove Cable. He turned the radiator drain with the pliers and let the water fall onto the pavement while he tested it with his hand. It was cool; tepid, rather. The car had been sitting there for hours.

He wriggled a little aside, allowing Dorothy to get her face beneath the spout. She opened her mouth and drank while the excess splashed over her face and chest. Finally, he said, "You'd better stop, Dorothy. You'll get sick if you get too much. Move over, let me have some."

He drank until his belly felt as if it would burst. Then he removed his handkerchief, soaked it, and told Dorothy to do the same to hers. "It'll help screen out the smoke."

When they were on their feet again by the car, he opened the door and squeezed into the front seat. "What're you doing?" Dorothy said.

"Looking for a container to hold water."

There was a glove compartment, locked. It looked as if it had been specially built. He couldn't remember if the old car was equipped at the factory with a glove compartment or not. It didn't matter. There was one in this.

He used the screwdriver to pry open the door of the compartment, though the effort made him pant. Inside, among other objects, was a flat silver-coated flask. On its bottom was stamped the name of the manufacturer and the date. 1930. Whoever owned the car was a genuine collector, a stickler for authenticity.

This was the type of flask carried in a coat pocket during the days of Prohibition.

Cable unscrewed its cap and poured the gin onto the floor. He thought, why in hell didn't I do this first? Now I have to get back under there. I'm not thinking straight.

At least, he had turned the drain off. Otherwise, all the water would be gone by now.

Again, he went through the excruciating process of crawling under and turning the drain valve. A pint of water wasn't much, but it might make the difference between death and life.

A few minutes later, they were on their way again, the flask in the front right pocket of his jumpsuit. As they stepped from the hood of a Polara onto a Caprice, he said, "We have about nine more blocks before we get to Lincoln. Then we have it made."

He didn't believe this. But he had to give her some encouragement.

It took them an hour to get to Lincoln. The wind was approximately fifty miles an hour by then, perhaps more. The fires on both sides were definitely nearer, yet not so near that he could feel as if he were standing by a blast furnace. When that time came, it would be too late. But it was hot, hotter than on the open desert of midsummer Arizona. The flames were a solid mass to north and south; the smoke borne by the howling wind was thick. His handkerchief, dirty with smoke, was around his face. Dorothy was using her handkerchief as a screen. They had soaked them in water from the radiator, but the hot wind had dried them off before they had gone two blocks.

The southern fire must have reached the Santa Monica freeway by now and would be creeping toward Olympic Boulevard. It would also be spreading out from the cities of Santa Monica and Venice eastward, though somewhat slowed in their advance by the winds blowing against them. Northward, the winds were speeding down the curve of the earth. Probably the city of Beverly Hills was burning south of Sunset Boulevard. Bel Air was all afire, and the campus of the University of California, Los Angeles, and Westwood would be on the point of igniting from the heated air above it. Anybody caught in Westwood would be dead by now.

Brentwood Heights and the Will Rogers State Park would be smoldering, too.

And all those people, the hundreds of thousands who were behind them . . . He refused to think of them. But he could not keep from wondering about Lee and Katie.

Were they behind him or ahead of him?

Their way was more open now. On both sides, on the top of the cars, ahead, behind, and on the ground, people had dropped and were dropping. Fatigue combined with heat exhaustion was striking on every side. Cable felt so light-headed that he was afraid that he would soon be one of the victims. But the water had given both of them an advantage; they might make it.

It was painful to step up, gain a foothold on the steeply slanting back of a small car, fighting the wind, pull yourself up with one leg while assisting Dorothy, cross the few feet of roof, step down to the hood, and begin all over again. He wanted desperately to let his aching woodstiff body slump down to a hood, lie down, even though the metal was hot, and just let everything go. Pray that the smoke would strangle him before the flames reached him.

There were many who were doing so. They weren't unconscious from heat prostration; they had their minds and the terror of a burning death to drive them on. But they were sitting down on the edges, heads low, or were just lying down, moaning and calling for water with cracked lips. Or gazing dumbly at him with red eyes as if their piteousness would force him to help them.

Then they were at Lincoln. He halted—there was no one close behind him to push them on—and looked south. About a mile away a solid sheet of bright orange and red roared upward. It was roughly along the stretch of Santa Monica Boulevard. Against its brightness he could see the dark bodies of aerial craft, helicopters and large four-motored airplanes with big bellies. Even as he watched, one of the large planes dropped its load. To the north were other planes dropping tanks of foam, too, hoping to keep the corridor open long enough for the refugees to get through it. But it would take the entire Air Force to unload enough foam to halt that holocaust. It was a valiant effort, doomed before it started.

Cable started again, holding Dorothy who was staggering even more than he with weakness and the impact of the wind. The fire storm was building up terrifyingly fast. In a short time—which he hoped was still long enough for them—the winds would be whistling by at seventy-five miles an hour. And the air would scorch the skin, sear the lungs. After that, it didn't matter what it did; make the skin and hair smoke, fry them, shrivel them up until they looked like the charred corpses of children.

Dully, he was glad that he had not elected to stick to San Vicente Boulevard. Though it was still about a half a mile from the fire sweeping through Brentwood, the heat from it must be intense enough to explode the gasoline in the tanks of all the cars along that area. Then he thought, what did that matter either? Before that, the people on the boulevard would have died.

They got across the junction of Alta and Lincoln. After what seemed an hour but must have been ten minutes, they were at the crossing of Alta and Seventh.

"One more short block and then two long blocks!" he shouted to Dorothy. The wind snatched his words.

The two blocks they had to traverse before getting to the Ocean Palisades Park were indeed long. Together, they were equivalent to six of the blocks they had just put behind them.

Cable thought of this and then began coughing and thought of it no more. Smoke sped by him, increasing the rawness of his eyes, slitted now. It was so thick that it should have made the night as black as being in a windowless cell. But the glare from the two fires surrounded them with a murky red, and they could see at least three cars ahead. He couldn't understand how he had been able to see the airplanes before. There must have been a momentary clearing of the air. No. More likely, something had just caught fire to the north and had added an immense amount of smoke. The gasoline in the automobile tanks along San Vicente? Or just one of those unexplained phenomena in the currents of the atmosphere?

Dorothy stumbled, and both sprawled on the rear of a Dodge Monaco. They caught themselves on their hands but fell heavier than they would have if they had not been so tired. Their feet slid back down, hit the bumper, and they crawled back up. He stood up first and helped haul her up. He felt a dull ache in his neck and back muscles now; he wasn't even strong enough to feel a sharp pain. No, that was stupid. He was getting stupid.

There was one good thing about the last two blocks. They sloped downward from the plateau to the shore. If it had been an uphill climb, it was doubtful that he and Dorothy could have made it.

He stopped again and pulled Dorothy's arm. She looked up and he pointed at the road to their left. It wasn't nearly as crowded as it had been some distance back. Too many had collapsed on the wayside. She nodded, and they crossed the lanes, and got down off the hood of a Chevrolet pickup. Now they picked up speed, pulled along by gravity, impeded only by people who had fallen before them.

They went across the Palisades Park, climbed once more across cars. These were sitting on the Pacific Coast Highway, Route 1. They went down to the beach through the crowds and waded into the ocean up to their necks. The water was cool, though the air was very hot, and they felt some life surging into them with the surge of the ocean. They even allowed some of the salty water to go down their throats. But the wind was pushing the surface waves southward, threatening to carry them toward the inferno.

When they got back onto the sand, they sat down. Dorothy said, in a voice like a crow's, "What do we do now?"

"I could lie down right here and go to sleep," he shouted. "But if we do, we'll fry."

"But the cliffs will protect us!"

"Not enough. Only thing we can do is walk north along the shore. Take to the water if it gets too hot. No choice."

He spat out the wind-blown sand and blinked hard. His eyes stung with gritty particles.

"I just can't," Dorothy said. "I just can't walk another step. I'm shaking all over, I'm too tired, I'm hungry and thirsty again, I just want to lie down and have nightmares . . . I mean . . ."

"The heat won't be as much north of here," he said, "and the Palisades will give us some protection. We have to get at least as far as Topanga Beach. And maybe, just maybe, they'll have rescue crews up there. Trucks, boats, choppers, everything to carry the people away."

He didn't really think so. And if they did have some sort of operation going there, how could they handle hundreds of thousands? Dorothy, however, needed encouragement, no matter how false it was.

"Let's rest just a while," she said. "Ten minutes, anyway?"

He looked at the multitude sitting or lying on the beach and at those still coming down Alta. He shook his head.

"We'll stiffen up too fast. We won't be able to move at all. These people are going to stiffen if they stay here. But that's their lookout."

He rose, wincing, bent down, seized her hand, and pulled her up slowly.

"Come on. We can drink from the flask as soon as we can find a place where nobody'll see us."

She stood swaying before him, her eyes half-closed.

"It's five miles to Topanga Beach!"

"They'll be easier than the last five miles."

Somebody spoke to him. He turned. Mrs. Adkins was standing behind him. She didn't look as if she would stand much longer. She was blackened with smoke; her hair hung limply down her shoulders; somewhere she had lost both skirt and blouse. Her slip was torn and blackened; she was still wearing hose but the knees were torn, exposing bloody bruises. Her shoes had gotten soaked in oil.

He stepped up close to her so they could hear each other. He gripped her naked scratched shoulders and said, "Where's Malone? And the doctor?"

"He shot the little black girl," she said. "He couldn't stand to see her lie there with a broken leg and scream. He got up then, and we went along. But after a while he said he was too tired to go on. He sat down, and he died. Just like that."

If she had any tears, she had shed them long ago.

"Williamson? Jenkyns?"

"I don't know."

"We're going on up to Topanga Beach," Cable said.

She sat down, forcing him to bend painfully over so he could hear her.

"Not me. I've walked fourteen miles at least. Maybe twenty, counting the ups and downs. I've had it."

"You don't understand," he said. "The heat's going to build up and so will the winds. The wind may get strong enough to suck us right up against the cliff. And the heat'll fry us there."

"That's too bad," she said. She lay down and closed her eyes and went to sleep.

He looked at the ocean. The winds were bringing the water in closer. After a while, they would reach Adkins. If that didn't wake her up, get her going, nothing would.

He took Dorothy's hand and began walking slowly through the people, going around those still standing, stepping over those lying down.

Dorothy came up beside him and shouted, "You can't just leave her!"

"Why can't I?" he said. "You and I are the only ones I care about. I haven't got strength nor will enough to take care of anybody else."

TWENTY

Almost fourteen million were directly affected by the fires of February 22–28.

The deaths were never exactly figured. It was estimated that at least four million had died as a result of the fire. Considering the number involved, the deaths were surprisingly low.

Part of this relatively low figure was accounted for by the pre-firestorm evacuation of the coastline corridor and the city of San Diego. The overpowering odor of the oil and the obvious danger from fire forced about four million to leave. About three million had been settled in the refugee camps set up in the California, Arizona, and Nevada deserts.

One of the factors that had kept the casualties down was the prompt action of the commanding officer at March Air Force Base. On hearing of the fires set in Rosemead and South El Monte, he had ordered all the planes he could muster to drop firefoam on the buildings. He had no authority to do this. But, instead of waiting until Washington had approved, he made the correct decision and acted. As a result, the San Bernardino freeway was not cut off. The fires were extinguished, and the various forces which had Skycrane helicopters available went to work. They picked up and dropped cars that were stalled or abandoned. While the fires raged elsewhere the frozen traffic was slowly thawed out. Vehicles began moving, though at an average of ten miles per hour. The cities of the eastern area, which also used other avenues of escape eastward and northward, were gradually emptied.

By the third day, the firestorm had reached Pasadena, Alhambra, and Monterey Park and a day later the cities east of them. But the majority of people were out. Approximately 200,000 died in these areas according to figures published a year later. Half of these, it was assumed, were people who just refused to leave. There were always such, and when the overhead air became so hot that even the most stubborn had to flee, it was too late.

The Riverside freeway suffered in the beginning from the same traffic-stopping elements as the others. Cars used the incoming lanes to go out; the lanes reserved for the police and ambulances were filled; cars broke down or were wrecked; cars drove onto the off-ramps; the streets feeding into the freeway were clogged. This occurred in the heavily populated Orange County and on the Freeport freeway feeding into the Riverside freeway. East, in the Chino Hills, although there was relatively little population, traffic was also stalled for a while. As the San Bernardino freeway traffic began moving, the police and the National Guard began easing cars into the San Bernardino freeway. The release of pressure allowed two lanes of the Riverside freeway to move for a while. Then additional breakdowns stopped that. People got out of the cars and began walking. They were a long way from the fire; it was two days before the air in that area started to sear the lungs. Skycranes cleared out the cars that were broken down in one lane. Guardsmen, police, and hastily recruited civilians were lowered from other helicopters. These drove the cars that were still operable, pushing the inoperative, abandoning them on hillsides where possible, sending many over down the hills and over cliffs to make way for others.

Similar efforts along the Ventura freeway, where the San Diego, Hollywood, and Golden State freeways fed into them, failed. The fires spread too rapidly, and all available personnel and machines were ordered to abandon traffic-freeing activities. They joined the battle to keep the flames from spreading into San Fernando Valley. After four hours, on the advice of meteorologists, who were experts in firestorms, the evacuation of the San Fernando Valley was ordered. The firefighting operation continued, but this was a delaying action only. At the end of the second day, all crews and machines were also evacuated.

Much of Ventura County left for northern California and western Nevada, where camps were being hastily set up.

The observer satellites showed solid smoke covering all of southern California, parts of northern California and Baja California, western Nevada and Arizona, and a vast area of the Pacific Ocean off the shore. The infrared cameras of satellites revealed that the fire was of much smaller extent. Yet, this was awe-inspiring, a bright blotch beginning three hundred miles off the coast of southern California and extending inland, raggedly, for approximately sixty miles. While the firestorm was at its height, the land area was three times brighter than the oceanic.

For two days, the winds rushed into the fire over the mountains and the deserts with hurricane force, attaining an average one hundred and twenty miles an hour speed.

The scientists expected the great wilderness of the Angeles National Forest in the San Gabriel Mountains to catch fire. It didn't, but the winds did uproot hundreds of thousands of trees.

The loss of life from the fire did not cease when the evacuation was completed. At least three thousand died from post-shock pneumonia because of the unavailability of medical care. Very few died of burns. A person either got away untouched by flames or burned up.

It would not be known for several years how much the property loss was. At least two hundred and fifty billion dollars was the estimate of a Washington authority.

Yet, as tragic as the southern California firestorm was, it was trivial in the eyes of the world outside the United States. Earth could survive the devastation of California. But it might not survive the Glory Hole.

TWENTY-ONE

Half-asleep, sometimes actually sleeping, they had trudged and stumbled to Topanga Beach. On their right the cliffs sometimes rose high, at other places became quite low. Always, they could see the red glow. Near their destination, however, the brightness was dimmed, and the wind carried the heat away from them. Later they would find out that it had taken the fire another day to reach the tops of the cliffs above Topanga Beach.

The winds pushed the ocean on their left higher and higher up the shore. By the time they had gotten to the beach city, they were forced to walk on the right side of the road, in the shadow of the cliffs. Spray wet them from time to time, making them wonder if they had escaped burning only to drown.

The spray did one good thing. It awakened and refreshed them.

Neither Jim Cable nor Dorothy Gill remembered much of that walk. They had been too dulled, and only an overall feeling came back to them. People ahead as far as the eye could see, which wasn't far, and behind, being shocked into wakefulness when they tripped over a rock or over somebody who had sat down or fallen. Jumping, heart racing, when a gust of wind threw water over them. The occasional cry of a child or a hungry baby or the scream of a woman as her husband collapsed. Lights and the chopping of a helicopter overhead.

At Topanga Beach, for the first time, they got cold. They were soaked with salt water. Their bellies were empty and growling. They were shaking from exhaustion and the aftereffects of terror. Their feet were blistered and raw. They reeled to a hillside on which there was some room for them to lie down. Despite being chilled, by the winds, they slept until dawn. They awoke to find that below them the cars were being cleared away. Two huge bulldozers were lifting out those cars that could not be started and were dumping them in the sea. Many still had keys in the ignition locks; these were being driven by volunteers or by people drafted on the spot. Property rights were being ruthlessly ignored. This, Cable told Dorothy, was the only expedient thing to do. Operable cars without keys were being swiftly crosswired. One by one, the lanes were being opened. And people were being piled into the vehicles so the area could also be cleared of refugees.

Down the road, a quarter of a mile away, was a canteen and an emergency medical station. Both were manned by U.S. Marines; two houses had been appropriated for their use.

Cable and Gill walked, limping, and got into a long line. A half hour later, they were handed a big mug of hot coffee, two doughnuts, and a bowl of vegetable soup. It wasn't enough, but it was all they could get for a while. Marines standing at the tables on the lawn in front of the house had stamped their hands with a large blue X so they could not return for seconds.

Some portable toilets had been set up by the houses. There were not nearly enough, and men and women had to use open latrine ditches dug by the Marines. These had been partially screened off by jerry built fences, but the wind had blown them down. It wasn't pleasant under these circumstances, especially since the wind carried the excrement onto those unfortunate enough to be leeward. But they were past caring about modesty or decency. They had more important matters to think about.

They returned to where the bulldozers were working. A Marine officer asked them if they'd like to drive one of the cars to the north.

"The camps at Oxnard and Ventura are full," he said. "But there's a big one being set up in the hills above Ventura. Take route 33. If that's full by the time you get there, take 33 on to Taft. Or maybe on to Bakersfield. The big one is at Bakersfield."

"My parents' home is at Santa Maria," Dorothy said.

"Yeah. Then take 166 from 33," the captain said. "You know the road. Only trouble is, you may run out of gas long before you get there. And don't try to pass. Stay on the right lane. There'll be military vehicles coming this way, and any smartass blocking them is liable to get shoved off the road. Understand. Hey, Sergeant," he said to the man sitting behind the wheel of a Dodge pickup truck. "It's ready to go?"

The sergeant nodded and got out. "It's crosswired," he said, "so you won't be able to shut it off unless you unwire it. Know how?"

Cable nodded. The sergeant said, "It's been filled up, we've been siphoning gas out of the throwaways, so you oughta be able to get to Bakersfield. That where you going?"

"Santa Maria," Dorothy said.

"Yeah, good luck! There's a camp there too, but it's been filled up, and people are being quartered in private houses. You may find yours occupied."

The captain shouted, "It doesn't take that long to give information, Sergeant! Hey, you, on the double!"

He was gesturing at a dozen civilians who stood behind them. Evidently they'd been sent by another Marine and had their orders.

A man got into the seat beside Dorothy before Cable could get behind the wheel. The others climbed up into the open back and sat down. The captain bawled out to a corporal that there was room for three more. A man, a woman, and a boy of about nine were called from a line. They got in without any help from the others, the corporal lifted the tailgate, and the sergeant said, "Get going!"

Cable put the truck into a low gear, and it moved slowly out and then was directed into a line. It never moved more than ten miles an hour after it reached Route 101, and it often had to stop for ten minutes or more. Cable wished he could have turned off the motor to save gas, but he could do nothing about it.

The man beside Dorothy was about thirty, had long frizzy ginger-colored hair, and a down drooping reddish Fu Manchu moustache. He was naked from the waist up. Torn blue Levis and tennis shoes completed his costume. He stank as badly as his companions beside him. For a while, he was silent, then said, "You going to Bakersfield?"

"Santa Maria," Dorothy said.

The man turned to look at Dorothy, and he shouted, "Santa Maria? Son of a bitch, that dogface told me it was Bakersfield!"

"No," Cable said.

"I gotta friend in Bakersfield who's got a pad. He'll put me up there. Shit! I don't want to go to Santa Maria. Listen, I know shitting well that Marine told me you were taking us to Bakersfield."

"There's a lot of confusion now," Cable said. "What's the difference? I'll let you off when 33 runs into 166. You can hitch a ride from there."

"Yeah, and what if nobody's got any room? You seen them cars and trucks. Jammed up their asses."

"O.K., we'll go to Bakersfield," Cable said. He had dug his right elbow into Dorothy's side to warn her not to protest. But she was already asleep.

"That's real nice," the man said. "Why'd you change your mind?"

"One place is as good as another," Cable said.

"If you say so," the man said. He fell asleep in ten minutes. After a while, Cable did, too. He awoke as the truck bumped into the rear of the Mercury ahead. The people in it looked back, glaring, one giving him the finger. There didn't seem to be any damage to it. The truck had probably been making not more than five miles an hour. And the Mercury must have been moving, too. A relative impact of one mile an hour, perhaps.

Dorothy and the man awoke at the same time. Cable said, "Staying awake's going to be a problem. We've got at least a hundred miles to go, part of it on mountain roads. I estimate it may take thirteen hours. Maybe more."

"Jesus!" the man said. "We gotta take a piss, eat something. What happens if we get out of line? How do we get back in? And what if there ain't no food?"

"They must have soldiers, somebody, stationed along the way to direct traffic," Cable said. "They seem to be getting organized. Maybe they have emergency food stations, too. We'll find out. Meantime, I'll drive for a while. When we get to Oxnard, you can drive. I'll sleep. Dorothy can take over then for a while. What's your name, anyway? Mine's Cable; this is Ms. Gill."

"Smith's mine," the man said. He wriggled around, reached in his back pocket, and brought out a package of cigarettes. It was flattened and bent and contained one cigarette. He pulled out a brown cylinder, held it with his left hand, reached into his pocket again, and brought out a huge switchblade knife. There was a click and a long blade flashed out. He held the cylinder against the dashboard and cut it in half with the knife. The knife and half of the cylinder, put back into the package, went back into his pocket.

"That's marihuana, isn't it?" Cable said.

Smith gave him a hard look, grinned wolfishly, and said, "Yeah, what about it?"

"You're not driving if you smoke that," Cable said.

"O.K., so I'm not driving. I'll enjoy myself."

Cable stopped the truck because those ahead had stopped for some reason or other. "Get in back," he said. "We need someone to spell us."

He put the truck in neutral, got out, went to the rear. The people jammed in there, sitting, their knees drawn up to their chests, looked at him apathetically.

Sitting by the tailgate was a woman of about thirty. Cable spoke to her because she seemed to be the widest awake. "Know how to drive a truck?"

"I never have," she said. "But I have driven gear shift cars before."

"That's all that's necessary," he said. "How about getting up there with us and spelling us on the driving?"

She nodded. Cable went around to the other side. Smith was still in the cab, drawing deeply on the stub.

"Get out into the back," Cable said.

Smith turned his head to look at him. "Go fuck yourself, man. I'm comfortable here."

"Do you want me to drag you out?" Cable said.

Smith brought up his left hand, showing the knife in it. "This talk loud enough for you?"

Dorothy turned half-around, picked up a big monkey wrench off the shelf, and brought it down against the back of Smith's head. He slumped, the cigarette and the knife dropping. Cable opened the door, pulled Smith out onto the ground, and placed him on his back. The woman came around the corner then, stopped, sucked in her breath, and looked wide-eyed at Cable.

"He was doped up," Cable said. It was an exaggeration, but he didn't feel strong enough to explain the entire situation. Besides, the line ahead had started, and the horns of the cars behind were blowing.

"He was going to use his knife," Cable added.

The woman said, "At a time like this," and got into the cab and slammed the door.

The people in the car ahead were turned around staring at Smith. The rear view mirror showed him that those behind were also looking at the form on the ground. Nobody seemed inclined to do anything.

"Thanks, Dorothy," he said.

"The son of a bitch felt my breasts while you were out," she said. "I won't repeat what he said. I told him that if he did it again I'd rip his balls off. I told him you'd break both his arms. He just laughed and said we could wait until you were asleep."

"Jesus, at a time like this!" the woman said. "You didn't kill him, did you?"

"I didn't have room to swing hard enough for that," Dorothy said. The woman looked back out the open window and said, "He's sitting up now, holding his head."

"Anybody stopping to help him?" Cable said.

"Not so far."

"That's a hell of a note," Cable said. "He could be innocent and just sick, and nobody's stopping for him!"

"What's the matter with you?" Dorothy said. "Would you stop? If you didn't know anything about him, that is?"

"If there was room for him, I would," he said. "At least, I hope I would."

The woman introduced herself as Sheila Grassetti, née O'Brien. She had managed the students' employment office at UCLA and also worked part-time as a cocktail lounge waitress. She had been putting her husband through school. He had been about to get his Ph.D. in electrochemistry, his specialty being fuel cells.

"It's the up and coming thing," she said. "He was always talking about electrically driven, fuel cell powered cars. Was. Everything's was, isn't it?"

Nobody answered. In a quavering voice, she told them how she had walked to her apartment in Westwood right after hearing about the evacuation notice. Her husband was home studying then. At least, he was supposed to be. But he wasn't there. After waiting for half an hour, and vainly trying to phone him at the laboratory in UCLA, where he might have gone, she had gone out onto the street. It didn't take her long to see that she was going to have to walk out of town. On reaching Sepulveda Boulevard, which ran along the San Diego freeway, she had turned north. But the transistor radio she was carrying warned her that the hills were on fire and that the flames were sweeping southward. She had gone about three miles up Sepulveda by then. But she had come back on Sepulveda and then had gone on Wilshire which was oceanward. Like them, she had finally taken the car roof route. She didn't even remember where or when she had lost her radio and handbag.

"Mike has a lot of explaining to do," she said. "Why wasn't he home? He was supposed to be working like hell on his thesis. Wait'll I get hold of him. Just wait!" And she burst into tears.

After a while, she wiped her eyes and blew on her dirty handkerchief.

"I wonder if I'll ever find out what happened."

"It may take some time," Cable said. He thought, if ever.

Outside Oxnard, they were stopped for a long time. The sweating whistle-blowing National Guardsmen directing the traffic were doing their best. Cable would find out that Route 101, just outside the northwest side of town, was getting the priority. Every fifteen minutes, his line would be halted so that fifty vehicles could leave Oxnard to take 101. This schedule was interrupted occasionally by military convoys going southward through Oxnard.

The truck crawled and stopped, crawled and stopped through the main street of Oxnard. Some of the people on the back of the truck got out and tried to get into the stores. These were jammed inside while crowds on the walk waited to get in. Cable could not wait for them, though he was going so slowly that they could catch up with him when he was two blocks away.

"I'm thirsty and hungry," Dorothy said.

"So'm I," Grassetti said. "And my bladder's about to burst."

"When we stop next time, we can get out and piss," Cable said.

"I don't think I can go with all those people watching me," Grassetti said.

"Everybody's doing it," he said. "You can't get into a service station."

"I'll die first," she said. But when the truck stopped, she got out with Dorothy and squatted by the open door. Cable stood against the right rear wheel, wetting it. Several more got down from the truck bed and stood by him or squatted behind him. The passersby almost brushed them, but they paid no attention.

Cable zipped up his pants and walked over to a cop on the corner. He waited until he was through talking to a man and a woman. Then he said, "Where can we get food and water before we go on?"

They were directed to a side street two blocks away. If they had waited, they would have seen a large sign on the corner. Cable did not want to stop; he wanted to keep pushing on until they got to home. Even if it wasn't his home. No use wanting. He had to let the others eat and drink, and if he had sense he'd do the same. Which he did.

It took an hour to park, get into line, eat the dish full of beans and bacon and bread, drink the coffee, go again to the place behind a billboard where the latrine was located, get back into the truck, and then inch forward while the line from the Air Force emergency station was let into the main stream.

It took another hour to get out of Oxnard onto 101. Beyond Ventura, he turned onto Route 33. The traffic here was somewhat faster, averaging about twenty miles an hour. Now and then he came to a complete stop, waiting until a broken-down or out-of-gas vehicle had been shoved onto the side road. Sometimes this wasn't easy. On this winding mountain road there often wasn't any available space.

Three hours later they were at the tiny village of Ventucopa. During a stop, Cable got out and went to the back.

"I'm going to Santa Maria, not Bakersfield," he said. "Anybody that wants to go to Bakersfield can get out at 166."

There were cries of protest. Cable waited until they'd subsided. "I was told at Oxnard that there's a camp being set up at the Twitchell Reservation. That's not too far out of Santa Maria. You can go there just as well. In fact, it's a much better place, in the hills, clean, with a lake, and not many people know about it yet. So you'll be among the first. It's not likely to be as disorganized as Bakersfield."

"I've got a cousin in Bakersfield!" a man shouted. "He'll take me and the wife and the boy in! How'm I going to get there! Nobody's going to pick us up!"

The others seemed apathetic. One place was as good as another.

"You can phone him or write him a letter and have him pick you up at Twitchell," Cable said. "We're going there, and that's that!"

The man opened his mouth again, undoubtedly to protest. Then he closed it. Perhaps he was thinking of how Smith had been dealt with. He didn't know the reason whereof, nor did Cable intend to tell him. He went back to the cab feeling somewhat like a liar and a heel. But he was too tired to be very ashamed.

On reaching the intersection of the two highways, he pulled off onto the side. An Army tanker was stationed there to provide fuel for vehicles. It took him about twenty minutes to get to the tanker. He disconnected the crosswires while the officer in charge checked his fuel gauge. He was given the gasoline because the officer figured he'd need it to get to Santa Maria. The officer thought the whole party was going there; Cable didn't inform him otherwise. He had a few bad moments when the officer first spoke to him, because he expected the protester in the back to say something. But the man either had not heard or was too exhausted to care any more.

Outside the Twitchell Reservoir, Cable stopped long enough to discharge everybody, including Grassetti. With a sense of relief which gave him some extra energy, he drove on. He did not go to the town of Santa Maria itself, which was on the west side of 101. He turned off into a development several miles east of the state route, situated on the high country overlooking the town. The houses here were in the $80,000–$100,000 bracket. Its owners were real estate agents, automobile agency proprietors, and oil company executives.

Dorothy's father was a wholesale food distributor who had retired at sixty after his cancerous lung had been removed.

Cable drove over some winding streets past large two-story and ranch houses with broad well-kept lawns. At the northeast corner of the area, overlooking a gently sloping hill at the bottom of which was a small lake, he turned into a wide cement driveway. He stopped the truck outside the two-car garage and disconnected the wires. The front door opened, and Mr. and Mrs. Gill came running out. Dorothy, crying, ran to them and threw herself into their arms. Cable followed her slowly, was introduced to her parents, made welcome, and went into the house ahead of them. He sat down on a huge sofa while Dorothy and her parents chattered away, interrupting each other, exclaiming over the horrors of the holocaust, asking questions which were only half-answered before another question came. He closed his eyes, and light and voices faded away. Four hours later, he was awakened for dinner.

TWENTY-TWO

For two days, Cable and Dorothy did little but watch the TV news, eat, walk a little and sleep much. Cable was uneasy because he felt that he should report to the Bureau of Crises. On the other hand, in his weakened and numbed condition, he wouldn't be doing the Bureau any good. It was better to get his strength back first.

Dorothy wasn't bothered with his conscience. "We should be in the hospital," she said. "That's where they'd stick us if we reported. So why not just rest here? By the time we're able to function, some of the mess will be straightened out."

Cable didn't argue. He was too tired; too much had been taken out of him.

Her father was upset about many things but mostly about his not getting his monthly pension check. It came out of Los Angeles, and nothing was coming out of there.

The TV had shown camera crews flying over Los Angeles. They didn't show much except smoke since the planes had been forced by the heat to fly at eight thousand feet or higher. There were many films of refugees and their problems and interviews of people who had gotten out at the last moment. And there were many televised conferences of officials who discussed the situation and their suggestions for remedies. The president made a speech in which he said that Los Angeles would be rebuilt. This would mean an enormous increase in taxes, of course, and L.A., like Rome, couldn't be built in a day. However, he cautioned, despite the plight of the refugees, the most important problem facing the nation, the world, in fact, was the Glory Hole. Unless that were solved, there would be no problems at all in the future.

Cable was especially interested in the interviews of the meteorologists.

"Well, Doctor Hesse, you say that the smoke is so thick that it has blocked out the sun as far east as Colorado Springs, Colorado. We know that already of course from the weather reports. What about the eastern part of the United States? Will they get much fallout? Or perhaps I should say *soot-out?*"

Feeble chuckles from the interviewer and Doctor Hesse.

"Well, I would venture a guess, a highly educated guess, if you'll forgive me . . . that the Midwest and Eastern states, not to mention the South, will receive considerable soot-out, as you so aptly phrase it. The citizens of Lincoln, Nebraska have already reported that the air contains a faint oily smoke. But that may well be, probably is, a subjective reaction. The molecular-counting devices there report that there aren't enough hydrocarbon atoms in the atmosphere to be detected by the human nose.

"Now, a dog's nose could detect that, but so far, we've had no reports from the canine population."

More feeble chuckles. Evidently the authorities had told the participants not to voice too gloomy a view. The president had been strongly and widely criticized for making a panic-inducing speech. The word for the mass media was: soft-pedal.

"Doctor Hesse, what about the global circulation of the smoke? Didn't you say in our preshow warm-up that the smoke will eventually circle the earth?"

"Ah, yes, I made some statement to that effect. But the smoke will be somewhat diminished when the areas of southern California have ceased burning. Just how much I cannot say, since it is too early for a considered study. As for my previous statement that the atmosphere will continue to be warmed up . . . if the Glory Hole burns indefinitely . . . and we can't have that of course . . . the smoke will have a counter effect. A somewhat beneficial effect. It will screen out some of the solar radiation. That means, possibly, one effect will nullify the other. The temperature of the atmosphere, on a global basis, will be about what it was before the Glory Hole and California fires started. That is, well, quite possibly. It's too early to determine for certain now, of course. Ahem."

Cable waited, in vain, for a statement about the effects of the smoke on the crops. They were not going to bring the subject up.

That evening he switched on the MPB program, which came on daily for two hours. When he had become aware of it, two days ago, he had mailed in the snapshot of Katie which he had carried in his wallet. This went to the MPB in San Francisco. But it would take months before the station could process the photograph and the information he'd sent in. He had no photograph of Lee, but he had typed out a detailed description of her. Meanwhile, he watched the program, rated among the top ten, because of its intense human interest. He also was looking for the faces and names of people he had known. What had happened to Doctor Williamson and Jenkyns, for instance? Did they have families or relatives who'd be looking for them? And what about Adkins? She had a mother in Phoenix. There were many others, people he'd worked with out of Cal-Pax, Angelenos he'd gone to UCLA with.

He watched for an hour and then got up to go into the kitchen for a beer. There were no commercials, but he could hear the audio. And, as he tore off the strip from the can, he heard a familiar name.

His own.

"Come quick, Jim!" Dorothy called.

He ran back to the front room down the hall in time to see his magnified photograph on the screen behind the announcer. Below it, in bright white letters, was his name and his address and his occupation.

". . . last seen on top of the Cal-Pax building on Wilshire Boulevard," the announcer said. "If you know of the whereabouts, or of the fate, of this man, please contact Doctor Tengel, secretary of the Bureau of Crises, Washington, D.C. Or the nearest police station.

"And now, another missing person, a little girl . . ."

The bureau was looking for him, though it hadn't occurred to him that he was a missing person. It wouldn't be concerned about him unless it was about something important.

It didn't take much imagination to identify that *something important.*

He sighed and took a sip of beer. It was time to go back to work.

TWENTY-THREE

The Lockheed WP-3DA Orion held a flight crew of four, a mission crew of twelve scientists, technicians, and observers, and seats for five extra passengers. A twelve million dollar craft, it carried six million dollars of instrumentation. It was owned by the National Oceanic and Atmospheric Administration, which used it for environmental and weather modification studies. It also often flew into hurricanes to wrestle with them for their secrets. So far, some wins, some losses, mostly draws.

Today, with Cable aboard as an observer, it raced at five hundred feet altitude over Los Angeles, headed for a fight with a new type of combatant.

At this moment they were sweeping over the city hall and police department of central Los Angeles. The once grayish-white exteriors were dull black, fire-seared and smoke-sootened, the upper parts fallen in. They looked like two rotten teeth, the crowns rotted away and collapsed, the glassless windows spots of decay.

The streets around the central sector and the Harbor freeway were clotted with twisted and black metal bodies. Their fuel tanks had exploded and then the chassis had been half-melted from the blast-furnace of the firestorm. The concrete of the streets and the sidewalks was cracked and buckled.

The Orion passed over the Harbor freeway and then over more burned, hollow, partly collapsed office buildings and department stores. There were no residential houses or small apartment buildings

195

left, no trees or shrubbery. The fire and the winds had swept them away except for the steel beams and blocks of stone. Here and there basements gaped, their bottoms scooped free of even the ashes by the wind.

They passed over MacArthur Park. Its trees and bushes had been totally consumed, and the little lake was dry, its water boiled off.

There were no bodies visible or at least none recognizable as such. Most of those caught in the fire would have been fried down to a small size. The winds had picked them up or rolled them along, lodged them against cars and buildings, where they had been buried under debris and litter.

Most of the fires had died out, their source of fuel exhausted. Smoke still rose from the largest of the La Brea Tar Pits. The bituminous pitch that lay close to the surface and oozed up, and the pool which had attracted so many tourists, burned with a low but steady flame. The wind, fifty miles an hour at this point, dissipated the smoke immediately. The concrete statues of the male mammoth and the baby were unrecognizable lumps by the side of the tar pool. The statue of the female mammoth in the pitch was gone, disintegrated by the fire.

The Cal-Pax building across the street was a black and empty shell. Cable thought briefly of Malone and his concern for his records. These would be ashes now, blown into the ocean, except for those in the file cases. The papers there would have shriveled up from the heat, though it was doubtful that they had burned. They were fireproof; there wasn't enough oxygen in them to permit combustion. But the cases would have melted and then fallen into the lower floors when the upper floors collapsed.

There, shooting up, was Beverly Hills. The Home of the Stars was leveled, its mansions gone, vegetation gone, the office and store buildings in its business center now mounds. The sidewalks and part of the streets were covered with stones and bricks from walls which had fallen outward.

The UCLA campus, broken shells and piles, passed by.

The Veterans' Cemetery was scorched earth and blackened markers. Cable thought of the drunken men in wheelchairs he had passed on his way to the sea. He shuddered, trying not to think of them. Maybe the smoke had killed them before their clothes began to send up wisps and their hair had started to smoke.

As they went over the interchanges at Wilshire and the San Diego freeway, Cable looked north. About a mile and a half up the freeway, bulldozers and giant cranes were working. They were clearing off the vehicles, lifting them up and dropping them off the sides, or pushing them out of the way. The men working outside the vehicles leaned against the wind. Later, trucks would come in to haul the wrecks off. They would end up in the steel mills of the north and the Midwest, and some of them would end up as part of the new Hoover.

Some of the main avenues would be cleared later, though only for the transportation of the personnel and the materials of the project. The news media and many politicians were calling for a massive cleanup and reconstruction project so that the Angelenos could eventually move back in. This, it was claimed, would give jobs for all the refugees. It would also boom the building and construction industries. In fact, about half of the industries in the nation.

It sounded as if it were a good idea. But, until the Glory Hole fire was put out, it was impossible. The wind made it difficult enough for the workers to get the wrecks off the streets. Men venturing outside the cabs of the cranes and bulldozers had to fight to keep from being blown away. Rebuilding the city under these conditions was unthinkable, and if it could have been done, it was unlivable, unworkable, and again, unthinkable.

North, where the San Diego freeway came over the hills, men were constructing high thick walls of stone and cement. This would follow the freeway to Olympic, curve west, and end up on the beach of Santa Monica. Between the walls sheltering them from the wind, trucks would carry equipment to Santa Monica. They would drive into high enclosures of cement and unload the equipment there. Later, a new pumping and storage facility would be built inside the walls. And then the oil would be pumped from the Hole.

That is, it would if the Hole were capped.

The Orion passed over Westwood, and Cable thought of Lee and Katie. Though an intense search had been made for them, they had not been found. They must be dead, one of the thousands of shriveled objects buried under fallen stone or brick. For a moment he felt guilt. If he had gone to Westwood . . . no, that was ridiculous. How could he have found them in that horde of refugees? And if he had looked for them, had used time that should have been used getting out of the city, he would be one of the victims. He would have died for nothing.

And then the plane was out over the ocean and crabbing even more against the wind. Powerful though its four jets were, it could not travel in a straight line without compensation. It had to point its nose somewhat to the north to go directly west.

Six hundred miles out in the Pacific the air picked up speed, sucked in by the inferno. As it neared the edges of the fire, its velocity increased, becoming seventy-five miles an hour. The waves were pushed to sixty foot heights at these points. The wind and the waves roared in, shattering the fringe of the oil stream, breaking up the thick cover. They tore and ripped at the heavy black shield and pushed it inward, crumpling it up. The oil was thus pushed in, piling up, the edges continually emulsified.

On the landward side the oil was shoved in toward the center, too, leaving a quarter-mile strip of whipped water between land and blazing oil. But the winds here were not as strong. The mountain trees that had not burned had been toppled, uprooted, blown along until they formed massive tangled piles that even the wind could no longer move.

The winds drove the smoke inward, leaving the edges of the stream exposed. The fires flickered here, sometimes went out, only to come to life again at night, when the winds weakened.

The fire was destroying itself, but it would never complete its work. The waves would eat into the edges, eat away until the flaming part was only half its original area. But as the fire weakened, so would the winds. They sprang from the fire in a reverse sense; their strength depended on that of the fire. Also, their very work in smashing the edges resulted in a smoothing out of the waves near the edges. The emulsified oil settled down on the waves like a great pacifying hand. The giant waves would become rollers.

For a little while, a few days perhaps, there would be a balancing. The fires would rage over an area perhaps no larger than Alaska and Texas combined. The oil would continue to pour out from the Hole, increasing the territory of the stream. The fires would spread. The wind would become stronger as the fires extended. The waves would climb toward their maximum height of sixty-five feet. The eating of the edges and the blowing out of the flames would wax.

And the whole cycle would start over again.

The winds had had another effect. They had completed the destruction of the area that had not caught fire. They had smashed apart the islands left uneaten by the bacteria, and then they had driven the emulsifications inward, adding to the central mass. At the southern terminus of the stream, the piled up oil had then burned, was still burning. The bacteria had been destroyed, of course, along with the oil. But they were no longer needed. If the calculations were correct, the terminus would not extend past a point off Ensenada, Baja California. Hawaii and the islands past them on the north equatorial current and the shores of Asia would never see the oil. Not, at least, as the vast solid shield originally envisioned. Some of it could reach their beaches as small slicks, though in great numbers. Maybe. The north equatorial current no longer existed because the winds were carrying their waters northeastward, toward the inferno.

"God, look at that!" Jacobs said behind him.

Cable said nothing. He had already been staring at the area of the Hole itself. There, where the flow was strongest, the giant waves did not have so much impact. They did manage to push the many-feet-deep mass ahead of the area just above the Hole. But the mass resisted the waves, and within a hundred yards past the Hole, the waves subsided into heavy rollers. There was no fire immediately above the Hole. A quarter of a mile south of it, as far as the eye could see, an orange plain stretched. Beyond, perhaps a mile, the smoke began to soar.

The smoke that was slowly killing the life on earth, would eventually do so, if the fire was not put out.

The scientists now said that there was even more to worry about. It was bad enough that the smoke would cover the earth and keep the sunshine out and so cause the crops all over the earth to fail. It was bad enough that the polar ice masses were melting at an even faster rate and that the sea level had gone up two inches in two months. No, so said the scientists, the hydrocarbon pollutants were creating excessive ozone in the stratosphere. This meant that respiratory ailments would zoom upward; emphysema and pneumonia would bring down their hundreds of thousands before the end of the summer. And if the fire continued until Christmas, perhaps the toll would be millions.

Cable had first heard this from Dr. Feesher during the second meeting after his return. The conference had taken place at the new HQ of the Bureau of Crises on Edwards Air Force Base.

"Isn't there anything we can do?" Cable had said. "Some counter-measure, I mean. I've read that freons destroy ozone. Could a study determine how much new ozone has been created and then a proportional amount of freons released to cancel the smoke effect?"

"Freons kill people, too," Feesher had said. "The remedy would be as bad as the disease. Anyway, why worry about that? Starvation caused by crop failure is going to take care of most of us."

"I hope you're not spreading that driveling pessimism around!" Meisser had said. "It could make for even more panic!"

Feesher stared at him for a moment. Meisser had been getting increasingly hostile to Feesher. Cable thought that his attitude was caused by more than personal antipathy. Meisser suspected Feesher of subversion because of his religious background. Yet, there was no evidence at all that Feesher had anything to do with the Soldiers of Jehovah. If there had been, he certainly would not have been allowed to remain on the staff. No doubt, Meisser had talked with his superiors about his suspicions. But they had been rejected. Or was it that Meisser suspected everybody?

"What I'm saying," Feesher replied coolly, "can be read in any scientific journal."

"Not if I had my way!" Meisser had said. "That kind of self-defeating crap ought to be suppressed. And I expect that it soon will be."

"Censorship!" Feesher murmured.

"Censorship?" Meisser said. "The Constitution is suspended, Feesher. You know that. This is a desperate emergency, and desperate measures are required. It won't be long now. Such loose talk won't be permitted."

"The situation is indeed desperate," Feesher had said. "But trying to keep its desperateness from the public isn't going to help a bit. Anyway, it already knows."

"Not about the effect of the smoke on the ozone, they don't!" Meisser had snarled. "That's something that might drive them off the edge."

"Gentlemen," Cable said. "You can discuss elsewhere anything you care to. We're here to consider the next step in solving the problem of the Hole. Now, General Arden, how soon can the Army Corps of Engineers start repairing the railroad lines in Los Angeles? We have to bring in a lot of storage tanks and God knows what else by rail, and all the railroads have been destroyed. How long will it take to build a new railroad, say one with four sets of tracks, for a starter, from San Bernardino and Riverside?"

"Well," Arden had said, "there's the matter of appropriation. We don't have the money for it. How soon can we get that, if we can get it?"

"Just a minute," Connor, the chief of the White House staff, had spoken. "You tell us how much you need, and we'll see that you have it. In other words, you do your job. Let Washington worry about the money. I can't seem to get into the heads of you military people that funds are unlimited, available on demand, in this crisis."

"Sorry, Mr. Connor," Arden said. "But it's you people in Washington who've conditioned us to think like that."

"Well, then, uncondition yourselves," Connor had said. "For the duration of the crisis, anyway."

"You two can discuss that elsewhere, too," Cable had said. "All I want to know is when you think you can get the line through to Santa Monica."

"Well," Arden had said slowly. "We don't have time to roll out new rails and cut new ties and transport them here. Not to mention we don't have the rolling stock or time to manufacture new stock. I suggest, and I hope you don't think this is too bold, I suggest we use what's on hand. The northern California railroads could be requisitioned. It'd be a lot faster if we just took apart the rails and use their Diesels and cars. Move the railroads lock, stock, and barrel down to the L.A. area, reassemble them there."

"Wait a minute!"

Caraman, the California State senator, rose to his feet. "The railroads won't stand for this. You'll be stripping Sacramento and Stockton and God knows how many towns and villages of vitally needed freight transportation. What're they going to do?"

"Use trucks, and tighten their belts," Connor said.

"The truck industry's overloaded now as it is," Caramen said. "They can't cope."

"They'll have to," Connor had said.

"Then how in hell are you going to get the parts for the second Hoover to San Francisco?" Caraman said. "Some of those pieces are so big trucks can't handle them. The railroads will just barely manage it, as it is. But there won't be any railroads there to carry the stuff."

"We'll strip from elsewhere, maybe Oregon, to put in the track we'll need for the Hoover II," Cable said. "There's plenty of time for that. The parts won't be coming for a month yet. And, hopefully, we won't even need the Hoover II. It's just a backup, you know."

Cable had sighed. No matter how often he and the staff scientists repeated that nothing mattered but capping the Hole, some could not get it through their heads. They would die trying to carry on business as usual.

He looked up then, aware that Jacobs was in the aisle and smiling down at him.

"Great news, Jim! The pontoons are on! The sub commander says they'll be ready to start towing in about six hours. I just heard it from the radio operator!"

TWENTY-FOUR

Williamson removed the stethoscope from Cable's chest.

"O.K. You can put your shirt back on."

Cable watched the technician walk away with the tray of specimens. After she had left the office, he said, "How am I doing, Doc?"

Williamson's eyes narrowed but he grinned. "I won't know until I get the reports back from the tech. Your blood pressure and heart seem O.K., chest is clear, and all that sort of thing. Except . . ."

Cable felt his heart turn over like a sluggish motor on a wintry day.

"Don't look so alarmed," the doctor said. "Physically, you're all right. Emotionally, well . . ."

"What're you talking about?"

"Your heartbeat increased about thirty per minute when I mentioned Meisser. It was no accident that I did that. I wanted to see how you reacted. It's been obvious to me that you hate Meisser's guts. Obvious to Meisser, too."

"He had no right to take Feesher off the job!"

Williamson raised his eyebrows. "Yeah? Apparently he has every right. He could remove you if he wanted to. Anyway, Feesher is lucky. Meisser could have had him arrested instead of transferred."

"Without evidence? He has absolutely none!"

"Jim, you're like too many people in this country. They still haven't caught on to the fact that the effect of the Hole has been and is going to be, as political as physical. The Constitution has been suspended because we're struggling for survival, and the only way

203

to get things done is to ride roughshod over civil rights. Economic rights, too. Property rights, and all that."

Cable said, "I know that."

"Sure, intellectually, you do. But the old conditioning is still operating. You haven't accepted it emotionally. Things like this have been going on for some time. But you've had your nose buried in your job so you haven't really been aware of what's happening. Otherwise, you'd not have been so shocked. Hell, Jim, I've suspected for a long time that Meisser was a secret government agent."

"So've I," Cable said. "But I thought he was FBI."

"Now you know he's BOAR. I'll bet that was the first time you ever heard of the Bureau of Anti-Revolution. If that, is in fact, its real designation. You can't believe anything anymore. Everything's secrecy and deceit. The open liberalizing effects of Watergate are dead now. Gone for a long time, maybe forever. For decades, anyway."

"The president's a good man," Cable said. "As soon as this emergency is over . . ."

"Ah, you suddenly saw the light! About time, even in your insulated situation. The emergency, as you euphemistically put it, isn't going to be over even if—when—you cap the Hole. If you put the fire out tomorrow, there will still be enough smoke in the atmosphere to ensure a global crop failure. Not just this year. Next year, too. There are rumors that the government is setting up a food rationing bureau even now. I hope so. Usually the government has to be going down for the third time before it even thinks of starting to swim. Of course, the usual shenanigans and under-the-table dealing will go on, and some are going to get more than their share of food and many will get less than their share."

"Well, I do know one good thing that's come out of this," Cable said. "The Mafia's been wiped out. They're all in jail or concentration camps."

"Sure," Williamson said. "The biggest industry in America and the most powerful. Smashed in one night. Everybody's happy about it, cheering the president, the attorney-general, our gallant FBI and local fuzz. Even the CIA was in on it, since the Mafia was declared an enemy of the state. And the casualties, among the Mafia, were remarkably high, didn't you think? Sure, some were bound to resist. But two thousand? Nonsense, and if the news media weren't suppressed, you'd hear plenty of screaming from them. What about Gennetti's death? Is it likely that a ninety-year old man, even if he is the chief godfather and undoubtedly directly responsible for hundreds of murders, would grab a shotgun and shoot it out with the CIA? And what about that alleged breakout at the camp near Winterton, New York? With the type of security they must have there, how could all those pistols get smuggled into the camp? Fifty prisoners killed, Jim, and two hundred wounded. And not a casualty among the guards."

"I can see where you're going," Cable said.

"Sure. Everybody's happy about this radical surgery. One of the biggest cancers in the body of the nation is excised. At the present rate of inflation, the elimination of organized crimes saves the governments and the citizens twelve billion dollars a year. Of course, the crime rate has shot sky-high. The supply of drugs has been cut off, and the addicts are breaking into hospitals and doctors' offices like crazy. But that won't last long. However, I'm digressing.

"The thing is, the public is pleased about this. But they can't see, or they refuse to see, that the next body to be trampled on will be the public. Oh, there'll be plenty of them who'll make excuses, as long as they don't personally suffer. After all, Mussolini did make the trains run on schedule, didn't he? And Hitler did build the Autobahn, didn't he? And Stalin did get rid of the kulaks, didn't he? And we can't survive as a nation unless we force cooperation and run over a few rights and maybe suffer a little injustice here and there, can we?

"Sure, the president *was* a good man. But he succumbed to temptation, a mighty strong one, I'll admit, and he got rid of the Mafia in one fell blow. Without due process of justice. But what about the next temptation? And the next? What if he convinces himself that there should be no elections until the crisis is over? And that he is the one who determines just when the crisis is gone? Or the political-economic setup becomes such that a cabal takes over? Or whatever?"

"That couldn't happen here!" Cable said.

"It couldn't? Where have I heard those words before?"

Williamson opened a drawer in his desk and took out a half-full bottle of bourbon. "Care for a drink? No. Well, I do."

He drank from the fifth, capped it, put it back.

"The time will come when I won't dare say to anyone what I just said to you. As a matter of fact, I wouldn't say this to anyone except you and about five other people I think can be trusted. I don't want my little speech to come back to haunt me in the future. And I wouldn't say it if I hadn't checked my office for electronic bugs."

"You must . . ."

"Be kidding?" Williamson said. "You stopped. You realized that I wasn't kidding and that I probably had good reason for saying that. No, the next step is to make all felons enemies of the state. Traitors, in other words. With death or life imprisonment the penalty. Oh, it won't be done tomorrow. Things will go gradually so the public will get used to it. Once that idea is accepted, and a lot of people will be happy if the crime rate goes way down—if it does—who's the next to be declared enemies of the state? Those who dare to criticize it? I don't think the death penalty will be legalized for them. But they'll get stiff fines at first. Then, later, jail sentences. I think I'll have another drink."

Williamson poured himself three ounces into a paper cup.

"See what I got in my hand? This may become illegal. What do I mean—may? It sure as God's little green apples will. Before the summer is over."

"I should get back to the office," Cable said. But he stayed in the chair. "Listen, Doc, how much booze have you had today? You must be out of your mind. Prohibition? It just wouldn't work. The government knows that. It was tried, and it didn't work. If liquor was prohibited again, the people would revolt."

"For one thing, the president is a teetotaler. Did you know that? He never said anything about it when he was running because the electorate, generally speaking, would be suspicious of a man who didn't drink at all. But it's become obvious that he doesn't like boozing. When he's forced to toast visiting dignitaries, he drinks grape juice and no bones about it. He'd like to see Prohibition back in—if he had a good excuse and it would work. And he does and it will.

"The grain used to make liquor annually in this country would feed a million people. Or a hell of a lot of cows and pigs. This coming crop shortage will give him all the excuse he needs. What, use the grain for booze when people are starving? And he'll be right, Jim. You can't deny that. Right as rain. But when the crisis is over, if it's ever admitted that it is, will Prohibition be repealed? And I, a pretty heavy drinker myself, ask myself, should it be repealed? Won't we as a nation be healthier and brighter? Won't traffic accidents caused by drunkenness and the homicides inspired by alcohol be cut to almost nothing? Won't absenteeism drop enormously? Won't . . . well, why go on? You see the picture."

"There's nothing I can do about it," Cable said. "Not now, anyway. If we have to go Fascist or Communist in order to save the earth, it's too bad. After things are back to normal . . ."

"They never are," the doctor said.

Cable stood up. "I don't know that it's been nice talking to you, Doc. You're not your usual cheery if irritating self today."

"How're you and Dorothy doing?" Williamson said.

Cable had started toward the door. He stopped, turned, and said, "We don't see much of each other either except when we're working together. She'll be flying in tomorrow from Santa Barbara. Today she's filming the docking of the Hoover."

"Yeah, I know," Williamson said. "Busy woman, isn't she? Have you received any of the films she made while she was on the *Lamprey*?"

"Not yet," Cable said. "I don't know that I'll take the time to look at them. The Hoover's been raised, and she's ready for refitting. That's all I'm really interested in."

"You were lucky that the *Lamprey* found her," Williamson said. "She could have been carried off the continental shelf, and even if she'd been located, you couldn't have raised her from a thousand feet depth. Or could you?"

"It would have taken longer, but it would have been done," Cable said. "It would have been faster than waiting for the Hoover II to be built. I'll see you around, Doc. Make sure I get the medical O.K. as soon as possible, will you?"

"If it is an O.K.," Williamson said.

Cable stopped again. "Why do you say that? Do you have any doubts?"

The doctor shook his head. "No. But there's always a chance. What if I did find something? What would you do if you couldn't go on the Hoover?"

"I wouldn't like it," Cable said. "I want to be in on the kill."

"The kill! What is the Hole, some sort of Moby Dick? And you're Captain Ahab?"

"I just don't want somebody else finishing a job I started. Especially one which is so important."

"Especially one which would bring you glory?" Williamson said.

"Quit trying to psychoanalyze me, Doc," Cable said, and he walked out.

The two men who had been outside the door followed him as he strode toward his office. They were big and tough-looking BOAR agents, packing .45 automatic pistols. They had been assigned to him the day of his return from Santa Maria. Though not until after he had been exhaustively, and exhaustingly, grilled by Meisser. Meisser had wanted to know in detail just where he had been and what he had been doing. He was especially interested in why Cable had not reported to the BOC immediately. Cable had explained over and over, though he didn't think he had convinced Meisser. Meisser had had his story checked out. Dorothy's stepmother had written about the visit of two agents at their home. The Gills had been thoroughly questioned. Also, Dorothy had told him that she had undergone a grilling by Meisser and two men who weren't introduced to her.

Garret Shattuck had had an even harder time with them. He had been held for two days while Meisser interrogated him. Meisser had made it evident that he was extremely suspicious about one aspect of Shattuck's handling of the Hoover from the *Sea Ichneumon*. That was Shattuck's accidental punching of the anchor-button on the control panel. Again and again, Meisser had said that it seemed strange to him that Shattuck's hand should hit the very control that ensured that the Hoover would not settle down over the Hole.

Shattuck, telling Cable about it, had said, "I thought sure for a while that I was going to be arrested. Meisser even showed me films of the operation. He had a dozen, all taken by newsmen and Dorothy Gill, but there was only one that showed me when the gas exploded. The other cameras had all been turned toward the explosion. Meisser said it looked to him like I had deliberately done it. But I knew he was just saying that to rattle me. I kept telling him that the film showed very clearly that I had been knocked down. Naturally, my hand flailed out. He let me go finally, but I didn't quit shaking for two days. I was afraid that even if I wasn't arrested, I'd be taken off the job."

"You weren't the only one," Cable had said. "I was afraid I'd be pulled off, too. I called Renzel and told him that, and he said he'd put pressure on the BOAR chief. That was the first time I'd even heard of BOAR. Renzel called back and said he'd told the BOAR chief that we couldn't be spared. It'd take too much time to train replacements. Besides, we were indispensable and all that. And it'd shake the public confidence if it suspected that subversives might have been in charge of the operation. I asked Renzel who the head of BOAR was, and he said he couldn't tell me that. It was top secret information."

"Well, we seem to have come out O.K.," Shattuck had said. "But we don't exactly smell like a rose. And God help us if something goes wrong the next time. We might get hung!"

"You're exaggerating," Cable had said.

"Not very much," Shattuck had replied.

Ostensibly, the BOAR men were guarding the BOC personnel against SOJ attacks. They were also reporting all the movements and conversations of their charges to Meisser. Cable was certain of that. He wasn't so sure that protection was their primary directive. They could be more interested in determining whether or not the guarded were SOJ members. But if this was true, the close and unremitting scrutiny ensured that the guarded couldn't possibly communicate with the SOJ.

The constant attendance, plus the certainly that his office and quarters were bugged, angered Cable. He had protested to Meisser, but Meisser had coolly replied that all the measures were absolutely necessary. Cable had then phoned Renzel, only to be told that Renzel could do nothing in this case.

"It's for your protection and for the country's. The world's, I should say," Renzel had added.

"They're driving me up the wall," Cable had said.

"Don't let them hear you say that," Renzel had said. "If your mental stability is in the slightest doubt, you won't be allowed on the Hoover. You *are* all right, aren't you?"

"Except for irritation," Cable had said. "And a total lack of privacy. Why . . ."

He hadn't finished that thought, since he didn't care to discuss his relationship with Dorothy.

Not that there was much relationship. They were both worn out from too much work and too little sleep. And the realization that both his and her quarters were undoubtedly bugged, that agents would be standing by outside any room they locked themselves into, cooled off what little passion they could summon. For all they knew, hidden TV cameras were filming their every moment. "Including the bathroom," Dorothy had said. "I sometimes wonder if my mirror is a one-way window, if dirty men, young or old, aren't standing behind it, watching me."

As Williamson once remarked to Cable, "You and Dorothy are having the most interrupted and inhibited romance of all times. Except for the sad affair of Heloise and Abelard. And he castrated himself, didn't he? Dorothy might as well be in a nunnery and you a eunuch, heh?"

Sometimes, Cable wondered if the world was worth saving. What kind of life was it going to be when the Hole was capped?

Of course, he worked just as hard despite these bad moments. He was an engineer, and engineers were basically optimists. They had to believe that any problem could be solved. There was always a way and a means.

TWENTY-FIVE

For once, Cable agreed with Meisser.

"I understand why you want to dramatize it, Connor, why you think the world should view it," Meisser said. "But all those TV people and officials milling around, the planes overhead? No. That'd make security impossible. You can't frisk the big shots, the congressmen and the foreigners. They'd be offended. But one of them could be an SOJ in disguise. And how do you know a TV camera isn't concealing a gun or bomb? And a plane that's supposed to be carrying a TV crew isn't loaded with explosives and piloted by a suicidal fanatic? Those SOJ are real kamikaze types."

"I think so, too," Cable said.

Meisser looked surprised but said nothing.

Cable continued, "We've had the air space off limits since the dry-dock was built. Why blow all that just for the PR value? What do we care about that? The only thing worth considering is the ultimate goal. That's getting the Hoover to the Hole."

There were eight sitting at the table. Cable, Meisser, Connor, Renzel, Admiral Greeg, General Arden, General Seymour of the Air Force, and Senator Amato of New Jersey. Amato was chairman of the Internal Affairs Security Committee. Cable suspected that he was also the head of BOAR.

Dorothy Gill and Chang were absent. Meisser had refused permission for any recording of this conference.

Connor said, "The whole world wants to see the Hoover when it is launched on the final phase. It'll want to see it when it submerges. And it's too bad we can't televise it while it's under water. Especially when it settles down onto the Hole. It's a great historic event, maybe the greatest, since the whole world depends on the Hoover for its salvation. I wish it could be covered visually from beginning to end. The simulations aren't going to satisfy the people.

"And also there's the matter of our national prestige. This is going to take some of the blame off of us. People'll be so relieved they'll forget the United States was the cause of this catastrophe. They . . ."

Senator Amato boomed, "Nonsense! We aren't to be blamed! It could've happened anywhere in the world. The North Sea, Arabia, Russia, anywhere where offshore drilling was taking place. I don't like to hear that kind of talk! But that's beside the point. What is pertinent is security! Mr. Connor, I appreciate the president's desire to show all the world that America can conquer any problem, no matter how vast. I understand fully the value of recovery of our prestige, of thrilling the entire population of earth with a drama that far exceeds that of the first landing on the moon!"

He lifted a finger.

"But! What if the mission fails because we succumbed to this desire for dramatics! What if we were unable to control the situation and the SOJ, or some fanatical individual, the SOJ isn't the only enemy of the state, you know, what if someone or some group did penetrate our defenses? And in some way aborted the mission? I say no! I say that we must not let down our vigilance by one micrometer!"

He paused again, smiled briefly, and said, "Unless you can convince me otherwise, of course!"

"I'm not proposing that we relax security measures," Connor said. "You know as well as I do that only authorized planes'll be in the air. God help any innocent who strays into the corridor. He won't be asked to leave; he'll be shot down. The TV crews in the authorized planes will be accompanied by special agents. The TV crews and their equipment in the air and on the ground will be thoroughly examined. As for any subversive kidnapping a foreign representative or a congressman and passing himself off as such, that's preposterous! Pure paranoia! Besides, what if one did? What could he do? Only the crew and a few other authorized people will be allowed within the enclosure. Everybody else is going to be outside the walls. Don't be paranoid, Senator!"

Amato scowled from under thick dark brows. "Are you really telling me I'm mad?"

"Of course not," Connor said hastily. "It's only a figure of speech. Overzealousness is what I meant. But the president, and the majority of congressmen, not to mention practically everybody in the world, want to see the mission from start to finish. The Hoover has been checked out twice, every inch of it. It's being inspected again, at this very moment. There's no way anybody could get a bomb aboard it or hide it there. It's been checked out electronically and mechanically. And Cable has made two test runs offshore. It'll be tested again during the trip down the coast. An aircraft carrier, a missile cruiser, and six destroyers will guard it until the seas get too rough for them. Thirty Naval aircraft, fighters and bombers, will be patrolling above it. A thousand Air Force and Naval planes will be patrolling the coastline. There'll be 25,000 men, police and military personnel, stationed along the coast. The two subs pushing the Hoover are equipped with sonar. They'd detect any unauthorized underwater craft, though that's unthinkable. The SOJ doesn't have any submarines, for Christ's sake. So, how could anything go wrong? Except for a malfunction in the Hoover, and everything possible has been done to prevent that."

Amato sighed and said, "Very well. Apparently I'm bucking too much clout. But I am going on record—the president and the news media will receive my formal statements—I'm going on record as opposing this. I don't want any unauthorized person within shooting distance of the Hoover."

So that was what that was all about, Cable thought. Amato making sure that he won't be blamed if anything does go wrong. He knows he doesn't have enough weight yet to overrule the president and the news media. And if he prevents the reporting of the mission, he'll be very unpopular with just about everybody. But if anything does go wrong, he'll have more authority the next time. He can say, "I told you so."

For a moment he wondered if Amato could be hoping that the SOJ would make at least a partially successful attempt. That would be just the thing to advance him one step higher, perhaps the only step needed to gain absolute control.

No, Amato wouldn't want that. Would he? Not when an attempt might be wholly successful. Not when a delay of two months might make the difference between survival and extinction for humanity. Two more months meant 5,126,400,000 more gallons on the surface of the Pacific. Five trillion, one hundred and twenty-six million, four hundred thousand gallons burning, burning. The world would choke. For certain.

"Very well," Connor said. "Go on record. Then—it's agreed?"

He looked at his wristwatch. "Are there any other matters to discuss? I have to be back in Washington in four hours."

"I have one," Cable said. "I was overruled by Meisser on something which I believe is very important. He insists on bringing a gun aboard. A .44 Magnum automatic pistol. I have excellent reasons for not wanting any firearms on the Hoover.

"In the first place, no one else will be armed. In the second place, the Hoover personnel are above suspicion. If we weren't, we wouldn't be on the Hoover. So, who's he going to use the gun on? In the third place, if he did have to use it, or if it is accidentally discharged, the bullet could hit the control console or a vital part of the life-cycle system. It could smash any one of a hundred components. A .44 Magnum bullet could conceivably penetrate the hull of the capsule and cause a leak. It could tear through whoever he might be shooting at and then through God only knows how many people in the line of fire.

"So, I object strenuously to any firearms. If Meisser has to be armed, let him carry a knife." He paused, then said, "Or a big sword, if that'll make him feel better."

"There's no need for sarcasm, Cable," Amato said. He looked at Meisser, whose face was reddening.

"Well, Meisser?"

Meisser bit his lip and said, "I've already explained to . . . to my superiors why I must have a gun. I thought it was a settled matter, arranged in the proper channels. There's no reason to discuss it here."

"Tell the gentlemen anyway," Amato said. "We don't want to appear arbitrary, do we?"

"Very well. In the first place, contrary to what Cable said, *nobody* is above suspicion. At least, to ensure one hundred percent security, that is what we must assume. I don't really think the operating personnel are in any way subversive. But you never know what . . ."

". . . evil lurks in the hearts of men?" Cable said.

Meisser glared. Amato said, "That'll be enough out of you, Mr. Cable. No more interruptions, please. This is a serious matter."

"Sorry," Cable said, but he grinned.

"You never know," Meisser said. "Aside from the operating personnel of the Hoover, there's the matter of the inspection crews. The first one thoroughly checked out the Hoover for concealed explosives and weapons and also for sabotage of the equipment. Then a second crew made up of entirely different personnel made another inspection. The third time, I personally supervised a still different crew. Every member of that was accompanied by a BOAR agent and a technician. Then I reran the inspections. I had each man show me what he did and explain his procedure in detail. I was aided by two engineers who validated each man's inspection and explanation. Still . . ."

"Yes?" Amato said.

"Still, how can I be sure some of the inspectors, and maybe one or both of the validating engineers, aren't members of SOJ?"

Renzel said, "This is too much! What *more* can you do?"

"Nothing. But, just in case, I want to be prepared. If I'm not armed, I'm handicapped. I can't perform my duties efficiently. I'm an expert in jujitsu, judo, karate, and jeet kune do. But what if, somehow, someone has smuggled a gun aboard? I'd be helpless. All those movies where the hero uses jeet kune do to kick the gun out of the criminal's hand are so much bullshit.

"And another thing. I find it strange that Cable insists I be unarmed."

"Are you accusing me of something?" Cable said.

"I find it strange. That's all."

"Mr. Cable's reasons seem justifiable to me," Amato said.

Cable was surprised. He hadn't expected help from this quarter.

"After all, he is also concerned about the safe operation of the Hoover," Amato said. "However," and he stabbed a finger at the top of the table, "Mr. Cable's only concern is engineering and operating. Very well. Let him engineer and operate. Let him make certain that the Hoover functions efficiently and achieves the goal for which it was built.

"But he won't be able to do this if any human agency interferes with him or his machine. It's the obligation, the function, of our security forces to see to it that he isn't interfered with.

"On the other hand, we don't want to be so zealous, so security-blinded, I might say, that we endanger operations. We don't want to be self-defeating. So, as in politics, gentlemen, we solve difficulties, seemingly conflicting interests, by compromise. Compromise. The grease that eliminates friction: social, economic, psychological, and political.

"Now, I can't see Meisser firing his weapon by accident. He's too experienced, too stable for that. Nor can I see him missing his target. He's a superb marksman, gentlemen. Take my word. He's deadly cool. I can't tell you of the incidents which prove that. They're top secret. But you can believe me. He doesn't rattle.

"On the other hand, Mr. Cable does have a valid argument. A .44 Magnum will go through a target, a man's body, I mean, and still retain considerable velocity. It could kill one or more people directly behind the target. It might punch through the half-inch steel plate of the crew's capsule. And it certainly could destroy the control panel or the life-system.

"So . . . Meisser will not carry a .44 Magnum. But . . . he will be armed with a weapon of lesser caliber, one that doesn't represent overkill."

He paused, then said, "I suggest a .32 caliber automatic. Any objections?"

Surprisingly, Meisser had one.

"I could use the .44 but I could notch the bullets, make dum-dums of them. They'd flatten out within the body of the target. They wouldn't go out the other side."

"We couldn't be sure," Amato said. "No, a .32 in your hands is just as deadly as a .44. But only for the target."

"I'd rather it was a .22," Cable said. If Meisser shoots as unerringly as you say he can, then he can put a bullet in the head or the heart. And a .22 there'll be as fatal as a .44. If he should miss, and I submit that no man is infallible, the chances for damage to equipment are much less. Not to mention the chances for killing one of the crew."

"I'm willing to accept a sensible proposal," the senator said. "Meisser, it'll be a .22"

Meisser tightened his lips. Cable saw that Amato also saw it.

"Meisser, your firearm will be checked before you go aboard."

"Sir, I wouldn't think of disobeying orders!"

"It's only a routine procedure," Amato said smoothly. "You know that. Well, gentlemen, I think that disposes of all discussion on this matter."

Cable thought of an objection, but he kept silent. It would be rejected. Anyway, what he envisioned seemed too improbable. And it was obvious that the matter was settled.

TWENTY-SIX

The sky at 12 P.M. was completely black, greasy-looking, and cold. Santa Barbara had not seen the beautiful blue and the sun for three months. Yet it was warm, unseasonably warm for April. The north wind brought heat which had circulated around the globe, a drying killing heat. The winter rye grass was yellow; the dichondra was dead; the palms were dying.

The band was playing, of all things, "Pomp and Circumstance," as if this were a high-school graduation ceremony. The music was loud but uninspired, as if the band was trying to overcome a sense of futility with a high decibel level.

The American flag on the pole over the gates of the high barbed-wire fence flapped frantically, tearing itself to shreds. It had to be replaced every other week, or so Cable had been informed.

Across the street from the enclosure, on a lot which had been occupied by a five-story building before the Naval demolition men had torn it down, was a temporary amphitheater. The less important dignitaries sat on wooden bleachers, holding on to their hats. In front of the bleachers, sixty feet away, were six rows of folding chairs. In these sat congressmen, foreign diplomats, a few governors, some colonels, generals, admirals, and heads of federal departments and bureaus. To one side, roped off, were the TV crews and newspaper reporters. Armed Marines stood by, ready to make sure they stayed within the set bounds. Other Marines formed a half-circle outside the area of the ceremony; armed soldiers completed the circle. The latter were here because the Army had insisted on being represented, just as it had insisted that at least one of its own be a member of the Hoover's crew. After all, the Army had borne a large share of the labor in the project. It was only fair that it should share the glory—though it had not phrased its insistence in so many words.

General Arden, the U.S. Army Corps of Engineers representative, had been proposed as a candidate for the presidency in the coming elections. His presence on the Hoover would make him a big public figure and enormously increase his prestige. That is, it would if there were an election. The country was still under martial law. Though there were few visible signs of it—no soldiers patrolling the streets—except in California—there was much uncertainty. The president had been challenged by some members of Congress on the question of holding elections, but he had not as yet replied. The unofficial word—which the news media had been allowed to report—was that he would make everything clear after the Hole was capped.

The president himself was present, standing now on the speaker's rostrum. He was a tall good-looking man of forty-nine who had often been compared to Lincoln by members of his party and the news media favorable to him. Physically, his only resemblance to the Great Emancipator was his huge hands. One of them closed over Cable's hand now in a strong grip.

"We're depending on you," he said. "All of us."

He smiled broadly and added, "God help us if you don't come through."

"We'll make it," Cable said. "If it's humanly possible. And I don't see why not."

"You'll have God with you," the president said. "He wouldn't let His people perish."

How would anyone know about that? Cable thought. His hand was released, and the president went on, saying goodbye and good luck to the other members of the crew. The band switched to "Nearer My God To Thee," which Cable thought was an ambiguous piece in the circumstances. A few minutes later, he filed with the crew down the wooden steps. Dorothy, close behind him, spoke loudly against the wind. "What did you think of the president's speech?"

"I got lost in the vague generalities," Cable said. "I really wasn't listening. He did talk a lot about the vast labor and expenses of the clean-up and what a burden it was going to be. And how necessary it was that strict controls be kept until normalcy is restored. And all that. I don't think he's going to allow the election."

"What did you say?" Meisser said. Cable looked back. Meisser was right behind Dorothy.

"Nothing you'd be interested in," Cable said. He turned his head away.

Marines formed lines around the crew, and they were marched across the street and through the gates. The band was playing "America" now, though the music got fainter with every step Cable took away from it. The wind caught the notes and hurled them southward. Cable looked back briefly. The president was talking to Renzel; much of the crowd was leaving despite the fact that the band was only on the fourth bar. No one seemed to be looking his way. It was as if they had been forgotten. That wasn't true, of course, but it certainly seemed that everybody had reverted to his own personal problems. Probably, they were intent at the moment on getting to the toilet. The ceremony had been overlong; Cable himself wanted to get to the latrine.

But first he and his crew had to be frisked. They endured this indignity, the only alleviation being that Meisser was also searched. The .22 automatic was brought out from the holster suspended from his belt under his coat tails, checked, and returned to him. The man who did this was dressed in charcoal gray civilian clothes. Cable presumed he was a BOAR agent. The man then reached into Meisser's pocket and brought out a big switchblade knife. Cable wasn't near enough to hear Meisser, but it was evident he was protesting. The man shook his head and put the knife in his own pocket.

The go-ahead was given, and the crew walked in the midst of the guards toward the vast curve of the Hoover. Cable, by Meisser's side, said, "They wouldn't let you keep your knife?"

Meisser looked suspiciously at Cable. "The damn fools! Apparently they had orders only for the pistol. Somebody goofed up, forgot to list my knife. So . . ."

"Too bad," Cable said. "But orders are orders."

"Don't be so smart, Cable," Meisser said.

They stopped before a wooden platform. A set of stairs ran up to it; just above it was the airlock port. They walked up to the platform, and Cable, according to the procedure determined upon, entered the lock first. Also, according to the program, he turned and extended two fingers in a V. This was recorded by the Navy photographer standing on the ground below. Cable turned and went through the lock and up the steep metal stairs in the narrow tube and emerged in the control room on the "bridge." One by one, the others joined him. Cable waited while Shattuck seated himself before the control console, a large cabinet bearing an array of dials, switches, pushbuttons and CRT displays. Shattuck spoke to Admiral Evans, the man delegated to close the ports of the airlock. There had been some jockeying for this post, since General Arden had wanted to be the last to enter and hence the last to be filmed. But the Navy was in charge of this phase of operation, even if Cable, a civilian, was captain of the Hoover. The TV viewers would see a Navy man close to the exterior port.

Evans reported in that the port was closed and secured, a redundancy since Shattuck could check this by the illumination of the panel airlock indicator. A minute later, Evans closed the port at the head of the staircase, which he insisted on calling a ladder. Shattuck spoke then to the captain of the tug fleet by the Hoover. Three minutes later, the structure was being eased gently out of the breakwater. The crew knew without being told when they were in the open sea. Vast and heavy as the Hoover was, it lifted and fell slightly in the waves created by the wind.

The control room was fifteen feet long and fifteen wide. Beyond a narrow doorway was a corridor sixty feet long. Its extreme end abutted against a wall ("bulkhead") behind which was the life-cycle and electrical generating equipment. The doors along the corridor on the starboard, or right, side led sequentially to the galley, the male crew's bunk room, and a small "rec" room. This held tables, chairs, shelves of books, and a TV set with taped shows. Proceeding from the control room, Dorothy's room, and the "head." The latter held two wash basins, one shower, and a toilet enclosed in a booth.

The whole was enclosed in a dirigible-shaped capsule of steel welded to the inside of the hull of the Hoover. It was counterbalanced on the other side of the hull by a capsule containing only air.

Cable went to the toilet, emerging from the booth to find four others, including Dorothy, waiting in line. He went back to the control room and took over Shattuck's post so that he could relieve himself. There was nothing for him to do except to listen to the radio operator on the command tug boat and the operator on the command cruiser standing by.

Shattuck returned before the tug boats had pulled the Hoover into line for the two cruisers. He took his post without a word—he was almost as taciturn as Meisser—and Cable stood behind Shattuck. The Hoover moved slowly and ponderously in a curve, heading finally southward down the channel. Hours passed as the tugs hauled their charge through the many navigational hazards of the oil platforms. When they were in comparatively open waters, the fleet captain sent the message that cast-off time had come.

The lines were released, and the tugs departed. The cruisers, the U.S.S Syracuse and Los Angeles, eased their bow into the huge Vs in the rear of the shell. A slight bump was felt in the capsule, and the cruisers slowly increased their power. In seventeen hours, if all went as proposed, the Hoover would settle down over the Glory Hole.

Cable went back to the rec room to talk to Dorothy. This was their first opportunity to be together for any length of time in months. Unfortunately, except for Shattuck and Meisser, everybody was at the card table. He wouldn't be having an intimate conversation with her. Still, it was better than nothing.

At the end of five hours of pushing, the cruisers pulled back. The waves were causing too much up and down movement even for the massive bodies of the Hoover and the ships. With all hands at their posts, the Hoover was submerged. Water was admitted into the giant pontoons until a depth of a hundred feet was reached. Since it was his watch, Cable manned the "helmsman" or pilot post. Dorothy was in a far corner of the room, supervising Chang as he swung the camera back and forth or held it. Meisser stood near the control console, intently watching Cable and Shattuck, who stood behind Cable, and glancing frequently at the others. Cable was relieved that Meisser kept the pistol in his holster. But then this was not the most critical phase of the mission. Admiral Evans manned the sonar communications equipment on the far right. He was in contact with the two submarines easing up on the stern of the Hoover. General Arden sat in a swivel chair while monitoring the CRTs and indicator lights of a panel. These signaled the state of the electronic and mechanical devices throughout the Hoover. An electronic engineer, Arden was thoroughly competent to troubleshoot and correct any malfunction of equipment. If he had not been, he would not have been allowed to be a crew-member. No amount of influence could swing that appointment.

Though Arden was checking on the state of equipment both inside and outside the capsule, he could do nothing if the extra-capsule devices ceased to work. They had no access to the anchor machinery and the sonar sets outside the capsule. On the other hand, these were stable and had been overtested. It was not likely that anything would go wrong with them.

The operation went as smoothly as it had in the two test runs made off Santa Barbara. Feeling with their sonars, sound pulses bouncing off the Hoover, reflected back to the receivers in the subs, the *Lamprey* and the *Coelacanth* simultaneously made contact. There was a slight shock in the control room from vibrations transmitted through the Hoover's hull and the capsule hull. A minute later, an indicator showed an increase of velocity. The atomic-powered engines of the submarines were applying all their power, pushing the Hoover up to the underwater maximum of 4.1 knots.

Two synchronized sonars along the bottom edge of the hull were counting the knots as the structure passed over the bottom. The count was shown in digits on the ROV screen before Shattuck.

While the ROV indicated a slow acceleration, the Hoover and the submarines sank another fifty feet. A depth of 150 feet would be maintained until sixty miles from the Hole. At this point the waves were so high that they affected the water even at this distance from the surface. The Hoover would then be lowered another fifty feet to escape the turbulence and would stay at two hundred feet until almost on the target. During this stage of the mission, the only post that had to be continually occupied was that of the helmsman. Shattuck and Cable were taking alternate four-hour watches.

After the cruisers had made contact, Arden suggested a poker game. Dorothy hesitated. Cable knew she wanted to stay with him on the bridge, but it was evident that Meisser wasn't going to leave him alone.

Cable said, "You go ahead. Shattuck'll relieve me in an hour. I'll join you then."

Dorothy shrugged, glanced at Meisser, and walked out.

At 8 P.M.—or 20:00—Cable gave up his seat.

"Get any sleep?" he said to Shattuck.

"A little. Too keyed up."

Cable left. Meisser backed up a few steps, presumably so he could have both of them in his field of vision.

Arden, Evans, Chang, and Dorothy were deep into a game of stud. She had the highest pile of chips; the admiral had one about half the height of hers; the other two were almost wiped out. Cable unfolded a chair from the rack and secured its legs with magnetic clamps to the floor. He sat down.

"Deal me in."

"Five dollars a chip," Dorothy said.

"Not bad for these days of inflation," he said. He looked at Chang's five chips. "I thought all you Chinese were keen gamblers?"

"Smile when you say that," Chang said, grinning. "This humble Celestial *is* a keen gambler, though I resent the appellation of Chinese. My ancestors were here a hundred years before yours, Jim. Yes, I'm a keen gambler."

He paused. "But I'm also a piss-poor poker player, to put it alliteratively."

Evans raked in his pot. Dorothy dealt Cable a deuce of clubs, face-down. Not much of a hole card. His next card, face-up, was a five of hearts. A bad beginning. Evans, an ace showing, opened the betting. The game did not go swiftly; there was much more banter than usually found among serious players. It was evident that they were more interested in socializing than in winning. Most of the remarks were directed at Dorothy. Cable liked it that they liked her. But he was also aggravated because it cut down his share of conversation with her. He wanted to monopolize her.

The admiral raked in his chips. "I'll confess something, Dorothy. I'm old-fashioned in many ways. I didn't like the idea of you being aboard. But you seem to have brought me luck."

She laughed and said, "What do you mean? Surely you don't hold with the old superstition that a woman on a ship is bad luck?"

The admiral was a tall thin man of fifty, gray-haired and eagle-faced. Smiling, he said, "Of course I believe it. I've made a study of it, gone through a list of books as long as a whore's . . . I mean, a very long list. I wanted to find out for myself if it's a superstition or if it might not have some basis in fact. And I found that there was a high proportion of ships wrecked, or lost, that had women passengers. So there must be some reason for the idea."

Dorothy looked at her cards, then looked up. "My God, Admiral! What about all those passenger liners? They must have carried thousands and thousands of women and never had an accident!"

"I'm not speaking of civilian craft. I'm talking about naval vessels."

"But there are plenty of women naval personnel now. Sea-going women!"

"My study stopped with 1918," the admiral said.

"But . . . but . . . !" Dorothy stopped, shook her head, and then said, "But when were women ever allowed on board naval ships?"

"Plenty of times. They'd pick up castaways or get them off foundering ships or take some official's wife aboard to transport her from one place to another. And you'd be surprised how many women have been smuggled aboard."

"You're pulling my leg," Dorothy said.

General Arden said, "That'd be a pleasant duty."

There was silence for a minute. So far, nobody had said anything the least suggestive to her. Cable wasn't surprised that Arden was the first to do so. He had a reputation as a womanizer. Dorothy had told him that, and he'd also heard it from a newspaper reporter. However, his remark was only lightly offensive.

"It could be pleasant," she said. "For the right man. You're not him, General."

Arden's face reddened. The admiral cleared his throat and said, "That'll be enough of that, General. She's just one of the boys, and I don't mean the cabin boy. Haw, Haw!"

Apparently, Arden abandoned any ideas he'd had about her. That is, if he had had any at all. Perhaps, in his fantasies, he envisioned sneaking into her cabin when everybody but the pilot was asleep. But no more.

Cable himself had thought about that but had rejected it. The chances of being detected were too high. And this was, after all, a sort of military mission. He should be thinking of only one thing.

At midnight, Cable was back in the pilot's seat. Shattuck left at once, but Meisser stayed. As far as Cable knew, Meisser had not left the bridge to eat or urinate. He was red-eyed and haggard-looking, but he never yawned, and he seemed vigorous enough. He would pace back and forth, his hands locked behind his back, his head low. He spoke only once, asking Cable if everything was all right. If he had been anybody else, Cable would have enjoyed the company. It was true that he could talk to the sonar man, but he preferred having a face to look at along with the conversation. Meisser resisted Cable's efforts to draw him out, responding only with a grunt or sometimes a long sniffling sound. Cable did not like him, but he thought that there must be something in him likable. He wanted to get him to talk about his childhood, his ambitions, his marriage, if he was married or had lovers. Somewhere in him was a human being, and Meisser and Cable might find a place where their nodes touched, where they could resonate on a human frequency.

That could only take place if Meisser permitted himself to move toward Cable, to come out from behind the insulation. But Meisser would not do that. He feared intimacy in any degree. To him it must be like touching an exposed electrical wire.

He could understand somewhat that attitude. Before he had met Dorothy, he had used his work as a shield. But he had never been as withdrawn or as unfriendly. Actually, he had been waiting for someone like Dorothy. And what if she had not come along?

At one, Meisser disappeared for ten minutes. Cable, looking back down the corridor a few minutes later, saw him coming out of the head. He went into the galley and presently returned to the control room eating a large ham and cheese sandwich.

Dorothy returned at three carrying a tray of sandwiches and a pot of coffee.

"Thanks," he said. "I thought you'd be sleeping."

"Shattuck's the only one in the bunkroom," she said. "We all tried it, but we're too nervous. At least, I can't keep from thinking about tomorrow. And the idea that only a half-inch of steel protects me from the dark cold water outside . . . I'm not claustrophobic, but I think I could develop a good case. Maybe it was just being alone in that little room. It's too much like a coffin."

"It's not tomorrow. It's today. It's only five hours until target time."

"Don't I know it? Anyway, I got up and looked in on you, but I decided I'd bring you something later on. I found the others shooting dice. They were tired of that, so we played more poker. And here I am, your faithful servitor."

They talked for a while, mainly about one of her stepmothers, who was thinking of getting married again. Meisser stood by, listening.

At ten minutes to four, he left again for the head.

"Maybe he thinks somebody's hiding in there," Dorothy said. "But more likely he feels an affinity with the contents of the bowl."

"Never mind him. I'll join you in a few minutes and get some of my money back."

She kissed him lightly on the side of his mouth and was gone. Some seconds later, Shattuck entered.

"You're early," Cable said.

"Didn't sleep well. I kept having bad dreams. Too tense."

"Meisser's going to be mad. He'll think you sneaked in when you saw him leaving."

"I didn't know he was gone until I came in here. I might as well take over now."

Cable got up from the chair. Shattuck seated himself and spoke briefly to the *Lamprey*, notifying them that the change of watch had been made. Cable hesitated. Why had Shattuck offered to relieve him early with Meisser absent? Then he thought, good God, Meisser's suspicions are rubbing off on me. It's like a disease.

Shattuck said, "I think Meisser is mostly suspicious about me. He still doesn't believe it was an accident that I activated the anchor controls on the *Sea Ichneumon*. Anyway, he hasn't quite convinced himself that it was an accident. It's a wonder he didn't convince the higher-ups, too. Up to the moment I boarded, I was afraid I'd be pulled off."

"He's crazy. He's killing himself from lack of sleep. It's a wonder he didn't equip himself with a relief tube and a bladder so he wouldn't have to leave the bridge to take a piss."

"I think he did," Shattuck said. "He just went to the head to empty the bladder, I'll bet. And he did that because he trusts you more than he does me."

"A saboteur could open the console and wreck the equipment in about sixty seconds," Cable said. "Of course, opening it would set off alarms. We'd be all over him in a few seconds. The bridge can't be closed off. I wanted a port in case we sprang a leak and had to close off the bridge. But Meisser overruled me. At least, somebody did, and I think Meisser was behind it."

"A saboteur couldn't cause any more than a twenty-four hour delay if he wrecked the console," Shattuck said. "He'd have to do it before we got close to the Hole, because everybody's going to be in the bridge when we get close. If the console should be damaged before then, we could put in a new console in less than twenty-four hours. A sub could bring one in and we could transfer it through the lock, and . . ."

"I know that," Cable said. "You must have done a lot of thinking about that situation."

"What do you mean by that?" Shattuck said glaring.

"Nothing, of course. I suppose we all think about it."

"Well, there's nothing else to do but think when you're here. That's the trouble with being around Meisser. You start to think like him."

"Attitude osmosis. Well, we only have thirteen more hours of this.

I think I'll go back and play some more poker. I'm three hundred dollars in the hole. Dorothy has most of it."

"Three hundred dollars!" Shattuck said. He shook his head.

"I'm sure glad I don't gamble. It's a fool's game, if you'll excuse me for saying so."

"No, you're right," Cable said. "But I enjoy it, and I can afford it. Anyway if Dorothy and I should get . . . well, never mind."

Shattuck looked up with a strange expression. "You mean, if you two should get married, the three hundred dollars will be yours anyway? Is there any chance of that?"

"I don't know," Cable said, wondering how he had gotten into this subject. Normally, he would never have said a word about it to anyone. Perhaps, though, he wanted to talk to someone, to unburden himself, however slightly. It must be the loneliness, the peculiarity of the situation, that had made him mention this. Or maybe he felt that he ought to tell Shattuck that he and Dorothy were contemplating marriage. Or at least had discussed it when they were at her father's home. He knew that Shattuck was aware that they had slept together. Shattuck had appeared very early one morning in the office in the Cal-Pax building only two days before the fire and had seen Dorothy come out of his quarters. Shattuck had not said anything, but Cable had gotten the idea, from Shattuck's stiff demeanor, that he disapproved.

Was he telling Shattuck this now so that Shattuck would know that it wasn't just an affair? No, what did he care what Shattuck thought? He was getting too self-analytical, too much like Williamson. Undoubtedly, it was Williamson's influence. The few talks he had had with the doctor had opened up something in him, a jack-in-the-box that popped out when he wasn't busy working.

"I don't know," he repeated slowly. "My ex-wife was too dependent. Dorothy is too independent. She's had several bad marriages, and she loves her work. She says she couldn't exist without it. I told her I had no objection to her working. But if she did, we wouldn't see much of each other, and so we might as well not be married. She agreed. Still . . ."

Still, it was none of Shattuck's business, and he had no right to be discussing personal affairs with him. Shattuck wasn't even a friend. He was friendly enough, but he had a reserve that cooled off any genuine warmth or intimacy. But, come to think of it, the only friend he had, aside from Dorothy, was Williamson. Was he himself also too reserved?

He looked up. Meisser was approaching in the corridor.

"I'm going now. The watchdog's back."

"It's a fool's game," Shattuck said.

"What?"

"Gambling. A waste of time and substance."

Cable shrugged and walked away. Meisser, entering, looked at the panel chronometer. Cable halted.

"I know he's early," he said. "But he couldn't sleep."

Meisser only grunted.

TWENTY-SEVEN

A ll hands were present in the control room at 07:00.

Shattuck, in the helmsman's chair, was monitoring all the indicators. He was especially intent on three, the depth gauge, the horizontal-level gauge, and the target-sonar receiver. The latter was a combination light-sound and distance indicator. It shone a steady bright orange and emitted a loud beeping. The target-sonar transmitter had been anchored on the sea bottom only forty feet north of the Hole a month ago. Two auxiliary transmitters had been placed near it at the same time by the *Lamprey*. If the one now transmitting should malfunction, either of the others could be activated by a pulse from a sonar on the Hoover.

A readout just beneath the light showed the distance of the Hoover from the target sonar.

Cable sat in a swivel chair close to Shattuck's left.

Admiral Evans was at the communications panel immediately to the right of the control console.

General Arden, a set of tools attached to his belt, sat in a chair at the northwest corner of the room. In a box at his feet were meters and probes. He was ready to spring into action if an electrical malfunction occurred.

Chang was near the entrance, his camera on its shoulder support swinging slowly. Dorothy stood to one side giving him directions in a low voice, and pointing a directional microphone at Shattuck.

Meisser stood a few feet behind him and to the left of Cable and

Shattuck. He faced toward the west, apparently to keep everybody in his sight at the same time. So far he had not drawn his .22 automatic, but Cable expected him to do so when the Hoover was near target.

Evans was in contact with another officer aboard the *Lamprey*. Actually, he had nothing to do unless an unspecified emergency occurred. His was a backup function. If some malfunction happened in the control console, one which interfered with communication with the submarine, he was to take over immediately. Cable had not originally designed the capsule to include the auxiliary communications unit, but the Navy had insisted on it. Evans had wanted to be aboard to represent the Navy, and he had won out. Cable had not fought this. He did not think that there was a real need for an auxiliary communications unit and operator. On the other hand, one never knew; it was best to be prepared for all emergencies. Moreover, if, because of some highly improbable reason, both he and Shattuck were put out of action, Evans could take over the helmsman's post.

There was little said by anyone in the room, except by Shattuck. Dorothy and Chang moved around, taking pictures from various angles. Meisser glanced at them from time to time. Arden took a cigar from the pocket of his jumpsuit and then remembered that Shattuck had asked that no one smoke during the final phase. He claimed to be allergic to tobacco, and he did not want to be sneezing during a crucial moment. Cable did not remember Shattuck ever having sneezed, but then Cable smoked only now and then. He had not been aware of Shattuck's allergy, since Shattuck had never said anything about it. Maybe Shattuck had sneezed, but he had paid no attention to it. Maybe Shattuck had not wanted to say anything about it because he did not want to displease his superior.

Whatever the case, Shattuck was in the driver's seat now. Even a four-star general had to obey his orders.

The Hoover was dead on course. The orange light shone steadily; the beeping maintained the same noise level. Shattuck spoke every five minutes, confirming to the submarines that all was well. The panel chronometer ticked off the seconds and minutes.

All eyes and ears were on Shattuck.

"Twelve seconds to break-off time. Eleven, ten, nine, eight, seven, six, five, four, three, two, ONE!"

"Contact broken, Hoover."

The submarines had reversed their screws, and the Hoover was on its own. If it went off course, it would have to depend on the pontoon screws to correct it. But that was not likely to happen.

"Received, *Lamprey*."

"God give you good luck, Hoover."

"Thanks, *Lamprey*," Shattuck said hoarsely. "I prayed last night; I'm praying now. We're in His hands now."

This was the first time that Cable had ever heard Shattuck mention God or indeed anything religious. But he was not surprised. At a time like this, even an unreligious person would feel that he would need the help of someone more powerful than himself, even if he didn't believe that someone actually existed.

Shattuck was sweating, despite the temperature of 68 Fahrenheit maintained by the air-conditioning. He looked strained, but his operation was smooth enough. After checking the console indicators, he punched a button which simultaneously activated all the rear propellers on the pontoons. The Hoover had started decelerating forty miles back. It took a long time for the colossal mass to slow down. The bottom current was 1.3 knots at this point. The schedule called for the Hoover to be going at 0.45 knots when it neared the target. The powerful battery-driven motors in the pontoons would slow down the Hoover to the speed desired.

Shattuck said "Velocity: 1.0 knot. Depth: 275. On horizontal. On course. Target sonar: 3400 feet ahead."

"Received, Hoover."

07:15.

Cable removed the chain from around his neck. At its end was a key which he inserted into a lock on the panel. Shattuck said, "Yeah," and he took a similar chain from his neck. He inserted its key into a lock next to Cable's.

"*Lamprey*," Shattuck said. "Both anchor keys inserted."

Out of the corner of his eye Cable saw Meisser move up closer.

It was at BOAR's insistence that double locks for release of the anchoring mechanisms had been installed. Undoubtedly, Meisser had instigated this. He wanted to make sure that there wasn't any accidental activation of the mechanisms.

"Meisser speaking. Anchor-key procedures correct."

"Received, Meisser. Anchor-key procedures correct."

07:18.

"Run the anchors down twenty feet," Cable said.

Shattuck turned his key. A red light flashed above the ANCH. rheostat. Cable turned his key. The ANCH. readout indicated the length of the cables unreeled. At 20, Shattuck pressed the ANCH. STOP button.

Cable turned his key; Shattuck left his untouched. Meisser reported to *Lamprey* while Shattuck bit his lip. He was even more annoyed than Cable at what both considered a totally unnecessary procedure.

07:20.

The submarines reported that they were even with the Hoover, the *Lamprey* on the right, the *Coelacanth* on the left. Their sonars were probing ahead, making sure that the bottom offered the same surface as during their run two weeks before.

Arden took his cigar out again, looked at it, looked at Shattuck, and stuck it unlit in his mouth. He chewed viciously on it.

Cable looked at the readout indicating the distance to the target-sonar.

"Less than one ship's length to go," he said loudly.

He looked at Dorothy. She happened to be turned toward him at the moment. She smiled, though weakly, and made a circle with her thumb and first finger. He hoped his grin was more convincing than hers.

Suddenly, the voice of the *Lamprey* operator shouted, "Hoover! Hoover! Unidentified object one thousand feet to port! Suggest you anchor until identity is established!"

Shattuck gave a little jump, then said, "Received, *Lamprey*. Unidentified object sighted."

He turned his head towards Cable. "What do we do? Anchor?"

Cable looked at the large relief chart of the sea bottom on the bulkhead to his left. "Commander Cable speaking. Could it be that protuberance—the one marked 12C?"

"It could be, Commander. But it's larger than it should be. It has a previously unnoted extension of approximately six feet and a height of approximately seven feet. It could be wreckage caught by the protuberance, but I suggest . . ."

"Received. I will anchor."

He turned the key in the ANCH. lock.

"O.K., Shattuck. All down. Hit the bottom."

Shattuck said, "But if we stop, we'll be a sitting duck."

"Damn it! I said let the anchors down!"

Meisser moved closer, the long-barreled pistol in his right hand.

Shattuck reached for the rheostat.

Meisser stepped toward Shattuck.

So suddenly that Cable had no time to react, Shattuck half-spun his chair and launched himself headfirst into Meisser. The pistol shot once, and the ricochet whee'ed by Cable's head. The others cried out. Meisser was on his back, and Shattuck was rolling away, the gun now in his hand.

Cable came out of his stunned state and rose from the chair. Shattuck, on one knee, fired. Evans fell back against his chair, his head lolling back. Blood trickled from a hole in his temple.

Cable froze. Shattuck was aiming the pistol at him.

"That's right, Cable," Shattuck said. He rose slowly and stepped back, then moved the pistol back and forth. "Everybody freeze."

Meisser groaned and rolled over and got to his hands and knees. Shattuck said, "Hold it, Meisser. O.K. Everybody down on your hands and knees. Crawl over to Arden's chair and then lie face down, hands behind your necks. Don't try anything. I'm as good a shot as Meisser. That's two rounds fired, I've got eleven left, and there's only five of you."

"My God!" Cable said. "You're an SOJ!"

Shattuck smiled. "From the beginning. The Lord God is on my side, you see."

Meisser looked up, his face twisted, and said, "So I was *right*!"

"You can't be wrong all the time," Shattuck said. "Now, quick, everybody! Do as I said! I can kill you all now. But it is my Christian duty to give you a chance to repent, truly repent, I mean, so that you, too, can live forever at His right side."

Cable became aware now of the voice of the *Lamprey's* commander. "Hoover, Hoover! Answer, for God's sakes! What in hell is going on?"

So that was why Shattuck had killed Evans. He had not wanted him to warn the submarines. Not that they could do anything anyway.

Cable sank to his knees. His brain was refusing to work. He was too stunned. What could he do? But there was no answer.

Dorothy was already on her hands and knees. Chang was placing the camera, very slowly, upon the floor. Arden was also down on all fours, the cigar on the floor by his side. He must have opened his mouth in astonishment and so dropped it.

Shattuck stepped back. He looked at the control console. Unless something happened to alter the course, he would not have to touch the controls. The Hoover would proceed on course, go on over the Hole, be caught in the swift flow of oil, and carried on past. And the oil would burn and burn, and the air of earth would become dense, the soot would fall, and the plants and the animals, including man, would die.

But maybe the Hoover now being built . . .

As if reading his mind, Shattuck said, "The Hoover II won't ever get here, Cable. Three groups of the Warriors of Gabriel—our striking force—will be striking now. One will be blowing up the train bringing in the capsule and other parts to Santa Barbara. The second will be blowing up the train carrying the pontoons. The third will be blowing up the warehouse in East Chicago where some of the big parts for the shell are stored while awaiting shipment."

Arden stopped and looked back. "They'll die, too!"

"They expect to die," Shattuck said. "But they are doing the Lord God's work, and they will get their reward."

"In hell!" Arden snarled.

"No, that is where you will soon be. Unless you truly repent. You'd better pray to God to make you see the error of your ways. You haven't got long."

Cable continued crawling until he was by Dorothy. She was still on her knees. Chang stretched out flat by them and put his hands behind his neck. Arden reached them, but he remained on all-fours. Meisser was moving toward them but very slowly. His eyes were huge, and his lips were drawn tightly back.

"Down on your faces, all of you!" Shattuck called. He moved to the auxiliary panel and then the console, flicking off the communications switches. There was silence for a moment.

Meisser, breathing hard, said, "What can we do now, Cable?"

Cable did not reply at once. He repressed the impulse to tell Meisser that if he had not insisted on the weapon, he would not have put them in such jeopardy. It wouldn't do any good to tell him that. Besides, Meisser must be only too aware of it.

Shattuck said, "In five minutes, we'll be right over the mines! You had better start praying, confess your sins, ask the Lord God Jehovah to forgive you."

Cable got down on his face and put his hands over his neck. But he lifted his head, feeling the strain in his neck and back muscles, and he said, "What mines, Shattuck?"

Shattuck laughed, and he said, "The mines that we planted, of course. You remember when the two Marcules, the sea bottom working craft, were stolen from Cal-Pax three months ago? The government searched for them, but it never found them. We had them all the time, underwater off Santa Cruz. Two weeks ago a group of the warriors moved them in near the Hole, and they buried six mines, mines they made, in the path of the Hoover. There's a transceiver buried by them, one Hoover-length from the Hole, and it should be transmitting now. The men in the Marcules will have started it; they have a passive detector that's picked up the pulses transmitted by the Hoover.

"An electrical line connects the Marcules, the sonar, and the mines. Three mines are placed so they'll be released inside the Hoover. I'll have the Hoover on the bottom then, and when the mines inside the shell float up, they'll explode when they reach the helium in the upper part of the shell. Their change of pressure detectors will make sure of that.

"At the same time, the three mines placed outside the exterior will float up. Just about thirty feet. Then they'll explode at a sonar signal from the Marcules.

"The mines inside will crush the capsule and twist the shell. The mines outside will make such a tremendous shock wave they'll crush the thin-shelled pontoons.

"So, you haven't much time. Start praying, you children of the lost!"

"Oh God!" Dorothy said. "He's crazy! He'll die, too!" Then, "There's only one thing to do. We have to rush him and hope some of us get to him before he . . ."

"Keep him talking while I try to think of something," Cable muttered.

Chang said, "Shattuck! How did those Marcules get down here! How'd they manage to get by all the subs patrolling this coast? And how did you manage to know all this? You've been closely watched, you know that. How'd they get any messages to you?"

"Never mind all that!" Shattuck said. "We have our ways. The Lord God Jehovah blinded our enemies and enabled us to carry out our work."

"You can shove that blasphemy up your ass, too!" General Arden yelled.

"And you'll die unrepentant and fall down to hell!" Shattuck shouted. "Pray, you sinner! Pray before it's too late! If you want to be with me on the Day of Judgment, pray!"

Dorothy said, "Then it was no accident that you punched the anchor-down button on the *Sea Ichneumon?*"

Shattuck nodded.

"Ask him where the other Marcules is," Cable said. "He only mentioned one." He lifted his neck again. Even at this distance he could make out the readouts. Within a few minutes the front edge of the Hoover would be within about 2900 feet of the Hole. But Shattuck would let the anchors down when about 1500 feet from it, would blow the gas out of the pontoons and admit water into them, would open the hatches on top of the shell to let the helium out and the water in. And then the mines would burst through the covering mud and float up, and . . . He shook his head, scraping his chin slightly on the floor. Then it would be all over.

But if the Hoover could be lifted to the surface, the effect of the interior mines would be softened. Maybe not softened enough, but there was no other alternative. The mines on the outside would be exploded at thirty feet up from the bottom, and so their shock waves might not crush the pontoons.

Shattuck, replying to Dorothy said, "Very well, if you prefer asking useless questions instead of making good use of the little time left to you . . . then that is the way you chose. I won't ask God to grant mercy to the likes of you. One of the Marcules had a malfunction in the life system. It couldn't be repaired in time, so the crew was transferred to the other Marcules. It put quite a strain on its life system, but the men could make it if they didn't burn up much energy. The malfunctioning Marcules was set to travel westward, and it must have gone off the edge of the continental shelf. The other, I was informed, was concealed behind a protuberance, some sort of rock. It was too long to be entirely hidden, but we hoped that it wouldn't be noticed. If it was, then I was to go into action sooner."

Cable wondered what the *Lamprey* and the *Coelacanth* were doing. With communication to the Hoover cut off, they must have realized that something was gravely wrong. And one or both of them must be proceeding towards the Marcules now. If only it could be torpedoed or rammed before the mine-release signal was sent.

He looked up again and noticed something he had missed during the confusion. Shattuck had cut off the reverse spin of the pontoon propellers and had set the controls for forward drive.

The Hoover was traveling at 1.6 knots. He must be planning on taking her down fast when he was over the mines.

Cable spoke softly. "Shattuck is going to have to operate the controls with one hand while he's holding the pistol on us with the other. And he can't keep his eyes on us all the time. When I give the word, get up fast. Split. Don't bunch up. And run zigzag, like broken-field runners. He's going to get some of us, maybe all of us. But if he doesn't hit a vital spot, he won't stop you. If you're hit, and you can do it, keep going. When I yell the word *go*, go!"

"No talking unless I can hear you!" Shattuck shouted.

"We're praying," Cable said.

Shattuck said nothing, but he looked disappointed.

At that moment a slight shock and a faint clang rang through the steel capsule. Shattuck looked startled, and he turned his head to each side.

"What the hell is that?" Meisser said.

Cable felt another vibration through the metal floor. And then he understood. The commander of one of the submarines was trying to make contact with the Hoover. He was placing his vessel alongside the structure, trying to match his airlock with the Hoover's. He was going to try to come aboard!

Whoever he is, he's a real Navy man, Cable thought. But if Shattuck realizes what's going on, he'll kill us all before he investigates.

"O.K.," he said softly. "Now's the time. Get ready!"

He drew in a deep breath, shouted, "Go!" and he started to get up.

Shattuck stepped back, crying "Hold it!"

Cable was on his feet, headed at an angle away from Shattuck. The gun sounded loudly in the small room, and he felt a numbness on his left side. He staggered sideways, almost collided with Chang, saw Meisser running straight at Shattuck. He recovered and started running, zigzagged, and he did bump into Chang this time.

Shattuck fired at Meisser, who reeled, and then he fired at someone else. Arden fell near Cable, face down. Meisser, yelling, charged into Shattuck as the pistol went off twice at point-blank range. But Shattuck was borne backwards and up and was slammed against the control console.

Meisser fell away from him, and he lay on his side.

Shattuck looked as if he had been hurt, but he lifted the pistol and pointed it at Chang. It exploded and Chang fell to the floor, clutching his knee and screaming.

Cable leaped upon Shattuck, felt the muzzle sliding along his shoulder, then his neck, was deafened as it went off, and felt a burning pain in his ear.

Shattuck, for a second, looked dazed. Cable tried to clutch at the pistol, but it danced away in a field of vision that was rapidly blurring.

Then he was falling, was looking up at Shattuck. And Shattuck was pointing the pistol directly at his head.

Something came from behind and over him and smashed Shattuck on the head. Shattuck crumpled. He fell heavily across Cable's stomach, driving the air out from it.

Near him lay the camera.

It wasn't until several seconds had passed, and not until he saw Dorothy's tear-streaked face, that he realized what had happened. She had brought the heavy instrument down on Shattuck's skull.

"Jim! Jim!" she cried. "Are you all right?"

"I don't know," he said. She seemed to be the only white object in increasing darkness. "Get him off me, for God's sakes. Then kill him."

"Kill him?"

"We can't take a chance he'll come to. Listen, Dorothy. We have to get the Hoover to the Hole. I may pass out. Do you think you could do it if I'm not able?"

"I've watched during the test runs," she said. "And I've studied the instructions."

She lifted Shattuck's two arms and then the upper part of his body. Shattuck's head dangled; blood was running from his forehead and down his face. Some of it fell on Cable's face as she carried the upper part of the body in a semicircle to Cable's left. It was a strange thing to do, he thought. Why didn't she just drag him on across? But then it was done, and he was trying to get up.

Some time later, he awoke. Dorothy was pouring water on his face from a cup.

"How long was I out?" he said thickly.

"About two minutes," she said. "You're wounded in the side and there's a gash across your thigh. And your ear is horribly burned."

"Don't I know that," he said. "But I didn't know he'd hit my leg. Listen, Dorothy, bend down, I can't seem to talk loudly. I think one of the subs is trying to lock into our airlock. That's easy when we're both on the bottom. But we're moving, and it'll take a hell of a sailor to do it. And even if it's done, they can't get in unless they cut through or unless you open the lock for them. Understand?"

She nodded.

"O.K. There's no time for them to cut through. The mines'll be going off in about . . . what time is it?"

She looked up.

"It's 07:30."

"Only ten minutes since this started? Listen, the airlock has a thick glass window. Get a big sheet of paper and write a note. Write MINES AHEAD. RELEASE US. Got that?"

She nodded.

"Get some tape out of the supply room, then run down to the lock and tape it up so they can see it. I hope the guy in charge of the boarding crew's a fast thinker. He must know that the sub can't stay attached to us. We're going down right now, Dorothy, we have to before we get over the mine field. But if the sub's locked in, it'll make one end tilt and God knows how it might deflect us from course. I . . . Dorothy?"

"Yes?"

"Where are you? Jesus, don't let me pass out now. There isn't . . ."

He awoke again. He looked to one side. Shattuck's face was near his. The mouth was open; the eyes were staring at him. There was a small hole in the center of his forehead.

Dorothy did it, he thought. I was hoping she'd have the guts. I wonder if I would have been able to do it, but where is she?

He tried to get up but was too weak. He wasn't so weak that he couldn't feel the pain of his ear.

Someone was moaning.

He called, "Who's that?"

The moaning stopped. "It's Chang, Jim. Everybody else is dead."

His heart seemed to stop. "Not Dorothy?"

"No. She went through the lock. Jesus, Jim, she shot Shattuck right through the head. Murdered him! Not that I blame her. But . . ."

"I ordered her to. It wasn't murder. It was war. If he'd recovered . . . How long has she been gone?"

"About three minutes. She didn't say what she was doing. What *is* she doing, Jim?"

"I don't know. Listen, Chang. I was trying to think clearly but I wasn't. I should have told her to set the controls to take us to the bottom, sub or no sub. We don't have time to wait until they cut loose, and when we started to sink they should have guessed what we were doing."

"What do you mean?" Chang said. "We *are* on the bottom! Dorothy set the controls before she went to get that paper."

Cable smiled. At least, he thought he was smiling.

"Yeah? She's one smart woman, Chang. A hell of a woman!"

Chang moaned. Cable said, "Did the mines go off? The ones set for outside, I mean?"

"I didn't hear them," Chang said. "Here comes Dorothy."

He waited, and then she was on her knees and bending down over him. There were other faces, too. Some of them he knew.

"I put her down and then I wrote they could come aboard," she said.

Lieutenant Hopedale's face came into view. It was smiling.

"We'll have you off here in a jiffy," he said. "Don't worry. We'll pump air into the pontoons, and she'll have enough buoyancy to float to the required depth. Twenty feet from the bottom will do it. It'll take a few days, sir, but it'll be a piece of cake from there on in."

"Damn it," Cable said. "I want to be aboard her when it happens. I haven't worked just . . ."

"Beg your pardon, sir," Hopedale said. "If you're conscious, you'll be there for the kill. We just want to get you on the *Lamprey* so you can get fixed up. Then we'll bring you back . . . if you're declared fit by the medic, of course. Oh, here he is."

The doctor was by his side and feeling his pulse. He looked a little like Williamson, which made Cable feel a little better. But as he was placed on the stretcher, he said, "Dorothy, what happened? The mines, I mean? And the Marcules?"

"Oh, they haven't gone off," she said. The *Coelacanth* got to the Marcules and rammed it, slid along the bottom and hit it and smashed it. The line to the mines was broken. It's going to be all right, Jim, all right!"

"That's just the first step, capping the Hole," he said. "If we ever get to survive this mess, do you think they'll learn?"

"By *they* do you mean *we*?" she said. "I hope so. But whatever they . . . we . . . do, things will never be the same."

"They never are," he said.

ABOUT THE AUTHORS

Philip José Farmer was born on January 26, 1918 in North Terre Haute, Indiana. He grew up in Peoria, Illinois where he spent much of his childhood reading everything from the Bible and books on mythology to the classics by Baum, Carroll, Cervantes, Defoe, Dickens, Homer, London, Swift, and Twain to popular works by Burroughs, Doyle, Haggard, Verne, and Wells.

He sold his first story, a mainstream tale titled "O'Brien and Obrenov," to *Adventure* in 1946 before he decided to try his hand at science fiction. His next published story, "The Lovers," appeared in the August 1952 issue of *Startling Stories*, and is noted for breaking the taboo on sex in science fiction, as well as for earning Farmer a Hugo Award for "Most Promising New Talent."

Married and with two children, he soon quit his job to become a full-time writer, but after selling several more stories to the science fiction pulps, his career hit a stumbling block when he "won" the Shasta Prize Novel Contest. The grand prize was four thousand dollars (a lot of money in 1953), but he never received his winnings. Instead, the publisher asked Farmer for rewrites while the prize money was invested in another book, which bombed. By the time the truth came out, Farmer had lost his house and was forced to take up manual labor full time.

Farmer left Peoria with his family in 1956 and moved around the country working as a technical writer for the space-defense industry, eventually ending up in Beverly Hills, California in 1965. All the while he continued to write and sell science fiction short stories and novels, launching his popular World of Tiers series and even winning a second Hugo Award for the novella "Riders of the Purple Wage." Then, just before the moon landing in 1969, he was laid off from his technical writing job, so he decided to write fiction full time once again. This time it stuck.

In 1970, Farmer moved back to Peoria with his family and again his career began to take off, this time with a third Hugo Award win, for *To Your Scattered Bodies Go*, the opening novel in his bestselling Riverworld series. For the next few years, Farmer sought inspiration from the popular literature he so loved, writing novels such as *The Mad Goblin* (a Doc Savage pastiche), *Lord of the Trees* and *Lord Tyger* (both Tarzan pastiches), *The Wind Whales of Ishmael* (a science fiction sequel to *Moby Dick*), *The Other Log of Phileas Fogg* (the "true" story behind Jules Verne's *Around the World in Eighty Days*), and *Venus on the Half-Shell* (written as if by Kilgore Trout, a character from the works of Kurt Vonnegut). He also wrote two "biographies" during this period: *Tarzan Alive: A Definitive Biography of Lord Greystoke* and *Doc Savage: His Apocalyptic Life*.

The next two decades saw the publication of the Dayworld trilogy, as well as further installments in the Riverworld and World of Tiers series. Farmer also fulfilled his lifelong ambition to write an Oz novel, and authorized Doc Savage and Tarzan novels, with the publication of *A Barnstormer in Oz*, *Escape from Loki*, and *Tarzan and the Dark Heart of Time*. Late in his career, Farmer switched genres with *Nothing Burns in Hell*, a detective novel set in his hometown of Peoria.

After Farmer retired from writing in 1999, new collections such as *Pearls from Peoria* and *Venus on the Half-Shell and Others* continued to appear, as did new collaborative works such as *The Evil in Pemberley House* (with Win Scott Eckert), *The Song of Kwasin* (with Christopher Paul Carey), and *Dayworld: A Hole in Wednesday* (with Danny Adams).

Farmer passed on February 25, 2009, but his fan base is as ardent as ever, ensuring that his works will continue to be reprinted and enjoyed by readers for generations to come.

Christopher Paul Carey is the coauthor with Philip José Farmer of *The Song of Kwasin*, and the author of *Exiles of Kho, Hadon, King of Opar*, and *Blood of Ancient Opar* all tales set in the lost civilization of Khokarsa. His short fiction may be found in anthologies such as *Tales of the Shadowmen, The Worlds of Philip José Farmer, Tales of the Wold Newton Universe*, and *The Avenger: The Justice, Inc. Files*. He holds a master's degree in Writing Popular Fiction from Seton Hill University and is currently the Head of Publishing at Edgar Rice Burroughs, Inc.

Sharman Apt Russell is a nature/science and science fiction writer who has won multiple awards for her fiction and non-fiction: the John Burroughs Medal, a Rockefeller Fellowship, the Mountains and Plains Booksellers Award, a Pushcart Prize, the Writers at Work Fellowship, and the Henry Joseph Jackson Award. Her recent *Knocking on Heavens Door* (Skyhorse Publishers, 2016) also won the New Mexico/Arizona Book Award for Science Fiction and the Arizona Author's Award for Fiction. Of this eco-sci-fi set in a "Paleoterrific" future, one reviewer said, "There's a spin on this story that is unlike any other I have read . . . I essentially inhaled this book. It has a wonderful flow." Sharman lives in the magical realism of the American Southwest and writes both adult and children's literature on a ridiculously wide range of topics, including citizen science, living in place, archaeology, flowers, butterflies, hunger, and pantheism. Her young adult fantasy novel, *Teresa of the New World* (Skyhorse Publishers, 2015), takes place during the plagues of the 16th century and First Contact. Her forthcoming *Within Our Grasp: The Revolution to End Childhood Malnutrition and Stunting Worldwide* (Pantheon Publishers, 2021) combines her longtime interest in both hunger and the environment. She is now writing about the test pilots of the middle twentieth century and about her father, Mel Apt, who broke Mach 3 in 1956. You can read more about her and her work at www.sharmanaptrussell.com.

Meteor House Titles

THE WORLDS OF PHILIP JOSÉ FARMER
Anthology Series edited by Michael Croteau
Volume 1: Protean Dimensions
Volume 2: Of Dust and Soul
Volume 3: Portraits of a Trickster
Volume 4: Voyages to Strange Days

The Best of Farmerphile edited by Michael Croteau
The Philip José Farmer Centennial Collection edited by Michael Croteau
Greatheart Silver and Other Pulp Heroes by Philip José Farmer
A Rough Knight for the Queen by Philip José Farmer

WOLD NEWTON SERIES
Doc Savage: His Apocalyptic Life by Philip José Farmer
Tarzan and the Dark Heart of Time by Philip José Farmer

THE KHOKARSA SERIES
Exiles of Kho by Christopher Paul Carey
Flight to Opar (Restored Edition) by Philip José Farmer
The Song of Kwasin by Philip José Farmer and Christopher Paul Carey
Hadon, King of Opar by Christopher Paul Carey
Blood of Ancient Opar by Christopher Paul Carey

THE PAT WILDMAN SERIES
The Evil in Pemberley House by Philip José Farmer and Win Scott Eckert
The Scarlet Jaguar by Win Scott Eckert

THE PHILEAS FOGG SERIES
Phileas Fogg and the War of Shadows by Josh Reynolds
Phileas Fogg and the Heart of Osra by Josh Reynolds

THE TWO HAWKS SERIES
Man of War by Heidi Ruby Miller

THE DAYWORLD SERIES
Dayworld: A Hole in Wednesday by Philip José Farmer and Danny Adams

SCIENCE FICTION ADVENTURE
The Abnormalities of Stringent Strange by Rhys Hughes
Airship Hunters by Jim Beard and Duane Spurlock

REFERENCE - CROSSOVERS
Crossovers Expanded, Volume 1 by Sean Lee Levin
Crossovers Expanded, Volume 2 by Sean Lee Levin

CHAPBOOKS
*Being an Account of the Delay at Green River, Wyoming, of Phileas Fogg,
World Traveler, or, The Masked Man Meets an English Gentleman*
by Win Scott Eckert
*The Adventure of the Fallen Stone: Being the First Part of the Account of
The Dynamics of a Meteor* by John H. Watson, M.D.
edited by Win Scott Eckert
Watch Your Back, Mr. Minamoto by Frank Schildiner

Visit us at meteorhousepress.com